A BEAUTIFUL PLACE TO DIE

Protector. Lover. Assassin. — *Kiku.*

Orphaned as a child and taken in by the Yakuza, Kiku swore an oath to serve and protect the organization. But, when Kiku discovers that the 13-year-old boy she has been assigned to guard may be the son of her lover and heir to the Yakuza throne, her pledge is put to the test.

With a price on the boy's head and a target on his back, Kiku must not only save him from the ruthless Russian mob but possibly from a traitor in the Yakuza itself. Torn between love and honor, Kiku must snatch the boy from the crosshairs before it's too late.

WARNING: If you have plans, cancel them! Call in sick to work, get a babysitter, do whatever you must to steal away with Kiku. You won't be able to stop reading, so get ready to strap in, buckle up, and hang on for the action-thrill ride of your life!

Praise for Christopher Greyson's
A Beautiful Place to Die

I loved every minute of it!

Move over Bond, here comes Kiku!

If you like Mission Impossible, you will love Kiku!

This book is so action-packed I had to remind myself to breathe!

A truly fun and face-paced read! Kiku is a kick-butt action hero, but her character is balanced by a vulnerability that adds depth and complexity.

From multi-award-winning *Wall Street Journal* bestselling author Christopher Greyson comes this spellbinding tale with jaw-dropping secrets, a colorful ensemble of characters, and a protagonist you'll root for from the first page to the last. Christopher Greyson's novels have been read by millions of readers.

ALSO BY CHRISTOPHER GREYSON

The Girl Who Lived

One Little Lie

Pure of Heart

The Adventures of Finn and Annie

The Detective Jack Stratton Mystery-Thriller Series:

And Then She Was Gone

Girl Jacked

Jack Knifed

Jacks are Wild

Jack and the Giant Killer

Data Jack

Jack of Hearts

Jack Frost

Jack of Diamonds

Captain Jack

Kiku - The Yakuza War Trilogy

A Beautiful Place to Die

Kindle the Fires of War

Dance of Death

This book is dedicated to Cindy Wilson.
A fan of Kiku, who encouraged me every step of the way.

A Beautiful Place To Die

WALL STREET JOURNAL BESTSELLING AUTHOR
CHRISTOPHER GREYSON

GREYSON MEDIA

1

Takeo's summer house

It is a beautiful place to die.

Kiku stood at the entrance of the traditional Japanese garden and drank in the delicate scent wafting on the breeze. The cherry trees lining the gravel path had flushed into bloom, their blossoms an unexpected, rare pleasure. Pink petals stirred in the late March air—it was much too early in the season for Takeo to return to his summer home, let alone summon Kiku here.

That was not a good sign. Neither were the men waiting to search her for weapons. Though it was standard practice for all visitors seeing the head of the Yakuza, Kiku was not a guest. She was Takeo's personal assassin and normally armed to the teeth.

She tried to hide her displeasure at the sight of Shin Uchihara, Takeo's head of security, awaiting her approach with arms crossed and feet planted. She stopped and stared off at a clump of cedars while Shin ran the metal detector wand down her arms, across her chest, and over her trim waist. The wand beeped when he reached her upper thigh.

"Glock," Kiku said simply, turning to him.

Shin held out his hand.

Kiku's eyes narrowed. Had Takeo insisted she turn over her weapon or was this a power play on Shin's part? Shin's typical smug, condescending smirk had been replaced with grim focus and the muscles in his forearms twitched like a gunfighter about to draw. The man standing beside Shin shifted his weight to his heels as his fingers tightened nervously on the machine gun in his hands. Kiku had never seen this man before.

Another bad sign.

She lowered her arms, and her widening smile slowly revealed her sharp canines. She'd always wondered if the stories about Shin's incredible speed were true. She doubted they were, yet part of her was eager to prove she was faster.

Let him try and take it.

Shin stepped closer to Kiku and locked his black eyes on hers. The veins in his temples throbbed across his shaved head. Most men in the Yakuza feared the fanatic, but Kiku wasn't most men.

"I'm just following orders." Shin took a step back but kept his hand out. "I need your gun." His eyes darted toward the other man and then back to Kiku. She smelled a musky scent in the air and glanced over at the man with the machine gun, confirming that he had broken into a sweat and his finger was on the trigger.

Following orders was something Kiku understood; in her line of work, to disobey an order was to sign your own death warrant. And the way Shin had lowered his gaze when he asked again for her gun was the equivalent of saying *please*. Kiku lifted the hem of her silky black dress and removed the Glock from her thigh holster. If Takeo wanted to kill her today, there would be no stopping it.

Seemingly satisfied with his search, Shin stepped to the side and let her pass. The arrogant smirk returned to his face as he said her name, "Kiku." He pronounced it correctly—KEE-koo—but the dismissive way he said it made her bristle.

Kiku bowed her head slightly as she walked past. Shin puffed out his chest. He believed she was paying him respect, but in fact it was the opposite. Angling her head as she had, she was hiding in plain sight the seven-inch titanium hairpin that held her charcoal hair in an elegant chignon—a delightful weapon and, in close quarters, as effective as a gun.

She knew her every move was monitored as she made her way through the garden toward the man standing at the back. With each step, her heels settled softly into the fine pea stones, the sound blending with the murmur of the waterfall cascading into the koi pond. The distinct *thunk* of a bowstring being released—followed by the shriek of metal tearing through metal—shattered the tranquility of this special place. Then, like the ripples from a rock tossed into a pond, all evidence of the arrow's flight was gone, and the garden was peaceful once more.

A curved wooden bridge spanned the koi pond. Guarding each side were two samurai statues. Their naginatas—long wooden poles each equipped with a single-edged blade that tipped up at the end—were crossed so that everyone who stepped onto the bridge had to pass beneath the arch created by the ancient weapons. Kiku looked up into the statues' eternally snarling faces and wondered what the medieval samurai would have done to her nine hundred years ago.

They would have tried to stop me.

A faint smile crossed her lips. She preferred to think she would have been an *onna-bugeisha*, one of the legendary female samurai like Tomoe Gozen. Gazing over the side of the bridge, Kiku glanced at her reflection in the water. With her high cheekbones and creamy white skin, she had a wolfish appearance, accentuated by her long canines. Something she had been told often: that she could be a model if it weren't for her eyes. It wasn't that they weren't beautiful—people said they were—but there was a coldness there that seemed to terrify everyone. At times the darkness behind them scared even herself.

Her heels clicked faintly on the wooden bridge, yet the man standing on the other side still didn't turn in her direction. His form was obscured by the trees, but surely he'd heard her approach? He pulled another arrow out of the quiver that hung from an old wooden post and notched it.

Kiku had expected to meet with her employer and sometimes lover, Takeo. But as she drew nearer, she realized it wasn't Takeo but his father, Kenzo. Takeo ran the Yakuza here in the States, but Kenzo was the head of the Yakuza worldwide.

That explains why Shin searched me. He was following Kenzo's orders. And Kenzo trusts no one.

She drew in a deep breath through her nose, readying herself. This was far worse than she had thought. The leader of the Yakuza seldom came to the States, and only under the direst of circumstances. Why was Kenzo here now?

A broad-shouldered man, Kenzo was ruggedly handsome. Where his elder son, Takeo, was built like a quarterback, Kenzo resembled an American football linebacker—thick, stocky, a bull of a man. The ancient Japanese longbow in his hands was wrapped in red, standing out in stark contrast against the modern elegance of his jet-black Armani suit. The hair at his temples had grown silver, but even at the age of sixty-five the muscles in his wide back bulged as he aimed another arrow. At the end of the archery range stood a mannequin dressed in samurai armor. Eleven arrows already pierced its breastplate. For a brief moment, Kiku wondered if Kenzo would turn and greet her with the twelfth arrow through her chest.

The bowstring sliced through the air and the arrow sank deep into the samurai's breastplate. Kiku bowed low and waited, while Kenzo stood as still as the statues guarding the bridge. A breeze rustled the trees, and the petals at Kiku's feet danced across the sand of the archery range.

At last, Kenzo inclined his head slightly. A man of tradition, he believed how deeply one bowed demonstrated the respect one had for a person. Which was why he demanded that his servants bend at least to waist height when addressing him. Kiku was surprised he'd bowed his head to her at all. Something was different. And in the Yakuza, different was *not* good.

Kiku straightened up and her back stiffened. If she had been in the Mafia, she would have expected there to be plastic on the ground and a hitman behind a tree. But this was the Yakuza. If Kenzo wanted her dead, he'd have a dozen of his best men rush in from all sides at once. The fantasy of a fight to the death, here and now, in this garden, made the corner of her mouth tick up.

That would be an honorable way to die.

Kenzo's eyes hardened. Although he'd never admit it, she knew he admired her fierce independence. Or at least part of him did. Like most powerful men, he was excited by rebellion—as long as it was soon followed by submission. But Kiku's spirit, like that of a wild horse, would never completely yield. It was a balancing act—one that even she couldn't continue forever.

Right now, Kenzo needed her for something. There was both safety and terrible danger in that fact. His need of her would keep her alive, but any assignment directly requested by Kenzo would come with the utmost risk.

"The Russian situation has escalated," he said coldly.

The feud with the vicious gang of former Soviets had been teetering on the edge of war for months now. But a turf war was beneath Kiku's skill set. She was a specialized weapon reserved for more challenging situations. Surely Kenzo wouldn't involve her in a boots-on-the-ground war.

"Cade Novikov's son was shot yesterday in New York while he was on one of our docks."

Cade Novikov was the head of one of Russia's most powerful and ruthless crime syndicates. If his son was injured, there would be hell to pay.

"Petr Novikov died last night. This morning, they sent that." Kenzo pointed to a box at the foot of the post holding the almost empty quiver of arrows.

The box was roughly big enough to hold a bowling ball, which limited its possible contents to a few possibilities, and Kiku didn't particularly welcome the images that came to mind. All the more reason to wait for Kenzo's explanation. She was well aware he might be watching for her reaction, trying to determine how much she knew. Kenzo had done such things before. After a failed assassination attempt on his own life, Kenzo had carried a briefcase back into the restaurant he had just exited and set it down on a table. The briefcase contained a pipe bomb someone had left in Kenzo's limo that had failed to detonate. His intention was to ferret out who planted the bomb by assessing everyone's reaction—because only the bomber would know what peril the attaché case contained.

Is he playing such a game right now?

Kiku waited.

"The Russians have Jiro."

Kiku didn't bother to hide a small jolt of surprise. Jiro was Kenzo's second son and Takeo's half-brother. Jiro, with his thick glasses and hearing aid, was the opposite physically of his dashing older brother, but he was brilliant and studious. Now twenty-four and brandishing an MBA from Yale, Jiro was the bookkeeper for the organization worldwide. He was the only one Kenzo trusted with such information, and if the Russians gained access to it, they could bring down the entire Yakuza. He was also second in line to the Yakuza throne.

"They have demanded a cash ransom."

The fact that Kenzo didn't state the amount could only mean he considered it insultingly insignificant. It also revealed the Russians' intent—an eye for an eye, a son for a son. The ransom offer wasn't genuine; it was merely to give a father false hope that his son might live. Really, they were twisting the knife in Kenzo's chest before taking Jiro's life.

The Russian situation hadn't just escalated; it had gone nuclear.

"Jiro, along with his girlfriend, was abducted while coming out of the VX nightclub in New York," Kenzo continued. "His girlfriend is in the box."

Kiku looked at the small box and tried not to imagine the several ways one could get a human being to fit into it. Perhaps it was just her head.

"They have given us a week to comply, or they will send a smaller box to demonstrate that Jiro will bear me no heirs." His hands tightened on the bow.

Novikov was hitting father and son where it hurt most. Kenzo's greatest desire was to establish a dynasty and Jiro, despite his physical shortcomings, was a wannabe playboy. To deprive him of his manhood would be the equivalent of cutting both of their hearts out.

Three things were immediately clear. First, the Russians had just unleashed Kenzo's fury. Second, if Kiku was unable to retrieve Jiro alive, that rage would be leveled against her. And third, she would accept the mission without hesitation. She owed it to Takeo to try to spare him her familiar agony of having a sibling murdered.

"I need to speak with Ross," she said. The former Mossad agent was the head of Jiro's security detail; he would have the best information.

Kenzo tilted his head away from Kiku, a Japanese sign of refusal. "That is not possible."

Kiku forced her expression to remain unchanged. She had to tread carefully; Kenzo's temper was as legendary as his brutality.

"How many were guarding Jiro?" she asked.

"Only Ross."

Kiku weighed her options. Questioning Kenzo's judgment was dangerous, but not finding Jiro was far *more* dangerous. "Then I must speak with Ross. He could have something to offer."

"He knows nothing." A vein on Kenzo's temple throbbed. He was getting angry.

"Are you certain?" Kiku pressed.

A low rumble thundered in Kenzo's throat. His hand flashed out, and with the speed of an Olympic archer he drew, notched, turned, and fired an arrow. Once more the arrow buried itself deep into the samurai armor, but this time Kiku recognized a difference in the sound. Metal scraped against metal as the tip of the arrow penetrated the armor, but now the screech ended in a wet smack. The wind shifted. Mixed with the sweet, fresh aroma of cherry blossoms was the unmistakable stench of blood.

The samurai armor strapped to the target at the end of the range had someone inside it.

Kiku stared at the dark streams of liquid pooling at the feet. Judging by the amount of blood and lack of movement, the person inside was dead.

Kenzo pointed at the target and lifted his hand.

A young man ran out from behind the fence and over to the target. He removed the helmet.

Ross.

Kenzo hung his bow on the pole. "You have a week to bring Jiro home unharmed."

Kiku bowed low and made her way through the garden, forcing herself to walk with a normal gait. She wouldn't hurry, nor would she look back. Either was a sign of weakness.

As she reached the exit, she was grateful Kenzo could not see her, because in spite of her best efforts, she felt the heat drain from her cheeks when she saw what had been placed next to the door.

A suit of samurai armor. Exquisite. Rare. Shaped for a woman.

If she did not find Jiro within the week, that armor would become her death shroud.

2

Five days later—Catskill Mountains

Kiku stood beneath the high-voltage power lines, calmly swinging a long metal chain in a wide circle to her side. Dressed in body-hugging black, with her raven hair in a sleek knot, she looked more New York chic than assassin. From her vantage point here on the small hill, the old mansion below her appeared impenetrable. Surveillance cameras and motion sensors wrapped the grounds in a virtual security bubble. She wouldn't make it a dozen yards before being cut down.

The mansion hidden in the Catskills had been transformed into a fortress. It was guarded by nine former Russian special forces—Spetsnaz—soldiers and outfitted with all the latest security measures. The security system itself was a force to be reckoned with, but all those cameras, motion sensors, and alarms had one thing in common: they needed electricity.

She still had two days before the deadline—plenty of time to act, but there was no reason to delay. The Russians were not known for patience; there was a very real chance they could jump the gun and kill Jiro before the week was up. It had already taken her four days to find their hideout and another to verify that Jiro was inside.

Anyone else would wait for help. One call would bring an army of *kyodai*—Yakuza brothers—led by Kenzo's personal security. She might as well let loose a pack of wild dogs. Jiro would die in the raid, and Kenzo would hold her personally responsible.

She'd take her chances the way she always had—alone.

The chain hummed as she spun it faster in her gloved hand. The sloppy soldiers frequently left doors open and curtains drawn back, so pinpointing Jiro's location had been relatively easy—third floor, in an interior room.

They had done nothing to hide their numbers or weaponry, either. Between the nine of them they were armed with at least a dozen pistols, two shotguns, and one PPSh-41 submachine gun with a drum magazine.

It was almost midnight and the perfect time to strike. The soldiers had finally settled down to sleep on the second floor after getting fired up by a televised soccer match. Kiku knew not to equate sleeping with being harmless, for when they did decide to sleep, these men kept their larger guns beside them like children with their favorite stuffed animals. Still, this was the best opportunity she was likely to encounter. Their boisterous celebration had included lots of alcohol, so their level of alertness would be especially low.

Kiku smiled to herself, building speed in the spinning chain. She didn't like much of what her work entailed, but she took great pride in the fact that she was excellent at it. Yesterday she'd knocked the power to the mansion out twice—once in the morning and once at night. Both times the state-of-the-art generator had turned on instantly; the lights didn't even flicker. After researching the generator on the internet, she now had a different plan. She looked up at the transformer attached to the top of the telephone pole. Every system, no matter how technologically advanced, has its weakness. A backup generator is a system designed to switch on whenever the main system is deprived of power. So Kiku wouldn't deprive it. Instead, she would provide the high-voltage lines with *too much* power and short out the transformer. The generator's breakers would be triggered to prevent overload. Those breakers would have to be reset manually.

The muscles in her shoulder burned. She let the chain fly. It arced high into the air before coiling around the wires and erupting in a shower of sparks and bluish smoke.

Kiku raced toward the building. The security lights rimming the mansion snapped off and a couple of Russian curses sounded from inside, followed by laughter and more swearing. Her Russian was rusty, but she caught that someone had been ordered to check the generator. The inferior American power grid was being blamed.

Grabbing the tall iron fence with one hand, Kiku slipped deftly up and over, and dropped quietly to the grass on the other side. Her seven-inch, fixed-blade knife slid easily from its sheath at the small of her back. She preferred to fight with the blade in her right hand, but tonight she kept it in her left and her Glock 19 in her right. The weight of the extended thirty-three-round magazine wasn't ideal, but it too was necessary.

Nine men. Three shots apiece. No need to reload.

The generator was housed outside on a concrete slab surrounded by gravel. Silently, she leapt over the rock and hid in the shadows beside the boxy unit. A rear door banged open as the low man on the totem pole took out his frustration on the door. Muttering and swearing, he approached, his boots crunching on the gravel.

Kiku hefted the blade in her hand. She wouldn't use the Glock until she had to; the goal was to remain undetected for as long as possible. She didn't question for a moment whether the knife would be enough. With the element of surprise and her striking capabilities, it wouldn't matter that her opponent outweighed her by a hundred pounds; he was at a disadvantage. People—men especially—neglected to realize the equalization that weapons brought to the table. They had forgotten that simple wooden spears, along with hunger, had made it possible for puny hunters to bring down mighty mammoths.

Kiku sprang forward like a lioness at its prey, spearing the man through his eye socket. He crumpled to the gravel without drawing another breath.

"Hurry it up, Pavel!" someone called from inside.

"The ballerina tripped," another man yelled, and others laughed.

Kiku slipped to the side of the door Pavel had exited. Footsteps approached, and she pressed herself against the brick wall and quieted her breathing. A hulking man stepped into the doorway, a cigarette dangling from his lips and a lighter in hand. He flicked the lighter, and Kiku waited until he took a long drag on the cigarette before plunging the knife between his ribs to pass through his lung and into his heart.

Smoke billowed out of his mouth and hissed from the hole in his chest as he coughed and sputtered. He tried to pull back his arm to strike, but he was already sinking to his knees. Kiku stepped back, keeping an eye on the man in case he reached for a weapon, but her main focus was on the active threats still in the house. She sheathed her knife and drew her gun. The knife had just saved her six bullets.

The man who had called out previously did so again, now yelling for Pavel and the man dying at her feet to stop screwing around and flip the breaker on the generator. Other men laughed.

As their laughter faded away, Kiku heard the faint sound of someone descending the staircase at the end of the hall. The footsteps were drawing closer. Kiku peered through the open doorway as the man reached the base of the stairs. The soldier in him must have become suspicious, but whether due to alcohol or lack of discipline, he was careless. His hand was on his holster, but his gun wasn't drawn.

It would be his last mistake.

Kiku put the first shot center mass and double-tapped him in the head. Three guards neutralized.

Though she had used a silencer, the six men on the second floor had heard the shots and were now shouting orders, swearing both at each other and at the situation they found themselves in. Kiku jumped over the dead soldier in the doorway and sprinted down the hallway in the opposite direction of the stairwell. The LED emergency lights were dim but provided enough light to see. A thick Persian carpet muffled her steps. Her plan was to circle around and attack them from behind. She took a separate set of stairs, climbing them two at a time, sticking close to the wall. As she neared the second floor, she slowed.

The traffic jam she'd expected in the upstairs hallway was in full swing. Five men stood in the passageway with their backs to her and their focus on the stairs at the opposite end. Like photographers on Groundhog Day hoping to get a front-page photo of Punxsutawney Phil, they readied for their shot.

Kiku waited and listened.

One man was unaccounted for.

The man furthest away from her but closest to the rear stairs shouldered his machine gun and prepared to breach the stairwell.

Kiku dropped two of the men with a single shot apiece.

The remaining three men spun to face her. The men closest to her were still dressed. One carried a combat shotgun, the other a pistol. The man furthest away from her was bare-chested and holding a PPSh-41 submachine gun. He wouldn't have to worry about accuracy; with that gun he'd shred anything in the hallway.

Kiku took her time aiming. It wouldn't matter how quickly she got her bullets off if they didn't hit the intended targets. She put two shots into each of the closest men's chests.

The shots knocked both men back a step, but neither one dropped.

Kiku's heart pounded.

Body armor.

The man on the left raised the shotgun.

Kiku put two rounds into his legs.

The man on the right fired.

The bullet passed so close to her face an errant strand of hair blew against her cheek. She aimed for the man's unprotected thighs and fired.

The man shrieked. The gun tumbled from his hand.

As they dropped to their knees, giving Kiku a clear shot, she pressed her body against the doorframe and aimed for the man behind them holding the PPSh-41. Three rounds slammed into his bare chest, and he stumbled backward, his finger involuntarily depressing the trigger as he died. The men in front of him screamed as the bullets sprayed into their backs.

The machine gun clicked off, and all five soldiers lay silently on the lush carpet. Kiku put two more shots in each body to be sure.

One threat left. She considered grabbing the PPSh-41 but decided against it. If the last man was with Jiro, she needed the accuracy of a pistol, not the firing rate of a machine gun. She loaded a fresh magazine.

She crossed to the end of the hall. Stairs led to the third floor, where

Jiro was being held. What she didn't know was where she would encounter the unaccounted-for ninth man.

Kiku silently ascended the stairs, then stopped outside the room where Jiro was and listened. The smells of the battle below clung to her. The scent of gunpowder tinged with blood and urine stung her nose. With her ears still ringing from the close gunfire, she strained to hear any sign of life or clue as to where her adversary lay in wait for her. She heard nothing, and yet . . . there was a presence here. Death itself had an aura, and she sensed it now on the other side of the door.

A familiar chill passed through her. She flicked on her gun's attached light, shoved the door open, and swept the small room from left to right. In the center were two people tied up in chairs, facing each other, not moving. A closet door to the left was partially open, but she couldn't see inside. She shined her light on the chairs.

Jiro was bound to the seat on the right. His head was slumped forward. The side of his face was battered and bloody. He didn't turn his head in her direction. But, to her extreme relief, his chest rose and fell.

Tied to the other chair, facing him, was Jiro's dead girlfriend. Or so Kiku assumed. The headless body was naked, and a basketball with a smile scrawled on it sat in her lap. The sick scene confirmed the Russians' reputation for enjoying acts of barbarism.

Kiku was about to step in when Jiro raised a shaky index finger and pointed at the closet. Kiku put seven rounds through the door. A Spetsnaz soldier staggered out, fumbling weakly with his shotgun. Two more rounds dropped him to the floor.

Kiku hurried to Jiro's chair and pivoted to keep an eye on the main door as she cut him free. She glanced quickly around for his glasses and spotted them, shattered and bent, lying beside his hearing aid. She picked up his hearing aid and placed it in his ear.

"Nine men?" she asked.

Jiro coughed and nodded. His left eye was so badly bruised it was swollen shut.

Kiku forced herself to give him a quick smile. She'd always liked Jiro. He'd grown into a handsome man in his own way, though not as tall as Takeo and much leaner.

Jiro rubbed his wrists as Kiku stepped away from the chair, keeping her gun pointed at the hallway door. She made no move to help him up. She needed him to be able to walk in case they were both incorrect about the number of men.

Jiro stared at the body of his girlfriend, then leaned forward and knocked the basketball off her lap. It was obvious that she'd been tortured. He lightly stroked the back of her hand and then, after clearing his throat several times, croaked, "Cut her free."

"She is already gone, Jiro."

"I'm not leaving her." Jiro stood up and swayed. He grabbed the arm of the chair and glared at Kiku.

"Getting out of this town without the police stopping us because of the way you look will be difficult," Kiku said. "Having a corpse in tow will make it impossible."

Jiro bared his teeth and for the first time she realized how much he looked like his father. "There was another scumbag here who left yesterday," he said. "Liev. He was in charge. Red birthmark running up his neck to his ear. He killed Jessica." He grabbed Kiku's arm. His fingers were cold and crusted with blood. "Promise me you'll find Liev. Promise me you'll make him beg to go to Hell."

Jiro was Kenzo's son, but he had no control over Kiku. He could ask . . . but she could refuse.

"Promise me, Kiku." Jiro's hand trembled. "Look what he did to my girl."

Kiku wondered if Jessica had been Jiro's first real girlfriend. She didn't need to look at the girl's body again to be reminded of what Liev had done. She would see it in her nightmares forever—one of a thousand images no one should ever have had to witness.

Kiku kept her gun trained on the door. "Liev will pay for what he did to Jessica. I swear it."

3

Two weeks later

Kiku lay back in the tub and let the water lap at her slender neck. Baths were her guilty pleasure, and the cast-iron clawfoot tub had been one of the biggest factors in her choosing this apartment. It was long enough for her to stretch out and deep enough for the water to reach her chin.

The water was as hot as she could stand it, to let the essential oils of lavender, sage, and cedar float up on the steam. It was as near as Kiku could get to the illusion of solitude and tranquility in Silver Spring, Maryland.

She let her right hand drape over the side and her fingertips gently touched the handle of the twelve-gauge shotgun affixed to the side of the tub in rip-away straps. Even in the bath, Kiku could never relax completely.

Not here. Not anywhere. Not ever.

She used her toes to turn the faucet handle and add another splash of hot water. She'd jogged five miles again this morning, pushing herself the entire time. Surprisingly, her muscles weren't at all stiff. Baths helped with that, too.

Letting out a satisfied purr, she stretched and smiled. She loved her body like this—its scars hidden beneath scented bubbles. Her wardrobe was carefully selected to conceal these mementos of her violent past. The scars marred her porcelain skin in five areas on her torso and legs; two from bullets and three from knives. She hated them —not because they disfigured her beautiful body but because they served as permanent reminders of her vulnerability. The men and women who had inflicted them were long dead—but, like past lovers, they had left their marks.

The burner phone vibrated on the little table next to the tub. Only one man had the number.

"Hello?"

The pause on the other end was disconcertingly long.

"I'm outside. I'm coming in." The tension in Takeo's voice was clear. His words caused a visceral reaction she was very unaccustomed to: she froze.

The phone went dead. She clicked it off and set it back down.

Why was he here? Whenever he called it was always to arrange a future meeting . . .

She hadn't seen him in person for two months. Not since their last tryst. She had broken an unspoken rule that the Yakuza had probably never thought needed to be established: *Assassins shall not seduce their bosses*.

The first time they'd made love, Kiku initiated it—a spontaneous flare-up of a fire that had been smoldering for years. She and Takeo had sex in his office like two lovers condemned to die the next day. She'd left him exhausted on his couch, thinking that her death soon after was a distinct possibility. But when they met to discuss business a week later, again in his Chicago office, neither of them mentioned it. Kiku believed that Takeo, while flattered, had viewed their night of passion as a onetime occurrence.

A month later he surprised her by flying out to meet her here, and that night his desire for her was insatiable. They made love until dawn, a passionate dance set to the rhythm of their pounding hearts and rivaling the wild beat of Japanese taiko drummers. For hours they spoke without speaking. Kiku had never connected with another as she had with Takeo that night.

But when he left, he made it clear that they could not be together. He did not explain why. Nor did he need to. Kiku already knew the reason. For those two nights in each other's arms, they had cast off their roles and let down their guards and allowed themselves to be consumed by the fire of their union. For a time, they shared a sense of freedom that neither of them had ever known. Lust may have started the blaze, but the fire was kindled by a feeling they had dared to let live—trust. There is a reason trust does not exist in the Yakuza: trust gets you killed.

The security light beside the bathroom mirror flashed. Takeo was coming up the front steps. Kiku grabbed her regular phone and checked the cameras. He was alone, and carrying a crate almost half his size.

Another gift for rescuing Jiro? Takeo's father—who could be as generous as he was ruthless—had already given her a hefty bonus. Perhaps the box contained another token of appreciation. Or was Takeo the giver?

Kiku pressed a button, unlocking the security bars on the front door. The door looked normal, but it was as secure as a bank vault. She heard it open and shut, then something heavy was set down on the floor.

"Kiku?"

She pressed another button, relocking the front door. "I am in the bathtub," she called out. Once again, she dangled her right arm over the side of the tub, her fingers closing around the grip of the shotgun. It was an instinctual move. Her heart may trust Takeo, but her mind sorted everyone into one category—potential threat.

Takeo swung the door open and stopped in the doorway. His handsome face was stamped with the stiff business mask he seemed to wear more and more often lately. A poker face, designed to hide his emotions and conceal his thoughts. He looked so much like his father at this moment. And she hated it.

His eyes focused on hers. "I have an important matter to discuss, Kiku."

Kiku sat up a bit to listen more respectfully and inclined her head. When her neck and shoulders emerged from the tub, dripping with bubbles, Takeo's eyes wandered down, taking in the steam rising from her rosy skin and the tendrils of hair clinging to her neck.

The color in his cheeks bloomed brick-red.

"It's personal." Takeo gave the slightest nod and stepped out of the room, shutting the door behind him.

Kiku grabbed both sides of the tub and nimbly hopped out like a gymnast dismounting the parallel bars. Grateful for her thick Turkish towels, she was dry in a moment, and she paused only to tie her robe before opening the door.

It's personal. So, Takeo wasn't here to talk about *them*. His reason for being here concerned him only. And that worried her.

As she walked into her living room, she noted that the three-foot crate he carried in had been deposited next to the front door. Takeo was facing the window, his arms crossed behind his lower back. Kiku tensed as she awaited the news that was so important that Takeo needed to deliver it personally.

"*Arigatou gozaimasu*, Kiku. I am grateful for Jiro's safe return and should have thanked you before now."

"*Kyoshukudesu*." With this one word, Kiku expressed that there was no need to thank her; returning Jiro was her responsibility. She stood staring at Takeo's handsome reflection in the glass, attempting to make sense of the cold demeanor behind his warm words. His unexpected visit, unheard-of thanks, and an uncharacteristic edge of nervousness . . . something was definitely very wrong.

He cleared his throat. "I need you to locate someone for me. It's urgent, Kiku. You need to go today. Now."

The need for immediate action was not at all out of the ordinary. Many times, Kiku had found herself stopping whatever she was doing and jetting off to destinations around the globe. And though Takeo may have made it sound like a request, Kiku knew that, like the hundreds of times he sent her out before, it was a directive.

Takeo continued, "I left a file on top of the crate."

"I will get dressed."

"Wait." Takeo turned toward her, his arms dropping to his sides and his hands tightly balled into fists. He looked so anxious that she expected him to spring forward and grab her. "This is different. The target is thirteen years old. His name is Alex Harris."

Kiku stiffened. Takeo knew she never harmed children. She met his gaze and waited for him to explain.

"I need you to go to New York. Get his DNA. Leave the boy unharmed."

The assignment was atypical, but nothing about its goal should be causing Takeo so much discomfort. There was more.

"Can I offer you something to drink?" Kiku strode over to the bar in the corner and reached for the crystal decanter. She poured whiskey into a tumbler and smiled, exposing her sharp canine teeth as she offered him the glass. He tilted his head away, and she set the whiskey down.

She had always found it difficult to read him. They had trained together for years, but looking into his dark eyes was like trying to see the bottom of a river after a typhoon. If the eyes were indeed the windows to the soul, Takeo's soul was in constant turmoil.

He folded his hands behind his back again and stood ramrod straight. In his three-piece suit and crisp white shirt, he looked like he was about to address a board of directors. The muscles in his chiseled jaw flexed as he chose his words. "Alex Harris claims to be my son."

Kiku was surprised at the sharp pang that shot through her at the thought of Takeo having a child. It was as if he had reached into her chest, taken hold of her heart, and squeezed. But defining the emotion that caused her pain was difficult. *Jealousy? Longing?*

She pushed the thoughts aside, marched over to the crate, and picked up the file folder lying on top. She did the math in her head. If the boy was his—and he obviously suspected there was a real chance of that, or he wouldn't be sending her after a DNA sample—Takeo must have fathered the child when he was at university. That was a period of his life she knew nothing about.

The folder's top page contained Alex's personal information. The next page was a request for Takeo's medical history by a Dr. Rogoff. Beneath that were the educational records one might expect for a typical thirteen-year-old . . . as well as a rap sheet three pages long. It seemed that Alex was no honor student, and his extracurricular activities weren't honorable either. He was a juvenile delinquent and had already been convicted of a number of petty crimes.

A multitude of questions swirled in her mind. How had this Dr. Rogoff managed to locate Takeo in order to contact him? Why would Alex believe him to be his father?

"I do not see any information regarding the mother," Kiku said. "I need to know about her." She closed the folder, walked right up to Takeo, and stopped well inside his personal space. Had she been a man, Takeo would have leaned even closer, forcing her away. But she was definitely not a man, as evidenced by Takeo's struggle to look away from the areas of skin exposed by her loosely tied robe. His nose twitched slightly as the perfumed aroma of her bubble bath reached him.

"She is irrelevant. She's not involved in his life," Takeo answered.

No detail was irrelevant—much less something as fundamental as the identity of the boy's mother—but Kiku let it pass for now and stepped out of his space. "There is no photo of the boy."

"He doesn't have an online presence."

A thirteen-year-old without social media wasn't that out of the ordinary. The answer could simply be financial. Kiku doubted Alex possessed the electronic luxuries afforded to most American teens. She hadn't failed to notice that Alex had moved many times in his young life, from foster home to foster home. His last known address was a group home, but there was no guarantee that he hadn't been moved yet again. With no photo, how did Takeo expect her to identify him?

As if reading her thoughts, Takeo said, "I'm sure you'll figure out something." He nodded curtly and started for the door. He stopped beside the crate and ran his fingers along its edge. "A reward from my father."

Kiku masked the tinge of disappointment that the gift was not from him with a bow. "Please convey my gratitude."

Takeo stopped at the door but did not turn around. "You're to keep this assignment between you and me. No one else." He walked out without waiting for her reply. He didn't need to. He knew she would follow his orders.

When the heavy door clicked shut behind him, Kiku pressed the button next to it. She heard the faint sound of the thick steel bars sliding into place, securing her home once more. Then she turned her attention to Kenzo's gift, a simple wooden crate a little over three feet tall, fastened with shipping cord.

She retrieved a *kaiken*—another gift from Kenzo on a previous occasion—from a drawer in the hall table. Due to its plain wooden mount and ordinary sheath, the average person would probably think the dagger no more than a trinket procured from a tourist shop, but in fact it was an ancient weapon, over two hundred years old. Still, Kiku didn't display it as an artifact; she kept it in the drawer as a last-resort tool for self-defense. Ordinarily it would be a dishonor to use the beautiful weapon in this way, but if she was correct about the contents of the box, this knife was the most fitting tool to open it.

As the cord dropped away, the front panel of the crate fell forward, revealing exactly what she had expected: the suit of armor that would have been her burial shroud had she failed to rescue Jiro —if she was even awarded a burial. Now, it would serve as a trophy of sorts.

Kenzo had indeed been very generous.

As she set the front panel aside, she noticed an envelope sticking out from beneath one corner of the crate. Takeo hadn't mentioned a letter. Kenzo would never leave a paper trail of any kind, and besides, his messages were always more than clear, so there was no need for words. She tilted the box back and picked up the letter. Maybe it had fallen from the folder?

She examined the plain white envelope. There was no address or markings of any kind on either side. The flap was tucked in, not sealed. She flicked it open and removed the single piece of folded paper.

IF YOU ARE THE GIRL FROM JAYU-UI MAEUL, MEET ME IN LEAVELLS, VIRGINIA, MOUNT HICKS CEMETERY, ON APRIL 19—7:00 PM.

Kiku's hand shook as she retrieved her phone and pulled up the security footage of the front door. Her security was top-of-the-line and should have detected someone slipping the envelope under her door. Her heart pounding in her ears, she rewound the footage until just before Takeo arrived. She watched him set down the heavy crate and enter the security code at the front door. He propped the door open as far as it would go with his foot, lifted up the crate, and stepped inside, completely oblivious to the man behind him.

The stranger was tall, at least six feet, with a medium build. His face was obscured by a baseball cap. He followed Takeo at a distance and waited until Takeo was inside Kiku's apartment, before he darted forward, slid the envelope under the door, and hurried back down the stairs.

Cursing Takeo's lack of situational awareness, Kiku switched to the exterior cameras. The camera at the end of the street showed Takeo parking his Audi. It also picked up the stranger in the baseball hat. He had been waiting there, watching the building. Had Takeo not ditched his usual security detail, they would have surely caught the mystery mailman in the act. But Takeo had come alone and was clearly preoccupied.

Kiku rewound the video further and started playing it again when the man first arrived. She watched him pace back and forth nervously on the sidewalk until Mrs. Branson, her downstairs neighbor, left the building. The man crossed the street and spoke to the elderly woman for a few minutes. At the end of the conversation, Mrs. Branson pointed up to Kiku's apartment. The man nodded and waved to her before heading back across the street.

Kiku had fabricated a story of being an abused spouse in hiding from her ex-husband. Until now, the story had worked to keep the neighbors on guard for any suspicious people. Kiku made a mental note to have another talk with her neighbors.

She watched the footage again. The man kept his head angled down the entire time he waited, and because of the baseball cap, there was no clear shot of his face. It had always bothered Kiku that something as simple as a hat could thwart identification, even for powerful organizations such as the FBI. But, as with all things, she didn't complain; she did something about it. In this case, she'd placed a short statue just outside her door: two smiling, cherubic children holding a welcome sign. Inside that statue she had set up yet another camera, this one pointing upward.

A still image from that feed now filled her phone screen. It showed the man's face clearly. Caucasian, in his forties. He looked like a worried businessman who'd thrown on a baseball hat for a block party and appeared woefully out of place. His face was lined with stress; you'd think he was dropping off a bomb and not an envelope.

Kiku didn't know who he was, but she did recognize him. Two days earlier she'd gone for her run in City Lake Park later than usual, and as she sprinted past a food cart, the man, then dressed in a business suit, dropped his coffee. At the time, she arrogantly thought it was her new running shorts that had distracted him so, but as she replayed the moment in her mind, she realized it wasn't lust she'd seen in his eyes . . . but recognition.

And fear.

She stared at the face on her phone, trying to match it to one of the thirteen men who haunted her by day and made nightmares of her dreams. White, early forties . . . he might have been the man sitting near the far end of the table that day. The one with the nervous eyes. But she couldn't be sure. It had been twenty years since she'd seen them.

Forcing her heart into submission, she took three long, deep breaths. She had to be on the way to New York by this evening at the latest and had no time for anything else. Even this.

She tapped her phone, attaching the man's picture to an email. If this man was who she thought he might be, she could not get Alice involved. There was only one person she trusted to help her with this. He owed her a favor, but even if he didn't, he was the kind of man who would come to her aid, no questions asked. In her world, he was the rarest of men—one who kept his word. In a way, he was like her—orphaned, abused, and abandoned. But somehow, the hell he had gone through had forged a heart of pure gold in him, unlike the charred heart that sat in her chest. If anyone would help her, Jack would.

Under the picture she typed in the few details she had, and then she clicked on her list of contacts, selected Jack Stratton, and sent the message into the ether.

The paper crumpled in her tightening fist. April 19 was two weeks away. Two more agonizing weeks before she could find out what the man in the hat knew about Jayu-ui Maeul and her sister's murder.

4

Washington Heights, NY

Alex huddled with five other boys in the shadow of the school, all staring at the hair comb in Jaiden's hands. To Alex it looked like an ordinary comb—black plastic, about nine inches long—but Jaiden was claiming it concealed a knife.

"You're full of it, Jaiden," Darnell scoffed.

Jaiden grabbed the teeth of the comb in his left hand and yanked. A four-inch blade emerged from the end, eliciting gasps from the group.

Jaiden grinned proudly. "It's my dad's."

"If it's plastic, it's gonna be wimpy, like you," Darnell said, shoving Jaiden's shoulder for emphasis.

Jaiden bristled and held the knife up. "This thing's legit."

Everyone except Alex stepped back.

"Keep it low, man," Alex said, putting his hand on Jaiden's arm.

The boys resembled a flock of startled geese, their necks lengthening and their heads pivoting as they scanned the area for adults.

"It's hard, like metal." To demonstrate his point, Jaiden tried to bend the knife. It stayed rigid.

"There's metal inside it then," Darnell said. "There's *no way* it'll get through."

After a senior had been caught bringing a handgun into school earlier in the year, metal detectors had been installed. Naturally, that had led to creative experiments to see what would set them off. And those experiments had quickly escalated into challenges of teen bravado.

Jaiden stuck out his chin. "It won't set it off."

Darnell crossed his arms. "Prove it."

Jaiden's eyes circled the group and stopped on Alex, who could see his friend's emotions written all over his face. Jaiden wasn't scared—he was terrified.

"It's my turn," Alex said, holding out his hand. Jaiden covered the blade and handed him the comb.

"Bye-bye," Darnell said, waving. "The cops are going to be all over you and you're going to get expelled."

Alex's fingers tightened around the handle. He hadn't thought this through. If the stupid comb did set the metal detector off, he'd get caught. And Darnell was right: he'd get expelled.

Darnell laughed. "Smell that? He's crapping his pants!"

Alex stuffed the comb into his back pocket and flipped Darnell off. Everyone took a step back. No one flipped Darnell off. He was a year older than the others, six inches taller, and twenty pounds heavier. The giant of the schoolyard, feared by all.

Except Alex. They had fought ten times this year. And Darnell had won every fight—until the last one. Alex had hung on and the battle dissolved into an odd truce. The last thing Alex's face needed was a rematch, but he wasn't going to back down.

"Stop stalling," Darnell said. But his voice had lost some of its intimidation factor.

Alex hoisted his backpack and slung it over his shoulder. The backpack was made of clear plastic and see-through—another new security measure. He had been sent to the principal's office just yesterday for drawing a pirate skull and crossbones on the back of it with a black permanent marker. That had earned him a week of detention. Still, they let him continue to use it. Probably because they'd run out of the free backpacks for the poor kids.

He really didn't want to take another trip to the principal. He was there so often last year the secretary joked he had frequent flyer miles. But there was no turning back now. He jogged up the school's front steps and got in the line for the metal detector. He hoped that Dion was working the machine today instead of Janice McCreevy, or "McCreepy" as everyone referred to her. She ran the line like a prison guard and relished her power over the students.

Alex pasted a smile on his face, ran a hand through his thick black hair, and squared his shoulders. *No worries. Chill. And if I get bagged, I'll do what I always do. Lie.*

He exhaled. He didn't know where he had gotten his lying superpower from, but it came to him as naturally as breathing. And not the stupid boastful type of lies that got you called out in the cafeteria, but the kind that got you out of trouble. And trouble was a place where Alex frequently found himself.

Alex approached the front of the line. It was Dion manning the security station. That was good.

"What's up, Dion!" Alex called out, and gave the middle-aged man a salute. The guard kept checking the student's bag he was working on, but the corner of his mouth ticked up.

Alex's chest tightened; his relief at seeing Dion instead of McCreepy was short-lived. It didn't matter if Dion was more laid-back. It didn't matter if Dion liked him. If the comb in Alex's back pocket set off the metal detector, he was toast.

"What's happenin'?" Dion asked.

"Same old, same old." Alex handed Dion his backpack and stepped calmly through the metal detector.

Red lights flicked on and an alarm blared. Alex's knees wobbled and so did his voice. "I've got nothing on me."

Dion set Alex's bag on the table, picked up his wand, and motioned Alex forward. "Arms out."

Alex raised trembling hands and Dion waved the wand down Alex's chest. When it reached his front pocket, it beeped. Alex looked up at Dion, puzzled. Then he remembered his new find.

"My pen!" He thrust his hand into his pocket and pulled out the fountain pen he'd found that morning. Dion turned the metal pen over in his hands and frowned. "I found it. On the subway."

Dion pointed at the metal detector. "Go back through."

Alex swallowed. *What if it wasn't the pen that set off the metal detector? What if it was the comb?*

He stepped to the edge of the metal detector, careful not to go all the way back through, and started forward again, but Dion shook his head and waved him farther back.

Alex looked at the line of students waiting behind him. On a normal day, the hallway was so loud you wanted to cover your ears, but right now he could hear his heartbeat. A hundred eyes watched him like NASCAR fans hoping for a big crash. Feeling like he was about to jump into a pool, Alex held his breath, stepped all the way back, and walked through the metal detector.

No flashing lights. No alarm.

"Have a good day, Alex." Dion smiled and handed Alex his backpack.

"I will." Alex forced himself not to run or cheer or pump his fist as he headed for his locker. "You too," he called over his shoulder. He gulped in air like he'd just plunged down to the deep end of a lake and had only barely made it back to the surface.

Jaiden caught up to him at his locker and punched his arm. "You did it, man! I knew it. I knew it!"

The rest of the boys were there as well—except for Darnell. They all clapped Alex on the back and whispered how certain they were that the metal detector wouldn't go off.

The first bell rang, and everyone but Jaiden headed to homeroom. Alex was about to hand the comb-knife back to him when Wendy Miller walked up to retrieve her books from her locker next to his.

Alex leaned against the lockers and smiled at her. He was invincible. Maybe not bulletproof, but right now he had enough confidence to look the prettiest girl in school right in her hazel eyes and say hello.

"What's up, Wendy?"

Wendy got so close to Alex he could smell lilac. "Is it true?" the blond teen whispered. "Did you get a knife through the metal detectors?"

Alex's chest swelled. "Yeah. Do you want to see it?"

Her cute nose wrinkled as she said, "No, you moron."

Alex's confidence came crashing down, but he kept his eyes locked on Wendy's. "What's your problem? I made it through."

"Yeah, and every kid in school *knows* you did." Wendy crossed her arms and glared at him and Jaiden. Even mad, she was really cute.

Jaiden swore under his breath.

"*Now* you get it, brainiacs." Wendy shook her head. "Somebody's going to snitch. Get rid of it."

"I'll throw it away in the boys' room."

Jaiden grabbed his arm. "You can't! I have to get it back to my dad."

"Then *you* take it." Alex pulled out the comb.

Jaiden leapt back like Alex had offered him a snake. "If someone told the teachers, they know it's mine, so they'll search me, too."

Alex glanced at Wendy, but before he could say a word she said, "Don't even *think* about asking me for help. You got yourself into this stupid mess; I'm not getting blamed for it."

The second bell rang, indicating two minutes to homeroom. The hallway started thinning out fast.

"It's now your problem, Alex," Wendy said. "When are you going to learn to stop sticking your neck out for someone else?" she added before dashing down the hallway.

Alex held the comb out to Jaiden again, but his friend shook his head, his eyes growing wide. "Hide it."

"Where?" Alex's panic was rising. "There's no . . ."

Then he remembered Marquis's locker. Marquis had moved last month after getting placed in a foster home. His locker was still empty, and Alex knew the combination. Jaiden approved the plan, and while he kept lookout in the hall, Alex turned the lock with shaking fingers and yanked open the door. The bare locker offered no hiding places, so he pressed the comb into the narrow, recessed strip at the side of the door. Someone would have to know to search the locker and then stick their head all the way in to see it. Not perfect, but it would have to do.

"I'll get it at the end of the day," Alex said as he slammed the door shut and spun the lock. Jaiden probably didn't hear him. He was already halfway down the hallway, running for homeroom. Alex took off in the other direction. The hallway was empty now, and he was sure to be late, earning himself yet another detention.

He passed Wendy's homeroom and glanced in. If the disappointed look on her face wasn't enough to make him feel bad, when she held her hand to her forehead, her finger and thumb in the shape of an L, that sealed the deal.

5

Kiku sat parked across from the entrance to the high school, blending in with the parents impatiently waiting to pick up their kids. She had purposely parked in a spot where she could follow Alex on foot if need be or by car if he took a bus.

Kiku reviewed the information she had gathered and memorized about Alex Harris. Life had not been easy for the boy. He had repeatedly been passed over for adoption and eventually been assigned to foster care, where he had been shuffled from home to home every ten months on average. There had been complaints from many of the foster families, as well as some from Alex. He had been removed from his previous placement four months ago, in December, after reporting the foster father for inappropriately touching a young girl under his care. During the investigation, the father found out Alex was the one who reported him and broke Alex's nose. Alex's most recent listed address had failed to pan out, so Kiku had settled on finding him at the hub of teenage existence: high school.

Somewhere inside the brick building a bell rang, releasing the students, and the doors flew open like the gates of a prison torn asunder by its inmates. Young people, their faces glowing with newfound freedom, chatted happily as they streamed down the steps. Kiku scanned their features as they went and occasionally looked down at the one photograph of Alex she'd managed to dig up. But as she glanced back and forth between the photo and the kids exiting the building, her hope of finding Alex today was fading fast. The picture from the local paper was grainy and three years old; all she saw was a typical ten-year-old with a mop of dark, straight hair. The photo was taken on a field trip, and Alex was joking with a group of friends, his eyes closed, his smile wide. But no doubt he looked quite different today—

A teenage boy appeared in the doorway, and immediately a dormant maternal instinct flamed on somewhere deep inside Kiku.

If Alex wasn't Takeo's heir, he was his clone. Tall, handsome, and bursting with adolescent exuberance, Alex bounded down the stairs and high-fived a fellow escapee. Kiku added agility to his list of attributes. The two boys moved out of the stream of kids and took up positions leaning against a brick wall. The other boy was showing Alex a piece of paper, and the two of them laughed loudly. Alex's dark hair was in desperate need of a trim, and he was constantly pushing it aside as he read the paper.

Kiku zoomed in and started taking photos, keeping her phone low and as obscured as possible. Pushing her feelings for Takeo and his son aside, she focused solely on her mission as high-spirited teens continued to pour from the school and disappear into the line of waiting cars. A harried crossing guard looked like a whirligig in a typhoon as she tried to direct the chaos. Kiku merely watched and waited, prepared to follow Alex on foot. Seeing as he was in foster care, she doubted anyone was picking him up.

Along the curb in front of the school, the doors of a dark sedan opened and two men got out—a uniformed policeman and a man in a black suit, both extremely large, wide, and pumped with steroids. They planted their feet on the sidewalk and the stream of kids moved around them like water flowing around two boulders.

When the two men began to lumber toward the school, a school security guard hesitantly approached them, his face growing pale as he blocked the pair's progress. The man in the black suit flashed a badge and engaged the security guard in conversation for a moment. Kiku was unable to read his lips from her angle. The guard nodded and pointed directly at Alex, who was still leaning against the wall, talking nonchalantly to his friend.

Like hot sand blowing across the desert, a wave of heat rose up her back, prickling the skin on her neck. Coincidences didn't happen in her line of work.

Kiku got out of the car and closed the door, never taking her eyes off the men. The last thing she wanted was a confrontation with law enforcement, but were these men real police officers? The man acting as the detective had flashed a badge, but they were easy to fake; she had one in her own wallet. There was also a hacking pocket on his dark-blue jacket. Why would an American detective have a British-cut suit? As for the police officer, his uniform was complete with the tools of the trade—utility belt, flashlight, handcuffs, baton, taser, Glock—and his patches looked real.

Kiku felt the familiar chill seep into her veins. These men were imposters. The dead giveaway was the police officer. The service tags every policeman wears were missing.

How had they found out about Alex?

She shoved the question aside and focused on the matter at hand. They were making a move on Takeo's son.

Children swarmed all around her.

Kiku swallowed. She couldn't start a gun battle here without innocents being killed. But she needed to protect Alex at all costs. She followed ten feet behind. With their backs to her, she could take them both out now, but chaos would ensue. The men had to know that, too. They wouldn't try to harm Alex here, in the open. They would take him elsewhere.

The man in the suit stopped in front of Alex and flashed his fake badge.

Alex and his friend froze, the smiles tumbling from their faces.

Kiku stopped, pretending to scan the crowd for her child, ready to kill the men if necessary.

Alex, his hands shaking at his sides, turned to the police officer and said, "Let me see your ID."

The fake cop's mouth opened and closed before he looked questioningly at the man in the suit.

"Shut up." The man in the suit grabbed Alex by the arm and yanked him away from the wall.

"I don't have to go with you."

"Shut up," the man growled again, twisting Alex's arm behind his back.

A bottleneck formed in the sea of kids and hundreds of eyes stared. Then hands grabbed phones out of backpacks and pockets and held them up to tape the scene unfolding before them.

Kiku kept her face turned away from the cameras.

The fake police were quick-stepping Alex to their car while teachers and security tried to herd the other children away. The students were swarming like paparazzi, yelling and pressing in on Alex and the two men.

A slender woman in a business suit appeared on the school's steps and loudly announced, "If I see a phone, it will be confiscated!" Between teachers and security, they cleared a bubble around the sedan.

The man in the suit kept hold of Alex's arm as he opened the door. The fake policeman walked around to the driver's seat.

Kiku couldn't risk letting the men take Alex and following in her car. Not in rush hour. Not when they could simply shoot the boy and dump him out the door. But nor could she gun down both men in front of the school. No one but her knew they weren't real officers, and the initial police response to a school shooting would cast a net she couldn't escape.

The man in the suit pushed Alex's head down, shoved Alex into the backseat, and climbed in next to him.

Kiku prowled swiftly and smoothly toward the car, but the school security guard stepped in front of her, his chest thrust out, blocking her way.

"You need to stop right there, ma'am."

Kiku flashed her own fake badge and said, "Step aside."

"Sorry," the security guard mumbled and got out of her way.

Kiku grabbed the door before it closed. "Hold on! I'll catch a ride to the station with you guys."

The fake detective slid over a little on the backseat before his face contorted in confusion. "We're headed . . . downtown. We can't take you."

Kiku shut the door and pressed the barrel of her Glock against his groin. "Of course you can." With her other hand she pulled the fake detective's SIG Sauer from his shoulder holster. Grateful for the car's tinted windows, she pressed the SIG Sauer into the back of the driver's head. "Driver, eyes front. Both hands on the wheel—now. Go."

The driver pulled out.

The sedan eased out into the line of traffic being ushered along by the crossing guard.

Alex sat on the other side of the fake detective. He was pressed up against the door, his eyes wide.

The sedan reached the first traffic light and slowed to a stop. The driver's lips were set grimly and the vein in his temple throbbed as he glared at the rearview mirror, trying to silently communicate with his partner in the backseat.

Kiku tapped the Glock against the fake detective's thigh. "Tell your friend if he tries anything, you die. Guaranteed. Even if I miss your groin, I will hit your femoral artery and you will bleed out before the car stops. Driver, with two fingers hand your weapon back to me."

"Do it." The fake detective's voice rose high as Kiku applied pressure to the barrel of the gun against his groin.

The driver swore. He did as Kiku ordered.

"Who are you people?" Alex asked. He'd scooted as far away as he could, pressing himself against the door. "You're *not* cops."

"Stop talking." Kiku set the gun down beside her but kept her focus on the two men.

Alex opened his mouth, but a cold stare from Kiku cut off any further questions.

The car made its way down the street, the afternoon traffic in the city tight. The windows began to fog as the tension in the car escalated.

The driver looked into the rearview mirror. "I can't see out the windshield." His head moved almost imperceptibly down. "I need to turn on the defogger."

"Reach for that button and you die," Kiku said. "With your left hand, open your window one inch."

She kept the SIG Sauer aimed at the back of the driver's head as he opened the window a little and the sweltering air in the car whooshed out.

The car slowed as it approached a red light. A police car coming from the opposite direction stopped on the other side of the intersection.

Alex shoved his door open and tumbled from the car.

The fake detective tried to grab him.

Kiku slammed the butt of her Glock into his nose.

Across the intersection, the police cruiser's lights flashed and its siren wailed.

Kiku could kill both of the fake policemen in less than a heartbeat, but with the real police coming, she needed a different plan. She pressed her gun close to the driver's ear and fired three quick rounds at the grille of the police car across the intersection.

Kiku's adrenaline pushed into overdrive and everything moved as if in slow motion. She stuck her Glock under her shirt, opened the door, and leaped from the car, dropping both of the guns she had taken from the fake cops on the ground. She raised both hands as she ran away from the car.

"They have guns! They're *not* police!" she screamed, trying to sound hysterical as she dashed for the sidewalk.

Two real cops jumped from the shot-up police car and leveled their guns at the sedan. "*Show me your hands!*" they bellowed in unison at the men in the car.

Scanning the area for Alex, she spotted him darting between the stopped traffic toward her side of the street. While the police focused on the impersonators, Kiku slid through the gathering crowd toward Alex.

He had stopped on the sidewalk. His whole body was trembling and he was panting. When Kiku came up beside him, his eyes darted wildly, presumably searching for a direction in which to bolt. The last thing Kiku needed was for him to start screaming.

She whispered in his ear, "Alex, those men are not the police. They are after you and more are coming. Follow me." She grabbed him by the elbow, spun him around, and marched him down the street.

From every direction, police cars swarmed, their sirens wailing.

"You're not a cop either," Alex said. He resisted and Kiku tightened her grip. "Who the hell are you? Let me go." He squirmed and tried to wriggle free from her grip.

"You are not listening. They will kill you."

"I don't know you!" His voice rose, and people turned their heads.

"Your father sent me."

That shut him up. He stumbled, but his legs were moving now.

Kiku wrapped an arm around his back. "Keep walking. Not too fast. We are going to my car, by the school."

She wanted to get them out of the area as quickly as possible, but stealing a car wasn't worth it when her rental was just three blocks away.

"You know my father?" The hope in the boy's voice was so intense it was palpable. "Who were those men? Why did they grab me?"

Kiku forced herself to keep a steady pace while ignoring his questions. Her answers would mean nothing to him anyway. She doubted he knew who the Russians were, and nor would he understand why they wanted to kill Takeo's son. But she had a pressing question of her own . . .

How did the Russians find out about Alex?

Kiku and Alex hurried down the sidewalk toward her car, which was still idling. The flow of cars picking up students from school had slowed to a trickle. A few scattered groups of kids hung around the front of the building and on the steps; the recent excitement seemed to have mostly passed.

Kiku kept Alex on her right, her arm draped across his shoulders. To the casual observer, she hoped they appeared like a mother comforting a son who had just flunked a test or lost a big game.

A group of kids stopped talking as the pair passed them. "Didn't he get arrested?"

Pretending she hadn't heard, Kiku opened the passenger door and lightly guided Alex inside with a hand on his back. As she slid behind the wheel, two patrol cars sped toward them from down the street. One raced by, but the other pulled over to the curb in front of her, its tires screeching as it skidded to a stop. A policeman jumped out and raced up the steps of the school.

Kiku put the car into drive and banged a U-turn. If the police were at the school, they were starting to connect the dots. Soon they, too, would be looking for Alex. This mission should have been a walk in the park. She'd even planned on trying a well-reviewed Thai restaurant this evening. That would obviously have to wait, and she couldn't call Takeo with Alex in the car.

His head was against the window and his eyes were closed. He'd been pretty quiet since she'd mentioned his father had sent her. She'd said *father*, not *possible father*—and now she regretted it. After all, there was a possibility that his DNA would not be a match . . . and then what?

Turning on the dashboard GPS, Kiku located a shopping mall, and she parked in a deserted area at the far end of the lot.

Shutting the car off, she turned to Alex and handed him a stick of gum. "Do you have a phone?"

Alex shook his head and took the gum. She was tempted to pat him down until she remembered his absence on social media and the depravations of a kid in foster care.

Kiku opened her door. "I need to make a call."

Alex's face lit up like a child on Christmas day. The brooding teenager seemed to disappear as his brown eyes grew large and his hands balled into excited fists. "Are you calling my dad? You said he sent you, right? Is he looking for me?"

The naive innocence of his questions made Kiku feel that pang of regret again. *The kid thinks this is the day he's always dreamed about. The momentous day when his father comes riding in to save him from his crappy existence.*

She forced her expression into a neutral mask. "Stay here." Taking the keys, she shut and locked the door. Kiku walked several steps away from the car and dialed Takeo on her burner phone.

She tapped her pinky against the phone. Or what remained of her little finger, plus a small prosthetic to cover the top third, which had been cut off. The price she'd paid for a past failure. Kenzo had wanted her entire hand removed, but Takeo had interceded. And though Kenzo had relented, he made his son wield the knife.

As Kiku debated what to say, she pictured the storm in Takeo's eyes that day. She'd never seen him appear so conflicted—but you could only tell by looking into his eyes. His face had been so close to hers, she could have tipped her neck back and kissed him. She didn't, of course. Nor did she utter a sound as he did what he must.

"That was fast," Takeo said. "How did you get the DNA sample so quickly?"

"There has been a complication." Kiku forced herself to choose her words with even more caution than usual. She spoke several languages fluently—but in all of them, she had trained herself to speak deliberately, making the selection of each word a clear and conscious choice.

"Explain."

"Two men, dressed like a policeman and a detective, tried to abduct Alex from his school. I believe they were Russian."

"Did they succeed?"

"I intervened."

Takeo exhaled. "Do you need a cleaner?"

"No. They are in police custody—alive."

"And the boy?"

"With me."

"DNA?"

Kiku's fingers tightened on the phone. Takeo was missing what was truly important. "Not yet. Did you inform anyone else about Alex?"

There was a long pause on the other end of the line. Takeo must have realized the implication of the Russians beating her to the school.

"I have only confided in you," he said.

Kiku stopped pacing. Had the good doctor reached out to anyone besides Takeo?

"Get the DNA sample now and send it right out," he continued. "It will determine what we do with the boy."

"Understood. I will be in touch."

She clicked the phone off and glared at the black screen. Alex's doctor had contacted Takeo, asking for his medical history. Why? And how had he tracked down Takeo in the first place?

Kiku stalked back to the car. Alex looked like a teakettle ready to whistle, and sure enough, he immediately unleashed a string of uncomfortable questions.

"Did you talk to my dad? Does he want to meet me? Did—"

"He was not in," Kiku lied. "We are going to go someplace and wait for him to get back to me. Spit out your gum." She held out her hand with the gum wrapper unfolded.

"Why?" He continued chewing.

"The gum is expired. I do not want you to get sick."

Alex spit the gum into the wrapper in her hand and he wiped his tongue with his fingers. "Gross! Why'd you give it to me?"

"I apologize. I did not realize until now." Kiku tucked the gum wrapper into a pocket and backed out of the parking space.

Suspicion rose in Alex's eyes. "Where are we going? Didn't you talk to my dad?"

"I left a message. He will contact me. In the meantime, I need you to answer some questions." Kiku turned down the exit ramp. "What kind of doctor is Dr. Rogoff?"

Alex shifted closer to the door, his hand moving across the armrest and nearer to the handle.

"You can relax, Alex. I am not here to hurt you. As I said, your father sent me. He told me all about you." Kiku ran down the little information she knew about Alex's background—the cold details of where he had lived and gone to school. It wasn't much, but she hoped it would convince him she had a real connection to the person the boy craved most: his father.

When his hand shifted back into his lap, Kiku repeated the question. "What kind of doctor is Dr. Rogoff?"

Alex gave a one-shouldered shrug. "He's all right. A little stiff, but at least he's not boring, and he doesn't lecture me."

Kiku drove toward the center of the city. "That is not what I meant. Is he your general practitioner?"

Alex stared blankly at her.

"Dr. Rogoff contacted your father because he wanted to know your father's medical history. Why? Are you ill?"

"Oh." Alex rolled his eyes. "No. I didn't know he was gonna do that. He just thinks I'm a little nuts. Rogoff's my shrink. The court ordered it. Maybe he wanted to see if crazy ran in the family."

"Did you give him your father's name?"

"I don't know it."

Kiku's eyes narrowed.

Alex swallowed and moved closer to the door. "I don't. Maybe the doc got his name from my mother."

"Have you reconnected with your birth mother?"

"I tried, but I just know her name. Karen Harris. She lives in Anaheim. That's in California. I peeked into my folder once, but that was all I learned before I got busted." Alex crossed his arms. His fingernails scratched into the skin of his elbow, raising red streaks.

Kiku nodded but couldn't think of anything to say. She would have liked to know more about his mother, but he would not be able to tell her anything. The most urgent priority was to find a temporary base of operations. They drove quickly down Broadway. The diversity of the population and their preoccupation with their own busy, overworked lives made it easy for the seemingly ordinary middle-class mother and son to blend in.

The GPS displayed a list of nearby hotels, and she was beginning to formulate a plan when Alex asked, "What's my father's name?"

The intimate question that should never have to be asked packed an emotional wallop. She couldn't imagine not knowing such a basic thing about one's parent. Kiku was an orphan herself, but at least she had a few brief, pleasant memories of life with her parents. They were not to blame for what happened to her and her sister.

"I will explain everything to you," she said. Another lie. "But first, we need to get inside."

"I live on 188th Street."

"They may be watching your home. It is not safe." She pointed at the grand hotel on their right. "We will go there. The Royal Chalice. If you will do everything I say, I will let you get room service and a movie." She tried her best at a reassuring smile.

"What do you think I am, five?" Alex's hand rested on the door handle once more. "I'm not going anywhere with you until you tell me what's going on."

Kiku tried to relax her smile into a more natural grin. She wasn't good with children, but Alex wasn't a child. He was a street kid, and she understood street kids—she had been one herself. Her bribe had served only to make him more suspicious, because he had already learned that people didn't give things away without a catch. She didn't have time for a long discussion, so she decided to tell him some of the truth.

"The two men who came to your school were going to take you somewhere, cut off your head, and send it to your father."

Alex paled and his leg began to shake.

Kiku winced. It was more difficult dealing with a child than she anticipated. She didn't need him panicking; she would try a softer approach. "You would not have felt anything. They would have killed you first."

"Are you *serious*?" Alex's leg was shaking like a drummer doing a solo, his heel tapping off the floor of the car. "Me? Why? I didn't do anything to them."

"They want to send your father a message."

"What? What did *he* do to them? When are you going to tell me who he is?"

"All of that is irrelevant. The point is, there are more of them and they are looking for you."

Alex's eyes darted up and down the street and he slid lower in his seat. "Shouldn't we go to the cops?"

"The police will not be able to protect you from these men."

Alex stared down at his feet and his fingers tightened on the door handle. "You really expect me to just go with you?"

"Yes. And I will explain everything about your father when we are in the hotel," Kiku said—another lie, but it was necessary. Alex had come with her this far at the mere mention of his father, and she hoped that dangling the same carrot under his nose would get him to go into the Royal Chalice Hotel.

She pulled up in front of the revolving doors and a valet hurried over.

"Get out," she said to Alex.

Kiku grabbed her leather bag from the backseat and handed the valet her keys and a twenty.

"Do you need assistance with your bags?" the valet asked hopefully.

"No, thank you." Kiku filled out the valet slip with the name Sato—the equivalent of Smith in Japanese.

The doorman held the large glass door open for them and waited while Alex stood frozen in the middle of the sidewalk, his eyes darting down the street.

Kiku put her hand on his shoulder and leaned close so she could not be overheard. "If you run, and they find you again before I do, you will die. Or you can come with me, and I will tell you about your father over a hamburger."

Alex eyed her suspiciously, but she knew he would come with her. He was scared, but somewhere among the fear that clouded his eyes, the fire of determination gleamed like a beacon.

She had also heard that adolescent boys were almost always hungry.

Alex nodded.

Kiku walked into the hotel, and Alex followed. She was eager to get him off the street. Once those two Russians failed to return, they were certain to send more.

6

Kiku stood in the bathroom of the hotel room. On the counter was an open bubble-wrapped envelope and a plastic vial. She dropped Alex's gum into the vial, closed the top, placed it inside the envelope, and sealed it. She checked her phone. The courier would be in the lobby in twenty minutes.

She exited the bathroom. Like a wild squirrel trapped indoors, Alex was scurrying around the large suite, poking his head inside every cabinet, looking for some hidden find. When he opened the mini fridge, he whistled, wiping his mouth with the back of his hand.

Kiku understood his reaction. In a city group home, food was kept under lock and key.

"All this is free?" Alex asked.

"No, I will have to pay for what you take from the refrigerator or the bar."

He held up a candy bar with a mix of disgust and awe. "Ten bucks?" He put it back and picked up a bag of chips. "Five dollars. And look, the water is twelve. It's gigantic, but *twelve dollars*? Who could buy this . . .?" He trailed off and gazed at Kiku. "You must be loaded."

Kiku tipped her head to one side. He had guessed correctly; she was compensated very generously for her work. And her payments weren't the only source of her wealth. It was Takeo's policy that the spoils went to the victor—and on several occasions, her targets had expired with large amounts of cash and valuables close at hand.

"You may have the candy bar and a soda," she said.

Alex grabbed the candy bar from the fridge like a dog snatched a bug from the air. As he opened the package, he looked over his shoulder at her. "You're not going to tell me to wait until after dinner?"

"It is your body."

A knock sounded on the door.

Kiku pointed to the bathroom. "Get in there."

"I don't have to go."

Her eyes narrowed, but Alex stood his ground, standing stiffly, his arms crossed.

Kiku wasn't used to having to explain herself, and nor was this the right time to start. She grabbed his arm, yanked him off balance, spun him around, and shoved him into the bathroom. "Stay in there and do not open your mouth or someone may put a bullet through it."

Alex's mouth fell open as she shut the door in his startled face.

The young woman with a slightly soiled apron and tired eyes was pleasant and quiet as she set out the room service tray, which Kiku greatly appreciated. She didn't understand why people felt the need to talk so much. Still, Kiku had plenty to worry about. Each time the young woman lifted a silver lid, Kiku was ready to draw her Glock. She had to stop watching so many spy movies; they were making her paranoid. If this woman wanted to kill Kiku, she could have attached a shotgun underneath the tray car and done the job without even having to draw and aim.

At least, that's the way Kiku had once done it.

After receiving a generous tip, the waitress found her voice and began chatting nonstop. She offered to come running no matter the time. She didn't stop talking until Kiku escorted her to the door and locked it behind her.

"You can come out now," Kiku announced.

Alex shoved the door open but stood his ground in the bathroom. "I'm not going anywhere until you tell me who those guys who tried to grab me were and who my father is."

Kiku strolled over to the bed. "Are you really going to eat your hamburger in the bathroom?" She took the silver cover off his plate. "The smell in there might affect your palate."

Alex scowled. He licked his lips as he eyed the hamburger, then crossed his arms.

Kiku was surprised he wasn't taking the bait. She considered dragging him out, but decided on a different tactic. "I need to know about you, Alex. What do you know about your mother?"

"Nothing." Alex shrugged. "I told you, I never met her."

Kiku opened a can of soda, poured it into a glass, and set it down next to Alex's hamburger. "French fries are best hot." She tapped the silver dome with her red nail and it rang like a bell. "You know her name is Karen Harris. And you said she lives in Anaheim. Did you try to look her up after you found that out?"

Alex sighed and walked over to the table. He grabbed the plate and glass and walked back to stand near the desk. "Yeah. I found her on Facebook."

Since Alex spoke with his mouth full of food, Kiku had to work on deciphering his response. "Are you certain she is your mother?"

Alex took a long swig of soda and wiped his mouth with the back of his hand. "Yeah. I catfished her." He took another bite of burger and again began speaking with his mouth full. "That's where you create—"

"Close your mouth while you chew, please. I am aware of what catfishing is. You created a false identity and befriended her?"

"Yeah." Alex swallowed. "The file said Dr. Rogoff had talked to her. He had some of her medical information. No allergies or history of family mental issues."

"Who did you pretend to be when you reached out to her?"

"Dr. Rogoff's secretary." Alex sat down in the desk chair. "But she figured out I was lying and wouldn't answer my question."

"What was the question?"

"I asked who my father is and how I can get in touch with him. She said she already provided that information to the doctor, then ghosted me. When I asked Dr. R., he wouldn't tell me. Said it was against the law because I'm a minor. That's total bull. How's it right that my doctor knows my father's name and I don't? That's seriously messed up. So—what *is* my father's name?"

Kiku picked up her bag. "I cannot tell you yet."

Alex's brows knitted together. "Oh, my freakin' *word*. You're such a liar. You said if I came here with you, you'd tell me."

"I never said I would tell you *immediately*." Kiku eyed the boy. He appeared ready to break for the door and chasing after him would bring unwanted attention. She debated whether to tie him to the bed, but dismissed the idea. He would surely yell his handsome head off. "First, I need to prove that you are my employer's son. Once I have done that, then I will tell you." Alex opened his mouth to protest, but Kiku cut him off. "In the meantime, I am keeping you alive."

"What more do you need to prove it? My mother already told Dr. Rogoff who my father is. If Rogoff reached out to your 'employer,' the guy's my dad." Alex stuffed a French fry in his mouth, but it did nothing to stop the string of mumbled swears which poured out.

"Perhaps Karen Harris is mistaken."

"I think she'd know who the father . . ." The tops of Alex's ears turned crimson. "Well, how are you going to prove it?"

"There are tests for such matters."

"Like one of those paternity test things? Wait, is that why you took my gum?"

Kiku studied Alex. He seemed more intrigued than angry. "You are very intelligent." She walked over to the table and picked up the package she'd prepared. "I will send your DNA to a lab, and if it is a match"—she forced herself to omit *which I am certain it will be*—"I will reveal his name to you. If he is not your father, then there is no reason for you to know my employer's name."

Alex stuffed more French fries in his mouth and mumbled something she couldn't make out.

"I cannot understand you if you speak with your mouth crammed with food."

Alex chewed and swallowed. "I said, he *is* my father."

Kiku tore a sheet from the little notepad on the desk and began to fold it into a tight square. "Why are you so sure?"

"I always knew my dad would be someone cool, like James Bond. And he sent *you* and you were totally badass in that car. You scared the crap out of those two guys and you got away from them *and* the cops.

Now I'm in a fancy hotel eating a hundred-dollar hamburger, so yeah, I'm pretty sure the guy who sent you is my dad, and maybe he really is like James Bond after all." For the first time, Alex smiled. "Besides, why would my mother lie?"

Kiku stood up, switching the package to her other hand. "Just stay here. I will be back in fifteen minutes. Don't answer the phone or the door. If you hear anyone, hide."

She picked up the "do not disturb" sign and exited the hotel room, pulling the door shut behind her. The lock clicking into place provided her with no relief. The door would do nothing but momentarily stall the Russians if they found Alex again. She placed the small paper square she'd folded between the door and frame, then hung the "do not disturb" sign on the handle.

Kiku would have to learn more about this Karen Harris. All she knew was that she lived in Anaheim and had gone to the university with Takeo. Did she know who Takeo was? Had he confided in this American that he was the heir of the Nakumora dynasty and the son of the leader of the Yakuza?

Kiku doubted it.

If Karen Harris knew who Takeo *really* was, and the power he wielded, she should have been too afraid to even whisper his name.

7

Kiku handed the envelope to the courier along with a hundred-dollar tip for delivering the package as quickly as possible. The middle-aged man with a pot belly ran out of the hotel faster than he must have moved in a long time.

She scanned the lobby as she made her way back to the elevators. Weary businessmen, two families on vacation, and a few bored but eager-to-help staff went on with their lives.

Kiku stepped inside the elevator, pressed the button for her floor, and stared at her reflection in the metal doors as they closed. Her eyes were darker than usual. So was her disposition. From the time Takeo had given her this mission, she'd been on edge.

Why?

Since she was a child, she'd performed hundreds of tasks that were far more dangerous. Even with the Russians' involvement, she'd faced worse odds.

Something was very wrong. She sensed it. Like an animal before a tsunami, the warning system that existed inside her on an instinctual level was blaring its siren and flashing its lights.

But she couldn't fly away to the safety of the mountains.

She had a mission.

The elevator doors dinged open. She strolled down the hallway and stopped. The folded piece of paper lay on the carpet.

Pulling out her Glock, she pressed her back against the wall and tried the door. It was locked. She slipped her card into the reader. A beep was followed by the mechanical sound of tumblers turning.

She cracked open the door with her foot and scanned the room. She slid inside, sweeping the room, the barrel of her pistol following the line of her eyes. The TV was still on. A few scattered French fries remained on Alex's plate, but the main room of the suite was empty.

She rushed into the bathroom.

The boy was gone.

Had the Russians taken him while she was gone?

She rushed back into the suite. Nothing was amiss. The lock on the bathroom door was intact. If the Russians had come to get him, the boy would have at least locked himself in the bathroom, wouldn't he?

Kiku opened the mini-fridge and swore. The Russians hadn't kidnapped the boy. He'd left on his own. She was certain.

All of the candy bars were gone.

Kiku's anger burned as she drove up and down 188th Street. She had let Alex get away. A mere child and he slipped through her fingers. She was guessing that he would head home, but Alex had said only that he lived on 188th Street; he never gave a specific address. All she could do was drive, block after block, looking for a house with a group of kids gathering outside. The plan was thin at best, but it was all she had.

She tapped the shortened pinky of her right hand against the steering wheel—her permanent reminder that in the Yakuza, excellence is not simply something to strive for; it is a requirement. She would receive no mercy if any harm were to come to Alex. This mistake could cost her her life.

Not only was Alex Takeo's son, but he was Kenzo's grandson and first-born heir.

Kiku tried not to think about the samurai armor, but the image forced itself upon her. She could see herself wearing it, a human target suspended in the beautiful garden. She could almost feel the impact of each arrow and warm blood running down her legs.

She gripped the steering wheel and shoved the macabre nightmare from her mind. If she didn't locate Alex—if the Russians got to him first—she was dead. Simple as that. It didn't matter how many she'd take to Hell with her. The Yakuza were a tide you could hold back for only so long.

She slowed down when she spotted a group of kids hanging out on the steps of a triple-decker. As she watched, a black teenager in a baseball cap came hurrying out the front door, past the others. A silent alarm rang in Kiku's head, and she studied the young man to figure out why.

He was dressed in jeans, high-top sneakers, and a bright-red shirt, with a backpack slung over his shoulder. He looked like an ordinary teenager. And then he shifted the pack to his other side, revealing the Magic Marker skull-and-crossbones hand-drawn on the back. She had seen those markings before—on Alex's backpack.

It would be too difficult to follow the teenager while she was driving, so Kiku pulled over to the curb, shut off the car, grabbed her purse, and stepped out. She immediately noticed the unmarked police car parked opposite the house, and turned her face away from it.

Alex was smart. Too smart for his young age, but he was a street kid. She had told him the Russians were watching his house. He must have asked a friend to bring him his belongings.

The boy walked quickly down the sidewalk, looking around like a frightened bird, staying in the shadows of the buildings. Kiku followed some distance behind him, easily keeping pace. She wasn't worried about him seeing her; the sun was low in the sky and directly behind her, so even if he looked back—which he didn't—he wouldn't see her through the glare. Unfortunately, this also meant she couldn't see whether she was being tailed.

If the Russians were watching the foster home, would they even have noticed the teenager leaving with Alex's bag? Not likely. The Russians were known more for brawn than for brains.

At the entrance to the city park, the teen sped up. He passed the basketball courts and headed straight for a skate park in the corner where several teens zoomed around wooden ramps and a dozen more watched. Kiku scanned the faces in the crowd. She saw Alex immediately. His black hair and defiant stance gave him away, even from a distance.

Alex's friend waved, the shadow of his arm stretching out across the grass, the fingertips touching another shadow. But that second shadow was circular, moving at the same pace as he was. Kiku looked up. The fading sunlight gleamed off the rotors of a drone. Alex's friend *had* been followed, and he had led them straight to Alex.

Kiku broke into a sprint as a white delivery van barreled into a parking lot beyond the skate park. Her long legs stretched out, her feet kicking up little puffs of dust as she raced across the field.

The van sped up and jumped the curb. All heads turned to stare at the vehicle tearing across the grass. Someone screamed and the crowd scattered.

Alex hopped over a waist-high chain-link fence and ran for the buildings across from the park. Kiku hurdled the fence with ease.

"Leave me alone!" Alex yelled. He cut right, trying to escape her grasp.

She caught his arm and pulled him forward. "RUN!" She didn't have time for more explanation.

The van smashed through the chain-link fence. One panel of the fence got caught under the front tire. The vehicle jerked hard to the right and stalled.

Alex pulled against Kiku's grip. "Let me go!"

"No. They will kill you."

Gunfire echoed off the buildings as bullets ripped into the ground around them. One of the Russians had got out of the van firing a Mini Uzi. Still over fifty yards away, he couldn't possibly make an accurate shot firing that fast, but with that much lead in the air, he just might get lucky.

Alex stopped fighting Kiku, but now his legs seemed to have stopped working. She dragged him over the small retaining wall that separated the park from the buildings. A utility road ran behind the shops here. Trash cans, pallets, and dumpsters stretched out in either direction.

Three more men got out of the van and dashed across the grass after them. An image of charging Russian bears flashed in her mind as the musclebound men quickly closed the distance.

Alex had gone limp against her side. She wrapped her arm around his waist and dragged him over to the first door she came to. She shoved Alex inside and pulled the door closed behind them.

"Where are you hit?" Kiku scanned the boy for signs of blood, but didn't see any. "Where are you hit?" she asked again. She spun him around and ran her hands over his head and back.

"I'm . . . I'm . . ." Alex's eyes were huge and his legs shook. He sagged against the wall and started to slide down it.

Kiku grabbed him and pulled him upright. "Are you just scared?"

"Those were real bullets . . . they were shooting at *me*!" Alex's voice cracked.

"And they will kill you if you stop running. You're not hit. Now move!" Kiku spun Alex around and shoved him down a hallway that led to a commercial kitchen.

Four men in chef uniforms stopped cooking and stared.

"You can't come in here," said one.

"Sorry." Kiku pushed Alex forward. "We got lost."

"Go back out the way you came!"

"A dog chased us. We can't go that way."

The back door flew open with a bang. Kiku drew her gun and spun around. She pressed Alex against the wall and moved in front of him, her sights set chest-high on the end of the hall.

One of the bulky men lumbered through the door. His Mini Uzi was held low and his head was still pivoting when Kiku pulled the trigger. She could easily kill him, but wounding him would better serve her purposes. Her first round struck him flat in his right shoulder. The Mini Uzi dropped from his hand. The second round hit his left thigh and dropped him to his knees.

The kitchen emptied as the horrified staff jostled each other to get out, and by the sounds of chaos in the dining room, Kiku didn't have much time before the police were alerted. Still, this was an opportunity for answers that she couldn't pass up. She sprinted to the fallen Russian, dragging Alex behind her. She planted her foot on the Uzi and dragged it out of his reach.

"Who told you about the boy?"

"Go to—"

Kiku shot the man in his other shoulder. "The next two bullets go through your wrists. You will never lift a weight again."

That got his attention. Like a cat rolling onto its back to signal surrender, the man tipped his head back, staring up at Kiku and exposing his throat.

"I don't know. No one told me. I swear—"

Kiku slammed the butt of her gun into his temple. His head jerked to the side as he slumped against the wall. Leaving him alive might slow down the other Russians because they'd have to carry their wounded comrade. She grabbed the Mini Uzi, popped the clip, and dropped the gun back onto the floor.

"Who are you?" Alex asked, his eyes wide.

"Move." Kiku seized his hand and ran for the dining room. They pushed through two swinging doors into a dimly lit Italian restaurant, now deserted. Kiku started to pull Alex toward the front door, but stopped when a police car skidded to a halt just outside the restaurant.

"Back!" Kiku spun him around.

Having the police after them was far worse than the Russians. They were a coordinated force that could seal off the area. And she had no desire to harm a police officer. Not after meeting Jack Stratton. Jack had saved her life, and more important to Kiku, something about the man had changed her. That change now limited her options for dealing with the police.

They ran back into the kitchen. Kiku pointed at a row of chef coats. "Put on one of those jackets." She quickly slipped one on herself, then grabbed a roll of plastic wrap. "Follow me!"

She sprinted back down the hall to the unconscious Russian, put the unloaded Uzi back in the man's hand, and used the plastic wrap to tie it in place.

A voice shouted from the dining room. "Police! Come out with your hands up!"

With the police so quickly on the scene, the other Russians would be making a hasty retreat, which meant the rear exit was now Kiku's safest egress. But first she needed to slow down the police.

She slapped the Russian hard across the face. His eyes opened and his legs twitched. She grabbed him by the hair and started pulling him to his feet. "Get up."

The man lumbered awkwardly against the wall.

"Tell your friends to leave the boy alone." Kiku shoved him into the kitchen.

He lurched away from her. With Kiku standing in the hallway, he only had one way to go, toward the swinging doors and the dining room. He limped forward, glaring over his shoulder. "You're dead! They're gonna carve your heart out!"

Taking Alex by the hand, Kiku hurried down the hallway and over to the exit door. She peered outside. The alley behind the restaurant was empty.

The sound of the swinging doors smashing open echoed down the hallway.

"Drop the gun!" the police shouted.

Kiku pictured the Russian, confusion spreading across his face as he held up his hands, unable to let go of the unloaded Uzi plastic-wrapped to his wrist.

The thunder of bullets echoed down the hallway.

Kiku draped an arm around Alex's shoulders, and they raced down the alley.

A policeman rounded the corner of the building directly in front of them. He took one look at them in their chef coats and waved them on. "Go! Go! Go!" He raced past them, focusing his attention and aim on the rear door of the restaurant.

Kiku and Alex moved quickly toward the main road in front of the restaurant. Two police cars were parked out front, and a half dozen more were speeding in from both directions. Kiku spotted the kitchen staff gathered in a clump to the left, so she headed right.

"Keep your head down."

Alex tilted his chin against his chest and Kiku had to steer him sideways to keep him from running into a telephone pole. Sirens wailed behind them and a crowd began to gather across the street.

After a block, she removed her chef jacket. "Give me your coat."

Alex hesitated, so Kiku yanked the jacket off him like a magician pulling a tablecloth.

"Hey!" Alex said.

Kiku tossed the coats in a trash can, grabbed his shoulder, and pulled him forward.

Even more police cars were now racing to the scene. They had cut it very, very close. As the cop cars passed, Kiku forced herself to look at them with what she hoped was a curiously concerned expression. She was a passable actress, but only because conveying emotions was mostly physical. Actually *feeling* emotions was another thing entirely. She couldn't remember ever feeling scared in the way that had sent the kitchen staff fleeing from the restaurant, for instance. Most emotions had been seared out of her. The ones that attempted to come to life, she killed.

As they approached a gas station, Kiku slowed, tightened her grip on Alex, and drew him closer. She was adept at stealing cars, and the fastest method was a jump-and-run. She was amazed how many people, even in the city, left their keys in the ignition. It was like offering your car to a thief on a silver platter.

A dented red Honda Civic zipped up to the pump. The car lurched to a stop and the driver hopped out and hurried inside. Kiku headed straight for the driver's side. Sure enough, the keys were still in the ignition. *Silver platter.*

She yanked open the back door. "Get in. And get down."

Alex got in the back as she slipped into the driver's seat. She started the engine and tore out of the parking lot, with no sign of the car's owner in the rearview mirror.

Alex started to sit up.

"Lie down."

"I'm not a dog," Alex grumbled. But he obeyed.

"The Russians, and now the police, are looking for a woman with a boy—"

"I'm not a boy. I'm thirteen," Alex snapped.

Kiku stopped at a traffic light. The police would contain the scene of the shooting, then fan out. They would be long gone before that happened.

But as the light changed and Kiku drove farther away, she was far from at ease. The delicate hairs along the back of her graceful neck prickled defensively.

The Russians had used a drone to track Alex's friend. It was an intelligent tactical move. Subtle. Cade Novikov's gang wasn't known for either attribute.

Someone else, someone smart, was hunting Alex.

Kiku needed to discover who and fast.

8

LaGuardia Airport

Kiku abandoned the stolen car in long-term parking and hurried out of the garage with Alex at her side. With each step closer to the airport, the boy's expression changed. By the time they reached baggage claim, he was smiling.

"I've never been on a plane," he said. "Where are we going?"

It was a fair question, and Kiku didn't have an answer. She was considering Florida, but she would most likely choose whatever flight was leaving the soonest. She needed to get in the air and out of the city as quickly as possible. And until she had the DNA results, she wouldn't be taking Alex anywhere near Takeo.

"Don't we get tickets first?" Alex continued. "Why are we at baggage claim?"

"To claim baggage. Wait here."

Kiku left Alex beside the escalator that led up to the main floor while she headed over to the baggage carousel. A flight had just come in, and suitcases were making their way around the conveyer belt.

When a nondescript black suitcase made it past all the tired travelers, Kiku pounced. She pulled the suitcase off the carousel, extended the handle, and returned to Alex, carefully circling the outside of the crowd. With everyone's attention on the carousel, it was a simple snatch-and-grab, but the last place she wanted to get caught stealing was the airport.

She ripped the luggage tag off, grabbed Alex by the arm, and started up the escalator.

Alex leaned in so close that his breath tickled her ear. "Why did you steal a suitcase?" he whispered.

She glared at him, making him lean away and stumble backward. "Appearances." She tightened her grip to keep him from falling.

Alex winced. "Ow. Let go."

The woman ahead of them on the escalator looked over her shoulder.

Kiku forced a smile at Alex. "Be careful, honey," she said, trying her best to sound motherly.

Alex wrinkled his nose and made a face.

At the top of the escalator, Kiku pulled Alex over to the board listing departures. There was a flight heading to Florida in an hour. That would work. She had a safe house in Naples.

"Listen to me. We need to get out of the city—now. If anyone asks, we are going to Florida . . ." Kiku paused to think of a cover story that Alex could convincingly repeat. She decided to stick as close to the truth as possible. "To visit your father. You are my son. But let me do all the talking."

Kiku ran down the script in her mind. She'd say the visit was concerning a custody dispute and Alex was upset and didn't want to talk about it. That should avert questions, and because of his age, he didn't need ID to fly across America.

Alex looked up at a TV, and swore. Kiku followed his gaze and silently repeated his expletive. Alex's picture was on the TV, accompanied by an Amber Alert. There was no way she was getting him on a plane now.

"Sit on this bench and face the wall." She yanked out her phone, opened Solitaire, and handed it to him. "Keep your head down." She squatted in front of him so he was looking directly into her eyes. Alex's lips pressed together and he tried to look away.

"Those men, and perhaps others, will kill you," Kiku said. "I will *not* kill you. I *will*, however, break your legs if you try to run again."

Alex paled. "Is that supposed to make me feel better?"

"No. It is supposed to make you cooperate." Kiku stood.

"Where are you going?"

"I need to pick up a few things."

She took in three hundred sixty degrees of the main concourse, where hundreds of travelers streamed past the shops, fast-food outlets, and news kiosks, and then Kiku marched up to the closest store that sold snacks, souvenir mugs, and NYC snow globes. She purchased a baseball hat and an in-flight blanket. Sunglasses might attract attention, so she decided against them.

Snapping the tag off the hat, she beelined past Starbucks and Swarovski for the wheelchair she'd spotted next to an abandoned luggage cart and rolled it back to Alex. He was so focused on the phone screen, he didn't even look up when she approached. Kiku frowned. It would be so easy to kill him.

"Get in," she said.

When Alex saw the wheelchair, his mouth fell open. "You stole a wheelchair?" His voice rose. "Somebody wasn't in it when you took it, right?"

"Of course not. Shut up and get in. Here." She put the hat on his head, pulling the brim low, and draped the blanket over his legs. "Keep your head down and your mouth closed."

"Did you get us anything to eat?"

"You just had a hamburger."

"I'm hungry."

Kiku opened her purse and took out a candy bar. She gave it to Alex and held her hand out for the phone.

Alex scowled at her. "I'm in the middle of a game."

"Fine. Keep your head down and play."

Towing the stolen suitcase while pushing the wheelchair was awkward, but it provided an adequate cover. People quickly looked the other way, afraid they would be asked for assistance or accused of gawking.

When they reached the parking garage, Kiku noticed two police cars slowly moving up and down the rows and immediately headed for the Hertz car rental office. The line was short, and they even got to move up when an elderly couple in front of them allowed them to go ahead. Kiku's fake IDs were flawless and the rental went smoothly. The clerk offered to bring the car to the door for them, and Kiku quickly accepted.

When the clerk drove up in a white sedan, Kiku wheeled Alex to the passenger seat. "I got you, sweetie," she said. She scooped Alex up in her arms and lifted him out of the chair.

"What are you—" Alex started to ask, but her fingernails digging into his ribs cut off his protest.

She slid him into the passenger seat, then met the clerk as he rounded the back of the car. She exchanged a twenty-dollar tip for the keys in his hand, then smiled and thanked him again. His eyes widened, but it wasn't due to the large tip. The clerk was staring at Alex in the passenger-side mirror. Alex had removed his baseball cap and was busy brushing his hair and checking his reflection.

"Thank you," Kiku said quickly. She smiled and waved.

But the clerk's stiff back and tight lips told her the damage had been done. He must have recognized Alex from the Amber Alert.

She moved into the driver's seat and drove to the exit booth. In the rearview mirror, she saw the clerk watch them go for a moment before scurrying quickly back inside.

Kiku grabbed Alex's hat off his lap and jammed it back on his head.

"Hey!" he protested.

"A disguise only works if you keep it *on*. The clerk recognized you. Keep your head down."

At the booth, Kiku put on a friendly smile as she handed over her paperwork. The bored-looking woman merely glanced at the papers. She pressed the button to raise the gate. The phone beside her started to ring, but she ignored it. "Have a nice day."

"You too." Kiku drove through the gate.

A line of cars waited to exit the rental garage and turn onto the main road. Directly in front of Kiku's car, a woman driving a gigantic SUV crossed over the anti-theft spikes and stopped to scan the confusing array of signs. She appeared lost but really had only one way to proceed because of the spikes behind her. Kiku hoped she noticed the warning sign: DO NOT BACK UP—SEVERE TIRE DAMAGE.

She didn't. When the SUV's reverse lights came on, Kiku laid on the horn and pointed at the sign. The woman gave Kiku the finger, but at least she put the car back into drive.

The two cars in front of the SUV pulled out onto the main road. The SUV would be next, and then it would be Kiku's turn. Her fingers impatiently tapped the steering wheel as her tires passed over the spikes. She pulled up behind the SUV and waited.

The sound of another vehicle crossing over the spikes announced a car arriving behind her. She looked in her rearview mirror and saw a police cruiser roll to a stop a foot away from her rear bumper.

"Cops," Alex whispered.

Kiku's fingers stopped their dance. She was trapped between the cops and the SUV. The SUV was twice the size of her rental; Kiku wouldn't be able to budge it, let alone push it out of the way. She eyed the narrow space between the SUV and the cement wall beside it. She'd never fit.

The SUV finally pulled out into traffic. At the same moment, the police car's blue lights flashed and its sirens blared to life.

Kiku slammed the car into reverse and stomped on the gas. She smashed into the front of the police car, then kept the gas pedal to the floor as she pushed the cruiser backward into the spikes. She shifted into drive and pinned the accelerator to the floor.

Horns blasted, cars swerved, and tires shrieked as frantic drivers jammed on their brakes.

The police raced after them, sparks erupting from the rear wheels as the shredded rubber flew off. The cruiser slid along on its rims and slowed to a stop, blocking off the traffic behind her.

Alex turned around in his seat, staring out the back window, a grin on his face. "That was awesome!"

"Get your head down," Kiku snapped. She doubted the police would fire a shot with a possible kidnapping, but she wasn't taking any chances.

"Their tires must have hit those spike things. You're so lucky."

"Luck had nothing to do with it. I did." Kiku swerved into the breakdown lane and punched it.

The police already had a description of her car, so there was no point in going slow. The guardrail and the grimy brick buildings beyond it were a blur beside them as she kept the gas pedal pinned to the floor.

She took the first exit, then slowed. Her best chance was to double back into the city and make her way to the safe house the Yakuza had on Warren Street. She grabbed her phone from Alex's lap and dialed.

It rang three times before Hwan answered. "Three Guys Morgue. You bag 'em, we tag 'em."

"Forty minutes out with a burner," Kiku said. "I will call again when we are a block away."

All humor left Hwan's voice. "West corner."

Kiku hung up. "Be ready to get out," she told Alex.

"Where are we going now?" Alex asked in a voice perilously close to a whine.

"You will see. Keep quiet. I must concentrate."

Though Kiku had a good sense of direction and had been in New York many times, she paid close attention to the GPS and stuck mostly to the residential streets, driving south through Queens, which seemed endless, then into Brooklyn, and to the Williamsburg Bridge, which would get her back into Manhattan and not far from Warren Street. She had no doubt the police had added her car description to the Amber Alert. On top of that, since it was a rental, they could track the GPS signal in the car. However, that would take time to coordinate.

Kiku's concentration and Alex bouncing in his seat like a puppy out for a ride made for a conversation-free trip into lower Manhattan, for which she was grateful.

When she reached the safe house, she circled around to the alley in the back. The old moving van was ready, and so were Hwan and two men waiting beside it. Kiku drove the sedan up the ramps into the back of the van. The tin walls of the van were perfect for blocking the LoJack on the rental until Hwan's men could torch it.

As soon as Kiku and Alex had hopped down from the van, Hwan and his men removed the ramps. Hwan's men started to close the doors.

"Do not close up the van yet," Kiku said. "The police may have locked onto the GPS signal already. They will look where the signal cut out and we do not want police coming here. Drive a few blocks before you close the doors."

The men nodded, got into the cab, and drove off.

Hwan crossed his arms over his belly. The portly Korean's eyes almost disappeared because of his large smile. "I let *Oyassan* know you were heading this way."

Kiku was grateful Hwan had followed protocol and used Takeo's title, *Oyassan*, in place of his name. Still, she would have preferred to have contacted Takeo herself. But Hwan was again following protocol.

"Nice to see you again." She reached into her purse and tossed Hwan a candy bar.

His smile sloped. She normally brought him two.

Kiku pointed at Alex. "He ate the other one."

"I—I didn't know it was yours." Alex moved fractionally closer to Kiku and away from the scowling man.

"I hope you liked it," Hwan snapped. "They're Swiss. Best chocolate in the world."

Alex nodded nervously. "It was really good. Seriously, she gave it to me."

Hwan shook his head and looked at Kiku. "Judging from your call, you need an exit?"

"Later." Kiku took Alex by the hand and started toward the back of the row house. Things were getting increasingly complicated—and fast. And she was worried about how much Alex had already learned. He'd met Hwan, seen the safe house. Did he know too much?

If she was wrong and Alex wasn't Takeo's son . . . would Kenzo let him walk away?

9

Warren Street safe house

Hwan jostled Alex's elbow and pointed at the couch in the living room, which was outfitted with anything an avid gamer could want, including cup holders and extra speakers built into the sides of the cushions. "The controller is charged and the latest *Call of Duty* is in the console. Don't touch my saved games." Kiku noted that Hwan hit exactly the right tone, somewhere between an order and a host's welcome.

Alex's face lit up as he picked up the controller. "Thanks! I won't."

Kiku and Hwan went into the kitchen and closed the door.

Hwan opened the refrigerator, took out a beer, and held it toward Kiku. "So, who's the kid?"

Kiku waved away the beer. "No, thank you." She leaned against the stove and listened to the house. It was quiet. That wasn't normal. Ignoring Hwan's question, she asked another: "How many men do you have?"

Hwan cracked his beer and dragged back a chair. When he looked up at Kiku, his expression had hardened. "Ten, but Takeo sent four to the Jade and four to the docks, and left only two here with me. The Russians are hitting us hard. They used a tugboat to tilt the *La Rosa*, and three shipping containers were dumped in the bay. Cops and feds descended on the boat and the captain panicked and torched over a million in knock-offs."

"What's going on at the Jade?"

"They're having a concert tonight and a waitress found a couple of grenades hidden in the VIP section. We're at war, whether it's been formally declared or not. You picked a bad time to visit." Taking a large sip from his beer, he asked, "Who's the kid? Yours?"

Kiku resisted the urge to kick the table into Hwan's chest. "I need to keep him safe. We will only be here one night."

She hoped that wouldn't be too long. With only her, Hwan, and two men on hand, the safe house didn't feel very safe. There was war all around, and this place could easily turn into the Alamo.

"You look . . . wary." Hwan smiled. "Don't worry. I've upgraded security. I was going to wait until we exchanged pleasantries, but I can give you the nickel tour now if you'd like."

Kiku reached into her purse and tossed Hwan another candy bar.

"I thought you gave the second one to the kid."

"I did. I normally buy two for you and one for myself."

"You were holding out on me." Hwan laughed and unwrapped the bar.

"And for good reason. You are the *last* person I would tell I had a candy bar in my purse."

Hwan took a bite and let out a satisfied moan. "Smart thinking. You want half?"

Kiku shook her head.

"You don't have *another* one in there, do you?"

Kiku narrowed her eyes. "If you try to go through my purse, you will lose a hand."

"That's not a no."

"The tour, Hwan."

Like a little kid, Hwan folded the wrapper over the remainder of the chocolate bar and put it in his pocket. "Entrance and egress doors have been reinforced, and we added keypad entry."

"Change the codes."

"Now?"

"Yes, as soon as we are done with the tour."

Hwan looked like he was about to say something about that but thought better of it. "Front and back windows have all been replaced with bullet-resistant glass."

In the row house to their left was one of Takeo's bookkeepers, and one of his lawyers lived to the right. "Are the neighbors home?"

"The Morgans are, but Jerry's on vacation." Hwan pointed with his beer to the right. "Alaska. Who in their right mind goes to a place where freaking polar bears are the only thing tough enough to live there?" He lifted his arms dramatically. "And if he wanted snow, Canada is only—"

"Sweep both houses."

Hwan froze with his arms fully extended. "I'd have to run that by Takeo."

"I am not making a request." She was well aware of the respect both the bookkeeper and attorney were due, but they still lived under Yakuza rules, and if Alex's safety necessitated inconveniencing them by making sure their homes were secure . . . so be it.

Hwan nodded. "I'll ask. But seriously, who *is* this kid?"

Kiku liked Hwan; she had let him ask that question twice without consequences. A third time . . .

Hwan quickly waved his hands in front of him, sending a few drops of beer flying out of the bottle. "Forget I even brought it up. I like all ten of my fingers, every one of 'em. And you're getting that look again. Come on. Let me show you the other additions."

He led her down the first-floor hallway and stopped beside two wooden panels in the wall. The last time Kiku had been at the house, there had only been one panel and it covered a hidden weapons cache. But she wasn't surprised there was something new; Hwan was endlessly working on the place. With Hwan in charge, the safe house was like *This Old House* and *Guns & Ammo* got together for a fixer-upper project.

"Check this baby out." Hwan grabbed the new panel and pulled it out. Mounted on a retractable arm was a Browning M2 .50-caliber machine gun on a turret. "It rotates three hundred sixty degrees. It'll lay waste to anything that tries to come through those doors."

"And you would explain its use to the police how?"

Hwan shrugged. "Home defense. I'll let Jerry worry about that." He tipped the gun up and slid everything back into place. With the panel closed, the hallway appeared normal. "Wait till you see the vault."

Kiku was familiar with what Hwan called the "vault"—actually a souped-up safe room. The original owner of the home, a banker, had a gigantic safe installed there in the 1920s. The safe had long since been removed, but because it was so heavy, that section of the house had been reinforced with steel girders and beams, which made it the perfect location for the enormous weight of Hwan's vault, complete with bulletproof walls and floor.

Hwan led Kiku upstairs and down the hall to the safe room, which was a bit smaller than Kiku remembered—the back wall was closer. And in that wall was a thick sliding door crafted to appear to be an ordinary closet.

Hwan gestured to the sliding door. "We upgraded the vault by adding . . . a vault," he said with a chuckle. "It's a room within a room, but I'm telling you, the whole block could explode and anyone in there is going to be fine. It'll even have its own air system when I'm done." Hwan puffed out his chest.

"Is it fully functional?"

"Almost," Hwan said. "I'm still finishing up the electrics. It'll have its own mini-generator."

"Almost is unfortunate timing. Right now, it has no air and no electrics. What other systems are offline?"

"Just those." Hwan cleared his throat. "So, for now . . . the locks don't work."

Kiku frowned. "An unlockable vault is an oxymoron."

Hwan shrugged. "The inner vault won't lock, but the big one still does. And I'm finishing up this week."

"We will only be here until I get word from Takeo. The boy stays in this room until we leave."

"Got it. Can I get you something to eat?" Hwan asked.

"Yes, please. I have not eaten a proper meal in days."

"Well, *I* consider pizza and beer a proper meal."

They both chuckled. Hwan was one of the rare people who could make Kiku laugh.

"That actually sounds really good right now," she said.

"A couple of Hwan's famous Italian pies coming up!"

She followed Hwan down to the kitchen and sat down. It could take days for her to get the DNA test results back. When she did, she would be faced with another dilemma—what to do with the boy?

Life in the ranks of the Yakuza was a cursed existence. Was it even really living? Made up of the outcasts, they survived—but they were constantly hunted by the authorities, their enemies, and their own consciences.

What kind of life would Alex have in the Yakuza? Takeo would try to protect him, but with Kenzo as his grandfather, what chance would the boy have? He was an innocent. His heart was still pure. Kenzo would be his ruin.

And if Alex was not Takeo's son? What then? She couldn't bring him back to his foster home. No matter what the DNA results were, the Russians believed he was Takeo's son and they wouldn't hesitate to kill him.

Through no fault of his own, Alex's world had been blown apart. He could no longer return to the old one, and if he knew the cost of entering the life of the Yakuza was his soul, he'd never choose the new one.

He wouldn't get to choose.

Kiku would be making that decision for him. If the DNA proved Alex was Takeo's son, she'd take him to Chicago whether he wanted to go or not.

There was no real choice. It all came down to the DNA.

But one thing was certain—Alex's life would never be the same.

10

Hwan finished setting up the Xbox in the spartan safe room while Alex sat on the bed sulking.

Kiku leaned against the doorframe, puzzled by the brooding teen's behavior. "It is the same game up here."

"I was in the middle of a match," Alex said, fiddling with the unconnected controller. "You didn't have to unplug it."

"I asked you to shut it off."

"And I asked you to wait a second." Alex thrust his chin out defiantly.

Hwan chuckled.

Kiku cast a sideways glance at Hwan. "Do not encourage his disobedience."

A warning alarm buzzed through the house.

Kiku drew her gun, but Hwan held out a cautioning hand and took out his phone. "It's probably Tommy and Gin. You had me change the door code." He flipped the phone around, revealing a camera feed. Two men stood waiting on the back steps. "I'll go let them in."

"I will come with you." Kiku looked over her shoulder at Alex. "Stay here. And keep this door shut."

"Uh-huh," Alex mumbled, his focus on the TV, his fingers rapidly pressing buttons on the controller.

As Kiku and Hwan started down the stairs, Hwan nervously wiped his hands on his jeans. "Listen, I'm always on full alert when you're in town, but I take it this is like DEFCON-1?"

"Yes." They reached the back door of the row house, and Kiku pulled Hwan to a stop. "Let me see the camera feed again."

Hwan held up his phone. Tommy, the man who'd moved the van, was standing on the rear steps, along with the other man, who had ridden with him. Both were puffing away on electronic cigarettes.

"Do you have another camera view of the outside?"

Hwan pressed a button and the screen switched to an overhead shot of almost the entire block. "It's mounted on the old antenna."

Satisfied that the men were alone, Kiku holstered her gun. "Do not tell them the new code."

"Why? They're my best men. I trust them."

Kiku handed him the phone. He met her dark gaze.

Hwan held up his hands. "Okay, no codes. I wasn't suggesting you were wrong. I was just trying to say that they're . . . I'll just shut up and do whatever you say." He managed one of his goofy grins.

"If I did not like you," Kiku said, "your next fix-it project would have been much harder with your arm in a cast."

"I'll try to keep my mouth closed. But for a fat guy who likes to talk, that's a little tough. You know what helps? More chocolate."

Hwan's phone rang. He looked at the screen and tipped his head toward the door. "It's Tommy again. Can I let them in?"

Kiku nodded. "Yes. But keep them downstairs."

Hwan let the men in and told them the new rules. They didn't appear pleased, but neither man so much as glanced at Kiku. There were few rules in the Yakuza, but those rules were strictly followed, because the penalties for breaking them were so harsh. And though these men did not know Kiku, she was certain they at least knew *of* her.

They were wise to keep their mouths shut.

Her phone buzzed in her pocket. It was Takeo. She turned her back on the men and walked down the hallway toward the front of the house.

"There was a shooting at a skate park." Takeo's voice was deeper than normal, and each word was clipped. “Were you involved? Are you alright?”

“I had another situation with the Russians. We are at the safe house now.”

“The shooting was all over the news. So is Alex’s picture. It’s dated, but every police officer in the city is looking for you two. Bring the boy to me—the penthouse in Chicago.”

“Without the DNA results, it would be unwise to tell the boy anything.”

“Karen said the child is mine.” There was hope in his voice.

Kiku had known Takeo since he was nine and she was eleven. His uncle had taken Kiku over to Kenzo’s house. Kenzo had requested the two children practice martial arts together. But the practice session had quickly turned into a battle. Even at her young age Kiku realized the fight wasn’t really between her and Takeo. Kenzo wanted to prove his son was a better fighter than his half-brother’s student.

Takeo was stronger and outweighed her, but Kiku was far more skilled. She’d soon beaten him bloody, but the boy kept getting to his feet. Each time she’d knock him down, but he kept rising.

None of the men moved to stop it. Instead, they cheered the blood sport like Romans at the Colosseum.

Takeo made it to his feet again. His knees wobbled and he could barely raise his arms, but he did.

Kiku lowered her guard. She wouldn’t kill the boy.

Takeo ran at her in fury. He knocked her to the ground and got her in a rear choke hold. His mouth was so close, his blood splattered her cheek when he whispered, “If you stop, we’ll both be beaten. Me for losing. You for quitting.”

“Then what do I do?”

“Win.”

Kiku broke the hold and struck Takeo hard enough to knock him out. As she stood there staring at the boy lying in the dirt, something inside her bloomed. It wasn’t love. Love had died with her sister. It was something primal that rose within. The boy needed her. Inside, he was good, but in this world the good die. On his own, that would be his fate—dead and bloody in the dirt. Unless she protected him.

She realized her second purpose that day. She would avenge her sister and protect the boy.

Takeo was no longer a child, but in some ways he was naive. He had slept with Karen Harris and now he believed her unquestioningly in regard to Alex's paternity.

"Karen said the child is mine," he repeated.

"She may be mistaken." *Or lying*, she thought.

"He will be safer here. Leave in the morning." Takeo's order snapped Kiku out of her thoughts. "Tell the boy nothing." Takeo hung up.

Kiku gritted her teeth. Alex had gone along with her up until now in the hope that Kiku would tell him who his father was. She doubted that would be enough to get him to accompany her to Chicago.

Footsteps sounded on the stairs above, and Alex stuck his head over the railing. His large brown eyes, wide, he looked surprised to see her staring up at him. "Is there any chance I could get something to eat?"

"Did I hear someone asking for food?" Hwan called out from the kitchen. "Hwan's famous pepperoni pizzas will be ready in ten minutes."

"That's dope!" Alex grinned, and for a moment Kiku felt as though Takeo himself were grinning down at her. They had the exact same smile. "Call me when the pizza's ready!" Alex shouted, and he thundered back up the stairs.

"I'll bring them up!" Hwan called back.

Kiku looked down at her phone. In a few hours she and Alex were expected in Chicago, and she had no idea what would happen when they got there. She had never harmed a child, and nor would she, but she was part of ruining this boy's life. What hope did he have for normalcy now?

She studied her reflection in the blank phone screen. It was no wonder that most people feared her. As she looked at her black eyes, it was like she was getting a glimpse of the darkness that lurked inside her. Some people think that every sin costs you a piece of your soul. After her first kill, it was a little easier and hurt her a little less. It took her a long time to figure out why. It was because each time, her victims

—as wicked as they were—had taken a part of her soul, until there was nothing left.

Kiku was suddenly reminded of the *onryō*—a type of vengeful spirit that harmed the living. These spirits looked like people, but they were empty inside. Hollow, like a shadow.

Like her.

11

Alex looked up from his video game as Kiku entered the room. He beamed, and her guilt grew.

The boy was on the run in a strange house with a ruthless woman, but the simple offer of pizza and a video game had somehow made everything okay. Was his home situation so sad that this was literally that much of an improvement?

"You want to play?" Alex asked. He nudged another controller that lay at his feet. "We've got time for a game, but when Hwan gets here, I promised him a chance."

"No, thank you."

Alex pressed his lips into a frustrated grimace. "I died." He frowned up at Kiku. "Why do you do that?"

Kiku crossed her arms. "I did nothing."

Alex focused on the screen as his game restarted. "You just did it again. Every time you talk, you give me this look like you're going to smack me or something."

"I have not struck you—yet."

"*That's* what I'm talking about. Normal people would say something like, 'I'd never hit you.' Not, 'I haven't whacked you yet but just wait.'"

"I would not hit you unless it was necessary."

Alex pushed back his hair and stared up at her like she was an alien.

"Are you hearing yourself?"

Kiku sighed and tried to smile. "Do not give me cause, and you have no concern." What did the boy want her to do—lie?

Alex shrugged. "Well, chances are, if you hit me, you'll get yourself jammed up."

"And why is that?" Kiku regretted asking the insolent teen the moment she spoke.

Alex sat up straighter. "If my father's gone to all this trouble, he has to think I'm his kid. And since he's your boss, he probably doesn't want you smacking his son around." Alex crossed his arms across his chest and smiled.

He is more observant than I gave him credit for.

"Who's up for a game?" Hwan called out as he climbed the stairs, two sodas in one hand and a bag of chips in the other. "We playing co-op, or do you want to get your butt kicked?" He stepped inside and flopped down on the floor like an overgrown teenager.

"Can we go through the campaign?" Alex asked. "It's split-screen."

"Hell yeah." Hwan ripped open the snack bag and set it between them.

As the two started to play, Kiku turned and headed for the stairs. She needed to plan their trip. The sooner she dropped Alex off, the better.

It was close to midnight when Kiku went up to check on Alex and Hwan. The electrified crackles of simulated gunfire filled the room as the two blasted away at virtual bad guys, their fingers dancing over their controllers.

"Just a few more minutes," Alex begged.

"We're on the last level," Hwan added. He grimaced. "On your left! Left!"

"I need ammo!" Alex called out.

Kiku had no intention of sending him to bed; she preferred that he stay up and tire himself out. It would make bundling him into the car and taking him to Chicago in the morning that much easier.

"Stay up as late as you want," she said.

"All right!" Alex and Hwan high-fived.

Kiku walked down to the living room, where Tommy and Gin sat on the couch watching an old action movie. She had no interest in the movie and wanted to go over her route to Chicago again, so she went to the kitchen, sat at the table, and took out her phone.

A news alert in her notifications caught her attention. A bomb had gone off near city hall. She clicked on the livestream. A reporter was giving her report, surrounded by a sea of police cars and emergency vehicles. It looked like every cop in the city was there. As the camera panned the scene, the hairs on the back of Kiku's neck rose.

Above the racket of the video, an electric alarm chirped. It took her a moment to place the sound. The front door. Someone had just entered an invalid code.

Kiku drew her gun and stepped into the hallway. Tommy was already at the door and peering out the peephole. He reached for the door handle.

"*Stop!*" Kiku shouted. But it was too late.

A shotgun blast knocked Tommy backward, his arms spreading wide. He landed on his back and didn't move.

Two men stormed through the door, the first holding a ballistic shield, the second a combat semi-automatic shotgun. In a millisecond, Kiku processed the situation. A professional hit team was sweeping the house, heavily armed and wearing full ballistic tactical gear. She might as well just throw her pistol at them for all the good it would do against that kind of armor and weaponry.

She ducked into the kitchen as more boots thundered into the hallway and another shotgun blast sounded. She didn't need to see the result to know that Gin, too, was now dead. Kiku slipped into the pantry and watched through the crack in the door as a different pair of men—these too in ballistic armor—swept through. Dressed in all black, the two men moved like one beast, the man in front carrying a shield and the one behind armed with a combat shotgun. The shield alone was enough to stop anything less than high-caliber rifle rounds. Add in the body armor and there was no way she could hurt them. But they could hurt her; the combat shotgun could cut her in half. They only had to glance in her direction, notice the slightly ajar door . . . and it would all be over.

Hiding in the darkness, Kiku took hold of her fear and slowly began to strangle it. Choking down all emotion raging inside her, she forced herself to exhale slowly and softly. She would not give these men the power to scare her. Kiku controlled Kiku—no one else could make her do or feel anything.

The men finished sweeping the kitchen and opened the back door, letting another pair of similarly armed men into the row house. Then all four moved into the hallway.

Kiku's heart raced and her mind scrambled to catch up. Six men. Full tactical. Between the alarm and the sound of the shotgun blast, Hwan would have been alerted and sealed the door to the safe room. But given the precision with which this team had hit the house, they were sure to be equipped with something to breach the safe room door.

And with the bombing at the convention center, the police would be delayed in responding to any emergency calls.

Kiku could see through the open rear door to the darkness and safety of the backyard. Most people in this situation would flee. They'd dash into the night to live another day. Kiku wasn't like anyone she knew. For her, living was the difficult part of life. This was simple. Fight. She'd either win or die, but there was no choice anymore. A sense of peace washed over her.

The echo of many boots climbing the stairs rumbled through the safe house.

As she slipped into the kitchen, the whine of drills began upstairs. They were drilling holes for explosives. If she didn't do something, they would blow the door, sweep in, and kill both Hwan and Alex.

Kiku crept to the back door, closed it, and locked it, then did the same with the front. If this crew did have backup, that would slow them down. She tiptoed down the hallway and stopped just before the stairs. Tommy lay dead at her feet, his headphones resting at an odd angle on his head. She peeked up the stairs. Two men had placed their ballistic shields at the top, forming a wall protecting the men as they worked to drill through the safe room door.

A head-on charge was useless anyway. Her Glock was too low a caliber to penetrate their armor.

Kiku looked to the panels on the wall and smiled. There was a more powerful weapon in this house. She yanked Tommy's headphones off and moved over to the wall. She pulled open the new panel and the Browning M2 .50-caliber machine gun swung out. It was too heavy for her to lift—but she didn't need to.

The second-floor hallway was above her, and at the end was the safe room. Six men were now standing directly over her. Kiku set Tommy's headphones over her ears and tilted the machine gun toward the ceiling. The Browning roared to life. Debris and bullet casings filled the air as Kiku methodically tore apart the ceiling, moving her aim down the hall. Even with the headphones on, she felt like she was inside a bell being struck with a giant hammer. The kick of the weapon was so hard her teeth rattled, but she didn't let up on the trigger.

The thuds of the bullets into wood changed to steel clangs when she reached the end of the hall. She had struck the flooring of the safe room. Kiku ran the gun back up and down the hallway twice more before she stopped firing, yanked the headphones off, and took the stairs two at a time. She couldn't hear anything through the ringing in her ears, but one look told her what she needed to know. A half dozen dead men littered the hallway. The bullets had gone all the way through the ceiling of the second floor, the roof, and everything in between, revealing glimpses of the hazy night sky and stars beyond.

"*Hwan!*"

The door to the safe room cracked open and Hwan peered out with an Uzi in his hands. "Alex is okay. He's in the smaller vault."

"You should not have opened the door." Kiku stepped over the corpses. "They might have captured me and forced me to call out to you."

Hwan laughed. She was surprised how genuine it sounded, and amazed that he could laugh when surrounded by such carnage. "As if someone could ever make *you* talk. I take it you used the Browning? I told you it was awesome!"

Kiku peered down at the full-face helmet of one of the attackers. She reached down to lift his tinted visor for a clue to the identity of these men. An explosion rocked the row house so violently she had to brace herself against the wall to keep from falling.

"*In!*" She pushed Hwan back into the safe room and slammed the door shut behind them.

"It's not over?" Alex asked.

"Don't worry," Hwan said, "the police are going to be here any second."

"No," said Kiku. "They will not. A diversion was created uptown. Any police response will be too late."

Alex's lip trembled. "We're trapped."

"No, you're not." Hwan stepped into the smaller vault room and grabbed the air vent. "This leads to the roof crawlspace. I haven't plated it yet, so it's still just insulation and plywood. All the row houses are connected. You could escape through one of the neighboring units."

Kiku grabbed Alex's shoulder. "Go!"

Alex looked at the small opening, then back at Hwan. "How's he going to fit?"

"He will be safe here," Kiku lied.

All three of them were knocked off their feet by another explosion —this one clearly just outside the safe room door. Kiku grabbed the wall and pulled herself to her knees. The pounding in her ears was now a roar. The backup team had arrived with military-grade firepower. The safe room door was bulging, its top bent and misshapen. She didn't know what they'd hit the door with, but it wouldn't hold against another blast.

Hwan grabbed Alex and pressed him toward the opening. "You have to go. I'll lock myself in here, in the small vault. I'll be fine."

Alex nodded and scurried into the vent.

Kiku patted Hwan's shoulder. It was a feeble gesture, but it was all she could think of to honor him. Their eyes met, and Hwan's watered. He was a man who loved life, and he knew his was about to end. With no lock on the vault, he wouldn't be able to hold them off for long.

As Kiku climbed into the vent, another explosion rocked the building.

Crawling ahead of her in the darkness, Alex began to cry.

12

Kiku used her phone to light the way as she and Alex wriggled through the tiny crawlspace.

"There's a wall!" Alex's voice trembled.

"Get on your stomach." Kiku shimmied over his back to get in front of him. She tore away the pink insulation, revealing a plywood panel.

"Move back." She twisted around in the tight confines. Using the heels of her shoes, she kicked and the old plywood board gave way. She held up her phone, the light revealing the adjoining house's crawlspace, which was identical to the one they had just passed through.

They continued on through several houses. Each time they reached the separating wall, Kiku kicked out the boards, opening access to the next building. Their passage had a toll—nails stuck out from the ceiling and occasionally the floor, and several deep scrapes marred Kiku's back and arms—but she scurried forward at a frantic pace. She knew they had precious little time, and not just because of the armed men behind them. The police would soon be on the scene. The bombing at the convention center had drawn them away and distracted them for a time, but the explosions outside the safe room would change that quickly and the entire block would soon be under lockdown.

After the fifth crawlspace, she pulled back the insulation to reveal a brick wall. They'd reached the end house. She felt along the wall, moving toward the street, until she hit drywall. Her heel quickly busted through it, creating an opening into a master bedroom.

"Stay," she whispered to Alex as she wriggled through the hole and into the room.

The house was quiet, but sirens blared outside. She'd taken too long. She pictured a sea of emergency vehicles and law enforcement swarming the streets below. It would be next to impossible for them to get out. Unless she came up with a ruse.

A quick scan of the master bedroom revealed that the homeowner was a single man. The closet was filled with men's clothes, there were no female toiletries in the bathroom, and only one side of the king bed had been slept in. The house was completely silent. With all the chaos outside, it was obvious no one was home.

"Come out." She reached in and helped Alex into the room.

His eyes were red-rimmed and a nasty scratch ran across his cheek. He shook some plaster dust out of his hair. "Where are we?"

"We reached the last house."

From the look of things, the man who lived here had left in a hurry when he heard the sirens. The blankets were thrown back and his wallet and keys were left on the nightstand.

"Strip down to your underwear," Kiku said, peeling off her own shirt.

Alex stood there with his eyes wide and his mouth agape as Kiku kicked off her shoes and pulled off her pants.

"Strip. Now," Kiku ordered. She grabbed one of the button-down shirts from the floor and pulled it over her head.

Once Alex was standing awkwardly in only his underwear, she pulled a blanket from the bed and tossed it to him. "Wrap that around you."

She fanned another blanket over the bed and piled their clothes and shoes into the middle of it. She wrapped it in a bundle, then grabbed the wallet and car keys off the nightstand. Taking Alex's hand, she said, "Do not say anything, and keep your head down."

"Wait. We're going outside? Like this?" Alex clung to the blanket around him like it was a life vest. Judging by the mortified look on his face, Kiku didn't have to worry about him talking. The kid just wanted to crawl into a hole and hide.

She dragged him down the stairs. As she peered out the front window, her heart hammered in her chest. It was as bright as day with all of the police cars and fire trucks lining the street. She took a deep breath, yanked the door open, and rushed outside, crying.

She was always surprised by how quickly she could fake-cry. She couldn't remember the last time she'd shed real tears, but she could let loose manufactured waterworks in an instant. And she poured it on now.

Sobbing into her hand, Kiku dragged Alex behind her. An officer directed her toward a group of EMTs and civilians gathered next to two ambulances. A different policeman waved them on and pointed down the block, away from the safe house—which, she saw, was on fire. Flames licked the evening sky and great billows of black smoke rose heavenward.

The officer's voice was kind but firm. "We need you to keep moving. Please go to the EMTs."

Kiku nodded, releasing Alex's hand to press the unlock button on the keys she'd stolen. Across the street, the headlights of a silver Lexus flashed. She changed direction and hurried toward it.

Another policeman moved in to block her off. "We're keeping everyone on this side of the street."

"My son needs his inhaler. My car's right there." For emphasis she pressed the unlock button again to flash the headlights. Alex started coughing and wheezing. It sounded so real, she cast a concerned glance backward.

"Okay. Okay." The policeman waved them on.

As they neared the car, Kiku said simply, "Passenger seat."

Alex nodded and moved around the vehicle. Kiku tossed the bundle of clothes into the back, then slid into the driver's seat, pulled it forward, and started the engine. Another fire truck was racing up behind them and threatened to block them in. Kiku backed up quickly, cut the wheel hard, and darted onto the side street just before the fire truck reached her. She was relieved to see the fire truck would block any other cars from following them.

They had escaped.

For now.

Slowing a bit, she looked over at the boy. The reflection of the streetlights sparkled in the tears rolling down his cheeks. "Hwan lied," he whispered.

Kiku looked away, steeling herself to handle the onslaught of another person's emotions. "Why would you say that?"

"He told me all about that vault. I just remembered what he said about the electrical system. He was going to put it in this weekend. The door won't lock without it. He lied."

Kiku stopped at a red light and stared straight ahead. She'd known Hwan for a decade, but she didn't feel any sadness at his death. In fact, she felt—nothing. Like a flower slowly dying, each time in her life that she experienced pain, another petal fell off. Her hardened heart was turning to stone.

"Why did he do that?" Alex asked.

"So you would leave."

"I know *that.*" Alex's tears stopped. The muscles in his jaw flexed, and his hands balled into fists. "I mean, why did Hwan give his life to protect *me*? Why do all those guys want to kill *me*? Who the heck am I?"

Kiku opened her mouth, but Alex continued, cutting her off. "I don't care if it's true or not, I just want to know who they think my father *might* be."

She nodded sharply toward the backseat. "Get dressed."

"Not until you tell me."

Kiku's hands tightened around the steering wheel. "No."

Alex slammed his fist against the door panel. "Tell me!"

"I cannot. Do you really want to sit there naked?"

"Fine." Swearing softly, he snapped off his seat belt and spun around in his seat. It took him several minutes to get dressed and fasten his seat belt again. When Kiku saw a convenience store, she pulled around to the back and changed her clothes. They were on their way again quickly.

They rode in silence until they reached the highway. Alex sat with his arms crossed, glaring out the window. When they reached the on-ramp and started to speed up, he asked, "Is my father Yakuza?"

The boy was more than observant; he was putting the pieces together. She tried to hide her surprise with a laugh. "You watch too many movies."

Alex shook his head. "I play too many video games."

"Did Hwan say something?" Kiku asked. Hwan had always had a problem keeping his smiling mouth shut.

"No." Alex shook his head. "You did."

"What?" Kiku laughed again, but this time it was real. She was certain she'd said nothing that would reveal who Takeo was or what he did.

"I saw your back when you took your clothes off."

Kiku's chest tightened. She went to great lengths to hide the tattoo that covered her entire back, but in the midst of hurrying to get out of the house she'd made a mistake and let Alex see it—a white Japanese sun bordered by blooming cherry blossom trees. "Having a back tattoo does not make me Yakuza."

"No. But add in the guns, driving a stolen car up a ramp into a waiting van, and all the other ninja crap you've pulled, and I'd bet you're Yakuza. And my favorite video game is Yakuza 2042 and the boss battle at the end is with a dude named *Oyassan*. That's what Hwan called your boss, so—"

Kiku's anger boiled over. She grabbed Alex's shirt, balling the fabric in her hand, and yanked him closer to her. He struggled to get away, but she held him in place and flashed her canines.

Alex's eyes widened in fear.

Kiku rarely displayed her rage, but when she did, people usually died. And those who lived told her it was truly terrifying.

"This is not a game. You will forget that stupid notion and never repeat it again," she said coldly. "I am not Yakuza. Your father is not Yakuza. Say it."

Alex stared at her with watering eyes.

"Say it!" She shook him so hard his teeth rattled.

"You're not Yakuza. My father's not Yakuza." He was crying now.

"Never let that thought enter your mind again—ever."

She let go of him, and he scooted as far away from her as he could get, pressing his body against the door panel, trying to hold back sobs.

Kiku wanted to scream. She wanted to jam her foot down on the gas pedal and drive so fast the car tore itself apart. Instead, she did what she always did: she cut off her feelings. She drove as calmly as if she were headed to the mall. A picture of peace and normalcy. On the outside.

On the inside, another part of her was dying. If Alex was not Takeo's son, what would she do with him?

13

The police had been unwise in choosing their location for a roadblock. Just before she passed an off-ramp, Kiku saw the cruiser partially hidden behind a tree in the distance. She cut the wheel hard, and the driver behind her lay on his horn and flashed his lights, but she made it off the highway in time.

Alex sat up in his seat but didn't say anything. He hadn't for a while now. His eyes were bottomless black pits of distrust and hurt.

Kiku's phone buzzed in her pocket. She'd been forced to leave her purse behind at the safe house but still had her phone and gun.

Takeo. She took a deep breath and held it, like a sniper taking aim, before answering.

"Are you okay?" His voice was strained.

"The safe house was hit. The assault team knew the layout of the safe house. Six men with a backup contingency. Only Alex and I made it out."

The distinct sound of breaking glass came over the line. Kiku had never known Takeo to break something in anger. His father, yes, but never Takeo.

"I will meet you both at the penthouse in Chicago," Takeo said. "What route are you taking?"

"Interstate 90."

"I will see you in two days."

Takeo hung up.

"Was that him?" Alex asked. He had shifted in his seat so he was facing Kiku. The look of hope blazing in his eyes burned a hole in her stomach. "He knows we're in trouble. He's coming for me, isn't he?"

"He will meet us in Chicago."

Alex's hands flexed. He looked like he wanted to open the window, throw his arms into the air, and cheer wildly. If he knew what might happen to him in Chicago, he'd probably throw up, or jump out the window and try to make a run for it.

"Are you going to get back on the highway?" Alex asked. "You told him you were taking the interstate."

Kiku shook her head. "There was a roadblock. Besides, I need to ditch this car." They were not yet out of the city boundaries. Penn Station was too risky, but Stamford, Connecticut, wasn't far, and from there they could get a train to Chicago. "We are taking the train," she announced. Although it meant disobeying Takeo, she couldn't risk anyone knowing the route they were taking.

"But you told my dad we're driving."

And that was precisely why they were taking the train. Someone had known Alex was at the safe house. They also knew its layout, which could mean only one thing: there was a leak in the Yakuza. Unless . . . Her inherent distrust of technology kicked into high gear, and she looked down at her phone like it was a venomous snake. There were many ways to track someone's phone. She had, of course, disabled all of them.

Or had she?

She pulled up alongside an eighteen-wheeler stopped at a light. The big rig was carrying large cement pipes and was getting ready to turn onto the highway. Kiku powered down her window and tossed the phone up and into one of the cement pipes. If someone was tracking her phone, they'd be headed in the wrong direction now.

"What did you do?" Alex looked as though she had just thrown a puppy out of the car rather than her phone. His lip even quivered. Kiku realized Alex had never been taught that technology wasn't a priceless artifact; it was disposable and could easily be replaced. And in her world, people were treated the same way.

"Keeping it would cost more than disposing of it."

Alex let out a gust of a sigh, felt his pockets, then pulled out a plastic comb and began brushing his hair.

"Put your hat on." There were cameras at every EZ-Pass, and others on innocuous-seeming streetlights—too many to count. Billboards were still flashing the Amber Alert every few miles.

Alex stopped brushing and stared fixedly at the comb in his hand.

Kiku frowned. "Put the weapon away."

Alex's mouth dropped open. "How did you know it was a knife?" He demonstrated by yanking on the handle and revealing the four-inch blade.

"It is my job to see things. Throw it away."

"Why? It doesn't set off metal detectors or nothing."

"Do not say *or nothing*. Double negatives make you sound ignorant. Throw that toy away because it is an inferior weapon. It would break after one thrust."

"It would not."

"Do not argue with me, and put on your hat."

Alex stuffed the comb back in his pocket. "Is my dad really going to meet me?" Alex yanked his hat down on his head, then took it off, brushed his hair back, and stuck it on again. He looked in the side mirror and started brushing back the hair sticking out beneath the rim, and the hat came off once more.

Kiku sighed. The way he was preening, there was no way he'd keep that hat on. She'd have to do something about that. She looked into the wallet she'd stolen from the row house. Fifty dollars. That should be enough. She saw a twenty-four-hour pharmacy, pulled in, and popped the trunk. The oversized gym bag inside was perfect for what she had in mind. She shut the trunk and tapped Alex's window. "Get out."

"I thought you'd want me to stay in the car."

"I will do the thinking. Come."

Inside, a few customers waited at the counter while a harried middle-aged clerk glared at the credit card scanner. An equally frustrated-looking manager hovered over his shoulder.

Kiku walked right up to them. "May I borrow the restroom key?"

The manager let out an exasperated sigh and handed Kiku a key attached to a long plastic stick. To the clerk, he said, "Just clear the transaction."

"I already did that," the clerk shot back.

While the two argued, Kiku and Alex headed for the beauty section. She grabbed a hair trimmer off the rack, then walked briskly to the bathroom.

"We can't both go in there," Alex said.

Kiku dragged him into the bathroom and shut the door behind them. "Shut up." She snapped the package open and pulled out the hair trimmer. She clipped on the shortest attachment and steered Alex to the toilet. "Bend over."

"I'm not putting my head over the—*ow*!" Alex winced as Kiku squeezed the pressure point on his biceps. "Okay, okay."

Kiku plugged in the trimmer, and Alex straightened up again. "You're not going to cut my hair!" he said as though she was removing his manhood.

"Sorry, Romeo." Kiku squeezed again, and Alex bent over. "It is too noticeable."

She made quick work of buzzing his head, making sure the trimmings fell into the toilet. When she was done, she could see his white scalp through a quarter-inch black thatch. Then she tossed the trimmer in the trash and covered it with hand towels and toilet paper.

Alex looked into the mirror and swore. "I look like a dork."

"You do not look like you. That is the point. Hat."

Grumbling, Alex pulled the hat back on. He now seemed happy to cover his head. *Good.*

They left the bathroom, and Kiku headed straight for a display of reading glasses and picked out two pairs of anti-fatigue computer glasses. She grabbed a large shoulder bag off a rack and turned to Alex.

To her surprise, he looked . . . extremely upset. Like he might explode in anger. Or tears. Or both. A tiny pang of guilt hit her. As a foster kid, he hadn't had much. His hair had obviously been a big deal to him.

She led him to the candy aisle. "Get some candy," she said. "And some water. For both of us." She picked out a protein bar for herself.

Alex scanned the aisle. "Can I get two?"

"Yes. The water is over there." Kiku pointed at the cooler two aisles over.

While Alex went to get the drinks, she spotted an old-school handheld video game on a rack. She snatched it up, along with a pack of batteries. This was not to be nice, she told herself. She just wanted to keep him looking down at the screen.

Alex came back with the drinks, saw the package in Kiku's hand, and grinned. Kiku scowled and pulled the brim of his hat lower.

At the register, Kiku handed over the bathroom key, paid in cash, and walked away with seven dollars in change. There were no longer any customers in the store, and she considered ordering the two employees into the back room and taking all the cash from the drawer, but decided it wasn't worth the risk.

As they exited the pharmacy, two motorcycles thundered into the parking lot. The bikers parked right next to the stolen Lexus and stared openmouthed, blatantly ogling Kiku as she and Alex approached.

The larger of the two hopped off his low-rider and blocked Kiku from getting in the car. "Well, hello there, ma'am. You need a hand with your bags?"

The other biker shook his head. "Just get your smokes, man," he said.

The big man smiled. "What? I'm just being polite to the lady." His laughter sent his belly bouncing, jiggling the chain attached to his belt and disappearing into his back pocket.

Kiku looked at Alex and spoke in a thick Japanese accent. "Go in car, Hwan." She hoped using the name Hwan would make Alex obey. Then she stumbled off the curb and crashed against the large biker. "Excuse me," she said demurely.

He wrapped thick arms around her, smiling so broadly all of his remaining yellowed teeth showed. "Whoa. Gotcha."

"Sorry. So sorry." Kiku bowed and skirted away. "Thank you." She bowed again.

The biker puffed up his chest and smirked at his friend. "I could get used to all this bowing."

The man stepped aside, and Kiku yanked her door open.

"Come on," said the other biker, waving his friend over. "Let's jet."

The large biker banged twice on the hood of Kiku's car, gave a mock bow, and laughed as he strode over to join his friend.

"Why did you do that?" Alex asked as Kiku backed out of the parking space.

"Do what?"

"That guy cops a feel and you say you're sorry? I thought you were gonna shoot him."

"Shooting him would bring too much attention. I intentionally stumbled into him." She held up the big biker's wallet, still attached to the chain.

"Sweet! How'd you do that?"

"Picking pockets is much simpler when the owner advertises exactly where the valuables are located." She handed Alex the wallet. "Count."

He pulled out a sizable wad of cash and flipped through it. "Whoa. Three hundred and forty-seven dollars."

"Any credit cards?"

"No."

"Typical. Put your glasses on. We have a train to catch."

14

They passed the Connecticut border without incident, and Kiku pulled the car over to the curb a block away from the train station, in front of a convenience store. A group of three men, dressed more like teenagers, stood at the corner of the building.

Kiku opened her door. "We need to get snacks for the trip." She got out of the car, dropping the keys on the sidewalk.

Alex frowned. "We have snacks."

Kiku leaned back into the car. "Bring your game and your bag." She added in a whisper, "We are leaving the car."

Alex's nose wrinkled, but he gathered up his things and followed her into the store.

Kiku got another bottle of water and shook her head when Alex started picking out candy bars.

"You said we're getting snacks," Alex protested.

"We have limited funds, and I do not know what our tickets will cost."

"Then why'd you say it?"

"So that they would hear." Kiku tilted her head toward the door. The three men who had been standing on the corner had picked up the keys Kiku dropped and were hopping into the stolen car. As they started it up and zoomed away, their whoops of laughter were so loud they filtered into the store.

Alex's hands balled into fists.

Kiku paid for the water, and they left, Alex kicking an empty soda bottle into the alley as they started walking.

"What is wrong?" Kiku asked. She reached out to take his gym bag.

Alex kept a firm grip on the strap. "I got it. It ain't heavy."

"Is not."

"What?" He lifted the cap off his head as if to brush back his hair. When his hand touched only stubble, his scowl deepened, but he immediately pulled the hat back down.

"You should not say *ain't*. You should say *is not*."

"Whatever. Doesn't matter what I say. I'm only walking with you because those guys jacked our ride."

"Why would that anger you?"

Alex made a face like a fly had flown up his nose. "It's our—well, you stole it, but it was *our* car. And they were laughing at us. How do you put up with that crap? You never let anyone laugh at you. That's what I live by."

"That is a stupid rule."

Alex stopped walking. "No, it ain't."

Kiku flicked his ear. "Is *not*."

"Ow! Knock off flicking me and pinching me and crap."

"Behave."

"Fine."

Alex started forward quickly, but Kiku grabbed his arm. "Slow down."

He seemed about to say something, but Kiku tightened her grip and he kept pace beside her, glaring down at the sidewalk, his shoulders hunched. Kiku wondered whether people would interpret that as typical teenage angst or whether it would raise suspicion.

"You should never let the actions of another dictate how you behave."

"What does that even mean?" Alex huffed.

"If someone laughs at you, so what? You cannot control what that person does."

"I can punch them in the mouth."

"And what would you gain? Believe me, I do find pleasure in hitting some people, but I only do it if there is something to be gained."

"What did you gain by letting them jack our ride?"

"The car will already have been reported as stolen. And because it has a built-in GPS location system, the police will swoop down on it soon. Those three will not be laughing for long. As for what I have to gain, when the car is located, I am hoping it will be a good distance from the train station and so hide our trail."

Alex went back to staring at the ground. His shoulders relaxed, then he nodded. "That's dope."

Kiku resisted the urge to ask what he meant by *dope*. From the way he said it, she understood that it was an expression of approval. She pointed to the train station, just ahead. "You are my son, Hwan. We are traveling to Chicago to meet your estranged father. Speak as little as possible. Understand?"

Alex nodded. Once again, the name Hwan had the sobering effect she hoped for. Even though the boy had only briefly known Hwan, the man's kindness and his sacrifice seemed to have touched him.

The train station was surprisingly busy for so early in the morning. Kiku breathed easier when she saw the board listing departures. There was a train that could connect them to Chicago leaving in only forty-five minutes.

"Stay."

Alex scowled.

"What now?" Kiku pushed her glasses up her nose and forced a motherly smile on her face.

"Can you say it like I'm *not* a dog? How about you say something like, 'Please stay here'?"

Kiku pointed at a bench. "Sit."

"Oh, *that's* better," Alex grumbled. But he sat down and took his video game out of his pocket.

Kiku would need an ID to buy tickets . . . and she didn't have one. Not a problem. She just needed to find the right mark. It didn't take long. A Korean businesswoman was leafing through a magazine at the newsstand. She would do nicely. Truthfully, the only similarities between Kiku and this woman were their dark hair, height, and the fact that they were both Asian. But Kiku was confident it would be enough. People did have difficulty seeing differences among individuals of other races. Scientists called it the cross-race effect.

Clutching her bag to her side, Kiku did her best to act meek and timid—two attributes as foreign to her as fear and cowardice. She moved alongside the woman and reached for a magazine on the top rack. She even made a point of smiling and added a slight nod before stepping away. She pretended to thumb through the pages until the woman headed for the register. Kiku followed, and got in line right behind her.

The Korean woman paid, then dropped her wallet back into her purse. Before she could zip it closed, Kiku stepped forward and knocked her into the counter, sending several candy bars skittering to the floor.

"*Xin lỗi. Xin lỗi,*" Kiku said in Vietnamese.

The businesswoman reared back and glared down her nose at Kiku. "I'm Korean," she snapped.

Kiku opened and closed her mouth like she was struggling to find the words. "Sorry." She bowed her head as she scrambled to pick up the candy bars. "Sorry."

The woman rolled her eyes and stormed away.

Kiku placed the last candy bar back on the shelf and turned to the cashier. "My apologies."

"Don't worry about it." The cashier gave her a sympathetic smile. "Just the magazine?"

Kiku nodded and paid. Then she walked over to a trash can and peeked inside the wallet she'd just lifted. License, credit cards, even a little cash.

Perfect.

She went straight to the ticket counter. Despite the early hour, the man in the crisp white shirt appeared wide awake and attentive.

Kiku dropped her timid persona, opting instead for a world-weary look. "Two tickets to Chicago, please. Round trip," she added, well aware that one-way tickets raised flags.

"Can I see your ID?"

Kiku held out the license and smiled. The man barely gave it a glance. "Who are you traveling with?"

"Hwan. My son." Kiku pointed over to the bench, where Alex sat with his head down, his focus on the video game. "I can't get him to stop playing that stupid game. All day long he's either tweeting or texting or Facebooking or—"

"Track Four. Change in Philadelphia." The man seemed eager to cut the babbling mother off.

Kiku hid her smile. She was fiercely competitive, and even little victories like this made her want to gloat. But she was well aware that pride truly precedes a fall. If she said the wrong thing, the man at the ticket counter would alert the police and Kiku's plan would slam into the ground as surely as a plane that'd lost its wings. She was also counting on the Korean woman who had unwittingly lent Kiku her identity not noticing her loss until she got wherever she was headed.

Kiku turned around and her breath caught in her throat. A policeman was now sitting on the bench beside Alex, who was oblivious, his attention on his game. The train schedule disappeared from the TVs scattered around the station, and Alex's picture flashed across the monitors, along with some kind of alert. Alex chose that moment to lift his chin and look up.

As the beat cop's eyes traveled from the video game to Alex, Kiku quickly hurried over. She stopped in front of Alex, put both her hands on her hips, and huffed. "There you are, Hwan. How many times have I told you not to wander off?" She thrust a finger up at the nearest TV. "Do you see that boy? He wandered away and someone snatched him up!" She looked directly at the policeman. "Officer, please explain to my son how dangerous this world is."

Alex's eyes went wide. He looked like a koi fish, his mouth opening and closing.

The policeman stood up, hooked a thumb in his belt, and shifted his weight. He cast a sympathetic glance at Alex. "You need to listen to your mom, son." His gaze shifted to Kiku. "But getting too nervous isn't a good thing either, ma'am."

Kiku scowled at the policeman and snatched the video game out of

Alex's hands. "You will get that back when we are on the train. If you wander off again, I'll break it and spank you."

"Yes, Mom," Alex said, his cheeks flushing a bright red.

"Thank you, Officer." Kiku grabbed Alex's hand and started marching him toward the train.

When they were a good distance away, Kiku whispered, "You did well."

Alex pressed against her to whisper back, "Yeah, I know. But ease up. You sounded like a psycho mom. Break my game and beat me?"

"I said spank."

"You might want to catch up with the times. Spanking isn't a thing anymore. And I'm an adult."

"You are a child."

"I'm thirteen, thank you."

"You sat there so focused on the game that you did not notice the police officer sitting right next to you. And he was in uniform. You may not *want* an adult to watch over you, but you do *need* one."

"Whatever. I did my part." Alex's fingers tightened around hers. "Will you tell my dad that? Tell him I'm doing a good job?"

Kiku forced herself to keep staring straight ahead. She knew Alex was looking up at her, his eyes large and round like a toddler's. "Yes. I will let him know."

Alex squeezed her hand. "Thanks. I can't wait to see my father."

Kiku's breath hitched. History was repeating itself. She'd been told the story so long ago that she'd almost forgotten it. Takeo had an uncle, Kenzo's half-brother, Daichi, born of a Chinese mother. Young Daichi showed up in Tokyo insisting his father, Kediri, the head of the Yakuza at the time, recognize him as his son. Kediri refused—he viewed Daichi as a mixed-blood child. He sent two men to throw Daichi back out onto the street, but Daichi killed them with a hammer. Kediri ordered four more men to kill the arrogant boy and watched the fight with Kenzo at his side.

Daichi killed them, too. He was only fourteen.

Alex was no Daichi. He wasn't a killer. Not that it would matter. If Takeo rejected Alex, he wouldn't send six men to do the job.

He'd send Kiku.

15

Kiku sat rigidly in her seat, ignoring the beautiful stretch of woods outside as the train rumbled down the tracks. Her focus was on the five other travelers in the compartment. Four appeared to be sleeping, while the fifth, a woman, typed away on her laptop, her belongings taking up the entire tabletop of a booth seat designed to hold six.

"Thanks again for this game," Alex said without looking up. "I had one like it before I moved. But they didn't let me go back to get my stuff after . . ." His voice trailed off.

"Was this the home where you defended the girl?"

Alex rolled his eyes and looked back down at his video game. "I didn't defend anybody. I made a phone call."

"You did the right thing."

"Yeah, well, I bet you would have handled it yourself." Alex rubbed his nose. Kiku suspected it was an instinctual movement. He flinched when he did it, probably remembering the blow and the pain of the broken nose.

"It was good that you called the police," she said. "You protected other children."

Alex's eyes blazed. "I didn't call the cops. That was my mistake." He set the game down in his lap. "The creep that owned the house was . . . he was doing bad stuff to the girls, so I called my case worker, Doug. I've known him since I was, like, seven. I thought he was legit, but . . . he didn't believe me. He organized a meeting between him, me, and the guy. The guy lied and denied everything. Doug bought it and left." Alex picked the game back up. "The neighbors called the cops when the guy went after me."

"That is when he broke your nose?"

Alex nodded. "I thought he was gonna kill me." The game beeped. He'd lost. Alex looked up, his black eyes cold. "I didn't care."

He turned away and Kiku stared out the window. She knew the feeling well. Or the lack thereof. Part of her fought like the devil to avoid death. Another part of her shrugged. That piece which wanted life to be over. It yearned for the pain to just stop.

They rode in silence, the miles slipping away beneath the railroad car as they sped closer to Chicago—closer to Takeo and the end of their journey together.

"Were you born in Japan?" Alex asked, looking up from his video game. He was sprawled out across the seat and did nothing to hide the yawn that followed his question.

"No. I was born in Korea. I am half Korean, but spent much of my youth in Japan."

Alex didn't miss a beat firing off another question. Clearly, he didn't know what being "half" meant in a place that valued pure blood . . . like Japan. "When did you and your parents move to Japan?"

"My parents died when I was five and my sister, Akari, was ten. We then lived in an orphanage in Korea for four years."

"Then you got adopted?" Alex exhaled loudly. "You guys were lucky. Usually, the older you get, the slimmer your chances of being chosen. People seem to want babies and the littlest kids."

Kiku looked down at the bright boy. "We were lucky to have been placed in a Christian orphanage, given our mixed race. I liked it very much there. The couple who ran the orphanage were kind and took good care of all of the children in their care...until they could no longer pay the bribes necessary to stay open. The local authorities beat them and drove them out of the country. The youngest children were taken to another orphanage. The rest waited for the kind couple to return until the food ran out. Akari was fourteen, I was nine, when we left for the city to find work and food."

"Work?" Alex's voice was a mixture of puzzlement and anger. "You just said you were nine and your sister was fourteen. What kind of jobs could you get?"

"We worked as food servers in a resort until she was killed."

"Sounds like you skipped most of the story," Alex said, then stopped himself. He put the game down. "I'm sorry I said that. That really blows. You lost your parents, the people helping you, and then your sister." He put his hands on his knees and leaned forward with all the intensity of a student. "And . . . then what did you do?"

The last thing Kiku wanted to do was discuss her past, but for some reason, it was easy to speak with the boy.

"After my sister's death, I was sold and shipped to Japan."

"Sold?"

Kiku gave a slight, stiff nod. "I did not make it to my destination, fortunately. I was to be a prostitute"—Alex looked away, embarrassed—"but instead I was selected to work in import-export."

Alex looked confused. "But you were still just a kid, right? That makes no sense."

"I was still young, yes. They made me a 'courier.' My appearance and demeanor were suited to transporting items through customs. Women and children are less likely to raise suspicions. There was a demand for my services, and I was capable. I excelled and was rewarded."

Alex raised his eyebrows. "What's that pay?"

Kiku shot him a look. "Not enough. And that is not a life anyone should seek."

"I'm just curious. I'm not talking about joining the—" He swallowed. "I mean, I didn't say I was going to do it."

The anger that always burned like a pilot light deep inside Kiku flamed to life at what the boy had almost said. What would happen to Alex if Takeo brought him into the Yakuza's ranks? What kind of life would he lead? What would he become? Would he follow in his grandfather's footsteps and rule a new generation with a bloody hand?

She shifted so she was suddenly right beside him. Alex tried to scoot away, but she pinned him against the cold window. "You want to know about my life and the life you will have if you follow that same path? I killed a man when I was ten. I poisoned him and watched him choke to death. When I was twelve, I left a heavy bag in a taxi. A family got in by mistake. There was a bomb in the bag and the entire family was killed. Do you know what an *onryō* is?"

Alex nodded, his eyes wide. "It's like a ghost."

"They are avenging spirits. Every night in my dreams I walk through a cemetery. As I pass the graves, the spirits rise and call to me. I know the names of only a few, but I remember the faces of them all. I am the one who put them there. By the time I reach the middle of the cemetery I am surrounded by a great number of spirits, pressing in from all sides. They grab me and drag me down. I told you I was raised in a Christian orphanage. I believed every word that the couple said, yet I have chosen a different path for my life. Hell awaits me at the end. And if you go down that path, you will join me there."

Alex gave a trembling nod and looked out the window.

Kiku scanned the car and stood, balling her shaking hands into fists. "Stay here."

She hurried down the aisle toward the bathroom in the adjoining car towards the back of the train. The few people who glanced up took one look at her smoldering countenance and quickly looked away. Her heart was pounding in her chest.

In all her years with the Yakuza, she'd never brought someone into its ranks. She would not wish that fate on anyone. Especially not on Alex. But it didn't matter what she wished. This train would take them to Chicago, but there would be no happy ending. When it got there, there was only one way this would end. Either Alex was Takeo's son and heir to the Yakuza, or the boy knew too much to let him go, so they would make him join.

Either way, the good boy in him would die.

16

Kiku stood in the bathroom, her eyes tightly closed. The train rocked back and forth, its vibrations traveling up her legs. But her shaking was not caused just by the movement of the train.

It was always difficult to speak of her sister, Akari, though she was never far from Kiku's thoughts. Kiku had no photographs of her, but she didn't need them. Long ago she had made a conscious effort to imprint Akari's beautiful face on her mind. And she remembered her voice so clearly, she'd still hear it from time to time.

She could hear that voice now, a steady stream of condemnation pouring out of Akari's pretty mouth. After their parents' deaths, Akari had been like a mother to Kiku, and she had taken on the responsibility with the utmost seriousness; so much so that even after Akari was gone, Kiku still felt like her sister was watching over her. Sometimes in the dark of night she'd feel the urge to click on the light, sure that she'd catch Akari standing in the corner of the room. But more often, it was in times of danger that she felt her sister's presence. It might come as a light touch on her shoulder or a gentle breeze . . . Akari's silent warning.

Right now, though, her presence was not gentle. It was angry.

Kiku knew that if Akari were alive today, she would be furious with Kiku for taking Alex to Chicago. Akari would never have done such a thing. Akari always chose the right path. She had believed everything they told them in the orphanage, too. Do to others what you would have them do to you. Akari would never have allowed Kiku to join the Yakuza. She wouldn't want revenge for her death either.

Kiku opened her eyes and glared at her reflection in the dirty mirror. Akari's opinion didn't matter. And neither did Kiku's. The fact of it was, she had a job to do. What happened to Alex in Chicago was out of her hands. His future, if he got to have one, was up to Takeo.

She opened the bathroom door and stepped out. A soft breeze brushed her cheek like a whispered lullaby, and time slowed. The three passengers who had been sitting in the rear of the car when she first entered the bathroom were gone. A conductor now stood at the front, his back against the door, his muscular arms crossed, and another beefy conductor stood against the rear door. The only "passenger" was a man in the seat directly in front of the bathroom, and the tight shirt covering his broad back did little to hide the gun tucked into his waistband.

They should have eliminated the target and left. Had she faced the same choice, she would have killed Alex and vanished. Instead, they had chosen to attack Kiku.

She would make sure they paid for their mistake. She had no time to regret her own. She should not have left Alex alone, not even to go to the bathroom.

The man rose from his seat like a hippo from a river and charged at her. He didn't draw his gun. They must want her alive. Another mistake. It gave her better odds of killing them all.

As the man reached for her shoulders, Kiku's gun was already in her hand. Unlike most people, Kiku did not draw her gun in a wide arc with a stiff arm. The second her gun was out of the holster, she rotated her wrist so the barrel of the gun was aimed at the target. He was slamming her back into the bathroom door when her first round blasted through his thigh. He screamed as the second struck him in the torso.

She didn't know where the third round hit, but he stopped screaming. Like a drunk passing out, he crashed into her, his dead weight dragging her down. She struggled to pull her gun hand free as both "conductors" ran toward her.

The conductor from the front of the car reached her first. He should have kicked her in the head, but he grabbed her by the hair instead. He pulled back his other hand to ready a punch.

So many mistakes.

For a split second Kiku thought about trying to shoot through the dead man's body, but her odds of success were uncertain. Instead she thrust her free hand forward, striking with the ridge of her hand the base of the man's bicep, just above the crook of his elbow. The blow forced his arm to bend and brought his face close enough for her to strike.

Given her slender frame, Kiku didn't win physical fights through sheer brawn. What she excelled at was extreme violence. For her, a fight wasn't some noble pugilistic outing in a ring with rules. It was raw, barbaric, and bloody, and the only rule was that she had to win.

She grabbed the man's ear and used it like a handle to pull his head forward and push her thumb into his eye.

The man shrieked in pain as Kiku's thick, manicured nail dug in. He tried to pull away, but Kiku held on and pushed harder. Her attacker turned into an unlikely rescuer as he backed away, dragging her free of the weight of the dead man pinning her to the floor.

She fired a round into the conductor's chest just an instant before the second one tackled her. All the air in her lungs exploded outward as her back hit the floor, the huge man landing on top of her. Her hand opened involuntarily, and her gun skittered off under the seats.

The giant's fist came down hard against the side of her head. The lights in the train shone brightly, popping like flashbulbs. He swung with his other hand, and this time she feebly tried to block it, but did little to cushion the blow. His fist knocked her head violently to the side, and she fought the darkness rushing to sweep over her.

His large hands circled her throat and began crushing her windpipe.

As darkness squeezed the edges of her vision, she saw a strange mark on the man's neck. A red birthmark.

She remembered Jiro's words after she rescued him. *"There was another one here. Liev. He was in charge. Red birthmark running up his neck to his ear. He killed Jessica."*

So. This was the man who had tortured Jiro and beheaded Jessica.

This was the pig she'd sworn to make pay.

Kiku grabbed Liev's hands, trying to wedge her fingers under his. His grip was like iron.

"Where's the boy?" he demanded.

Kiku's fingernails raked down his arms, drawing bloody streaks.

He held her throat with one hand and punched her again with the other.

She jerked her head sideways to lessen the impact, but the pain was still intense. And she was getting no oxygen. The darkness was overtaking her.

She swung hard and fast. Three rapid blows to the man's face.

A drop of blood appeared on his cheek. Liev was used to getting punched in the face. He shook off the blows.

The door to the compartment flew open and Alex jumped forward yelling, "Let her go!" The comb knife clutched in his hand shook. He swung the blade in an arc, aiming at the man's shoulder. The plastic blade snapped with a twang.

Liev backhanded Alex across the face.

Alex ricocheted off a seat and tripped over the body of the dead conductor. He landed hard in the aisle.

Liev's grip on Kiku had lessened just a bit. She punched him in the face and felt like she was slamming her fist into a brick wall. Liev blocked her second punch and squeezed harder with the hand wrapped around her throat.

"Leave her alone!" Alex screamed. The boy was kneeling in the aisle, his trembling arms thrust straight out, a gun aimed at Liev. He must have taken the weapon off the dead man beside him.

"Shoot him," Kiku gasped.

"Put the gun down or I kill her," Liev growled. He tightened his grip once more.

Alex looked like he was trying to pull the trigger, but nothing was happening. Kiku saw confusion in his eyes.

He doesn't know guns. He's left the safety on.

Kiku tried to tell him, but she had no air. If her attacker would loosen his grip again, just a little . . .

She set her feet against the floor and tried to heave herself upward.

The Russian barely moved. Her fingers clawed at his. She could feel the blood vessels in her eyes starting to rupture.

Alex seemed to have realized his mistake. He was fiddling with the gun. He pressed the magazine release. The magazine fell from the gun and bounced under the seats. His eyes went wide.

Kiku twisted her neck. She wanted to scream *There is one in the chamber!* but only managed to croak out one word: “Chamber.”

She didn’t know if he understood, but he didn’t give up. He found the safety, flipped it . . . and pulled the trigger. The bullet tore into Liev’s back and came out his side. He didn’t scream, but his hold on Kiku lessened.

She punched him in the exit wound as hard as she could.

Liev shrieked in agony.

She punched him in the throat and Liev’s screaming was replaced by gasping.

Alex was wailing. Over and over the boy cried out something that sounded like “I’m sorry!”

Another punch in the exit wound, and the Russian finally tumbled off her. Kiku scrambled back, grabbed her gun from under the seats, and rose woozily to her feet. Her legs shook and her vision was still blurry. The train’s slight sway felt like the deck of a ship tossed in a storm. A commotion was brewing in the compartments in front and behind; she heard doors opening and closing and distant screams as well as Alex’s crying.

Alex fell to his knees beside the man he had just shot. “Is he dead? I didn’t mean to kill him! I tried to shoot his shoulder.” He let out a twisted cry that pulled on Kiku’s heart. She had a sudden urge to rush to him, to cradle him in her arms. His pain was so raw. So innocent.

She wiped at her blurring eyes with the back of her sleeve. “You did not kill him.”

Liev’s hand was sliding down his thigh. His pant leg had hiked up, revealing a pistol in an ankle holster. Kiku shot him in the head.

Alex screamed as Kiku pulled him to his feet. “As I said, you did not kill him. I did. Now stop screaming.”

Alex stopped screaming, but his eyes widened at something behind her. Kiku shoved him into the seats and spun toward the new threat. A gunshot echoed through the car and pain sliced into her side.

Another Russian stood in the open doorway at the end of the car. He fired another round and it whizzed by her ear. She returned fire. Three quick shots knocked the man back.

The train started to round a corner and Kiku stumbled and swayed. She pressed her hand against her wet side. "Alex, are you hit?"

"No. But you are!" Alex sobbed.

The car lurched and rocked as it suddenly began to slow to a stop. Kiku braced herself against a seat back, sending fresh pain radiating through her abdomen. "We need to get off the train."

Alex started back toward the front of the train.

"No. This way!"

"I'm just getting the bag." He grabbed the gym bag from the aisle, where he'd dropped it when he bravely—and foolishly—came to her rescue.

Kiku pushed past him to jam the door shut behind him and then rifled through Liev's pockets. He wasn't wearing a jacket and he had no phone on him. She motioned for Alex and they strode to the rear of the car. Kiku kept her gun trained on the body of the last man she had shot. She didn't relax until she saw his head wound and was sure he was dead. His gun was a few feet away; a phone lay at his feet. She picked up the phone and pressed his thumb against the sensor. It unlocked.

She handed the phone to Alex. "Keep this phone active. We cannot unlock it again if it goes dark." She considered removing the man's thumb . . . but the boy had already seen enough. And they had to move quickly. She pulled the rear door open and lifted the heavy metal plate to reveal the stairs. "Go!"

Alex grabbed a first-aid kit from the wall and looked at the wound in her side. "I think we might need this." His voice was ragged and his eyes were wild as he descended the stairs, but at least he'd stopped crying.

"That is good thinking." She looked outside. Beyond the tracks was nothing but farmland and woods. "Are you ready?"

"I guess."

"Do not guess. JUMP!"

17

Heavy rains had made the ground boggy, which slowed their pace. Alex panted heavily, struggling to keep up, and the pain in Kiku's side felt like her flesh was being seared with a branding iron, but she didn't slow until they were well away from the train. When she finally stopped and motioned for Alex to sit down, the boy dropped to his knees, his back rising and falling as he gulped in air.

She took the first-aid kit from him, opened it, and frowned. It was nothing more than bandages, gauze, and some antiseptic wipes.

"You need to get to a hospital," Alex wheezed.

Kiku shook her head as she lifted her shirt. Fresh blood oozed from the wound on her side. "It's a through-and-through," she said.

"A what-and-what?"

"The bullet only hit muscle and fat."

"You don't got any fat."

"I need stitches, but that's it. No need for a hospital."

Alex shook his head. "You need a doctor."

"That will not be necessary." Kiku opened the largest pack of gauze pads and slapped one on her side. It began to soak through almost immediately, so she placed two more over the top. "You will patch the exit wound."

"Me?" Alex's face wrinkled as he swiped the phone's screen with his thumb. "But I have to keep the phone going."

"Give the phone to me." Kiku took the phone and handed him the bandages.

He grimaced. "Oh, man. There's a lot of blood."

"Just wipe away as much as you can, then place a bandage on it." She was successful in keeping her voice calm and neutral. She took a breath and added, "You will do fine." He would be able to perform better if he was not in a constant state of panic.

While Alex, his mouth set in a grim line, fumbled to open an antiseptic pack and began to wipe away the blood from the exit wound, Kiku checked the call log on the phone. It had only one number. Most likely Liev's, since he'd coordinated the team. She opened the text messages. Again, only the one number, and two pictures.

Each picture was labeled. The picture of Alex was labeled SON. The picture of her was labeled GUARD DOG. Her teeth ground together and she growled.

"I'm sorry," Alex said. "I'm trying to be gentle, it's just . . . my fingers are all sticky. This is so gross."

"With all the violent games and movies a teenage boy watches, I would think you would be desensitized to blood."

"News flash, that's not real."

"Well, you are doing fine."

He finished wiping and applied a gauze bandage. "The blood is coming right through. I really think you need a doctor."

"You are my doctor. Thank you." She set the phone down, wrapped the Ace bandage around her waist, and pulled her shirt down.

Alex opened a water bottle and tried to wash his hands. "You need to swipe the phone again soon, or it's going to lock."

Kiku shook her head. "I have seen what I needed to see." She picked up a rock and smashed the phone to bits. "Take your shoes off."

Alex looked puzzled. "What? Why?"

With a lightning motion, Kiku reached for his feet, and Alex scooted back. "All right, all right. Just give me a second." He pulled off his sneakers. "Can you at least tell me why?"

"Are your shoes the only thing you have from your foster home? Do you have anything else?" She pulled up the insole and peered inside the shoe.

"No. And why are you killing my sneakers?"

Kiku handed them back to him and held out her hand. "Belt."

"What are you, TSA?"

Kiku grabbed his belt and pulled him to his feet, grimacing as she did.

"Whoa, chill out. You don't look so good."

Kiku scowled as she checked his belt. Then she patted him down from head to toe.

As her hands traveled over him, his face turned bright crimson. "Uh . . ." he said, "boundaries."

Kiku ignored him and finished her search. "Someone is tracking you," she said. "That is the only way they could have found us on the train."

"Oh yeah? Who says they're tracking *me*? Maybe it's you."

Kiku narrowed her eyes. Besides her clothes, the only thing she'd kept on herself was . . .

Her gun.

The holster was clean. She ejected the magazine and looked inside. There was no room for anything larger than a sticker but . . .

She turned the Glock over. All Glocks have a backstrap channel, a small cavity between the magazine and the backstrap. Kiku removed the cap and peered inside.

A tracker.

The boy was right. She was the one they had been tracking all this time. She started to rip out the chip, then stopped. Closing her eyes, she inhaled deeply through her nose and let the breath out slowly, evenly.

Calm. Focus.

Someone was hunting her. They were in Indiana, traveling west. The last station stop they had passed was South Bend. Less than a hundred miles to go. The corner of her lip curled upward as a plan formed in her mind. She set the gun down and started to dig through the gym bag.

"Did you find something?" Alex asked. He'd been gawking over her shoulder. "It was some kind of locator chip or something. I was right, huh? It wasn't on me. It was in your gun?"

Kiku pulled out the two large bags of potato chips that Alex had gotten for snacks. She opened one and poured the chips into the gym bag.

"Hey!" Alex protested.

"Hold out your hands." Kiku opened the other bag and dumped the chips into Alex's outstretched hands. Most of them still fell on the ground.

"Crap! You're wasting all the chips!"

Kiku reinserted the magazine and stuffed the Glock in the first chip bag, then stuck that bag in the second chip bag.

"You wrecked my chips to hide your gun?"

"The aluminum foil should block the GPS. I will shield it with something better later."

"Why not just destroy the locator thing?"

"I could do that," Kiku said. "But there are ways to gain more advantage from this situation."

Alex's eyebrows arched and his eyes widened. "You're gonna use it to lure them into a trap!"

Kiku nodded. "Take the gym bag."

While Alex stared at the pile of chips in his hands, Kiku picked up the bag and draped it over his shoulder. "Walk and eat."

They started walking at a moderately fast pace, Alex nibbling at the chips in his hand, Kiku hiding both the burning pain in her side and the ice-cold clarity of her new understanding. There was only one time and place when that tracker could have been planted in her gun—at Takeo's summer house. It was highly unlikely that there was a Baikokudo in the Yakuza—yet not impossible. The fact remained: the chip had to have been placed there by someone inside the Yakuza. And that traitor had shared her location with the Russians. Kiku was collateral damage. Alex was their target.

"Hey," Alex said, struggling to keep up and eat his chips at the same time. "Why are you smiling? Those guys have attacked us three times. I don't think they're going to give up. Don't you think they're going to send more men?"

"Yes, I do think so. In fact, I am certain of it." Kiku's canines flashed.

"Then why are you smiling?" Alex asked again.

"Because I am looking forward to killing them all."

18

Fireflies danced among the bushes and trees as Kiku stood at the corner of the shed, watching the postcard-perfect little white farmhouse and the red pickup truck parked next to it. Other than the fireflies, the only light was from the glowing kitchen window. It had been fifteen minutes, and she'd seen no movement inside. The driveway sloped away from the house, so she could put the truck in neutral and roll it silently down the hill, then start it up once they were a safe distance away.

She turned to Alex, and was surprised by the look on his face. She'd expected the teen to be bored out of his mind having to wait for so long, but his expression was one of true wonder. "This place is beautiful," he whispered.

She held up a silencing finger and scowled. Placing her mouth next to his ear, she said, "Stay on the far side of the truck, away from the house. I am going to roll it down the hill and—"

She was cut off by the distinct sound of a shotgun slide being pulled back and a round being loaded into the chamber.

"Hands up high." An older man in worn jeans stepped out from around the shed holding a twelve-gauge shotgun leveled at Kiku's chest.

Kiku made sure her hands shook as she lifted them high and mentally reviewed the story she had concocted. "Please don't shoot."

She assumed a local would be more comfortable with someone from the area, so she adopted a flat Midwestern accent.

She stepped in front of Alex and sized up the man. The farmer looked to be in his seventies, yet his arms didn't sway and his back was stiff. He stood in a strong shooter's stance. He knew how to fire the gun, and at this distance she had little hope of disarming him. Much better to draw him in.

She took a step closer to the old farmer. "We're lost, can you help us?" Tears rolled freely down her cheeks.

Footsteps sounded from behind them, and Kiku turned her head. The farmer's wife appeared around the other side of the shed with a shotgun of her own. "Take another step, lady, and it will be your last. Get your hands up, too, boy."

"Both of you walk away from the shed a couple of feet," the farmer said.

"Keep your hands up," the wife added.

Kiku winced as she lifted her hands higher and allowed a deliberate, small yelp to escape her lips. She didn't need to act; the pain in her side was intense. Yet she was playing a role. Kiku would never normally allow herself to show pain, let alone verbalize it. She'd rather stuff it down or choke to death on it trying.

The farmer looked at his wife. "The woman's hurt."

"Then I'll call an ambulance, as well as the police."

"Please don't call the police," Kiku pleaded. Her mind raced. "My husband's a cop."

"Then he can help sort this out." The farmer's wife shot her husband a concerned look.

"But"—Kiku glanced down at her side—"he's the one who did this."

The farmer started to lower his gun, but his wife gripped hers tighter. "What police force is your husband on?"

"South Bend. We just moved there."

The wife's eyes narrowed. "Son, this question is for you. Missy, don't you answer. What branch of police does your father work for?"

Alex's mouth dropped open, and he turned to Kiku.

"Don't look at her. What's his badge look like?" the wife pressed.

"He doesn't know," Kiku said. "He's never met him."

The wife's face scrunched up like one of the fireflies blinking on and off around them had flown up her nose.

"I gave Hwan up for adoption. I never told my husband." Kiku's lip trembled. "He's not his son. Hwan showed up at our house, and I had to tell my husband that before I knew him, I had a child and . . ." Kiku's shoulders shook with sobs. "He went crazy. He pushed me and I fell . . ." She glanced down at her side and looked pleadingly at the farmer. "Please don't call the police. He has friends in the state police and the sheriff's department. I just want to get away. My college roommate lives in Chicago. I need to get us there."

The wife finally lowered her shotgun and walked forward. "Any man who does that to a woman should be castrated. And I'd be happy to be the one to do it."

"Betsy!" the farmer admonished. He pointed his gun at the ground and Kiku let her hands drop, wincing as her left hand cradled her wound. "That must have been what all the fuss was about on the news. They even had a helicopter fly over. It spooked the horses so bad, we had to come out here and check on them."

"Hush up." Betsy angled her head toward her husband. "Help her up to the house."

"Thank you. Thank you," Kiku said, and took Alex's hand.

"Yeah. Thanks for not blowing our heads off," Alex said, rolling his eyes. Kiku squeezed his hand tightly, and he added, "I mean . . . thanks."

As they walked toward the house, Betsy frowned at Kiku's bloody side. "Tim, I'll go grab your med kit."

"Are you a doctor?" Alex asked hopefully.

"I was one, before I retired." The man held the kitchen door open. "Tim Masterson. Welcome to our home."

The large, tidy kitchen was bright and cheery. A sign hung on the wall behind the kitchen table. *Bless all who enter.*

Tim led Kiku to a chair, and Betsy returned shortly with a black bag and a white sheet.

Tim eyed the bloody bandage and said to his wife, "You may want to show the boy the living room."

Betsy patted the sheet. "You cover her up." She waved her finger at her husband like a schoolmarm. "And no peeking."

Tim blushed. "Of course not."

Betsy took Alex by the hand and led him down the hall. He cast a questioning look over his shoulder, but Kiku just lifted her chin to signal he should go with Betsy.

Tim pointed at the sheet and turned around. "If you could, uh . . . reveal your injury, I'll take a look and see what I can do."

Kiku lifted her shirt and draped the sheet over her. She didn't care who saw her naked, but the last thing she wanted was for Tim to see her tattoo-covered back, or ask questions about her older bullet scars. Nor did she wish to be the cause of a fight between the farmer and his wife.

Tim took a pair of scissors out of his bag and began cutting away the Ace bandage. The blood had congealed, and he had to pry the bandage and the gauze pads away from the wounds. Kiku grimaced and grabbed the edge of the table.

"I'm okay," she said, forcing a smile.

"You're one tough cookie." Tim winked and opened a cabinet over the refrigerator. He raised himself up on his toes, reached back, and took down a bottle of whiskey two-thirds full. "Betsy and I are teetotalers, but we keep this on hand in case of emergencies. I'd say this qualifies." He got out a teacup and poured Kiku a shot.

She gulped it down eagerly. Too eagerly. Tim's eyes widened. Quickly remembering her character, Kiku coughed and puffed out her cheeks. She could have used three more shots, but her host put the bottle back.

His lip curled as he examined her side.

"My husband didn't mean to hurt me. He shoved me against the wall, but there was a metal hook and . . ." She clamped her mouth closed like she was fighting back tears.

Tim looked more closely, but she knew he had bought her story when he said, "Ain't that somethin'? Almost looks like a bullet clipped your side and went right through you."

Kiku decided to try a joke. "I'd hate to think what a bullet feels like if an old hook hurts like this."

"You're going to need stitches and a tetanus shot if you haven't had one in a while. Let me take you to the hospital."

Kiku reached across the table and took the old man's hand. "Sir, I can't take the risk. Please patch me up. I'll go to the doctor's when we get to Chicago."

"Your husband should be fired and tossed in prison. Do you really want that man running around with a badge and a gun?" Tim's face turned a splotchy red.

Kiku let out a little sob and shook her head. "No. I promise I'll go to the authorities as soon as we're safe in Chicago."

Betsy appeared in the hallway. "That's enough, Tim. Mimi has been through the wringer."

Alex stepped out from behind Betsy, smiling impishly. Apparently, he knew that *mimi* was the Chinese slang word for breasts.

Kiku forced herself to coo maternally, "I'm fine, honey. Don't worry."

"She'll be good as new in a few minutes," Tim said. He hitched his thumb toward the living room, and Betsy led Alex away again. "I still think you should go to a hospital. If I stitch it, you'll have a bad scar."

"It's fine. Please." Kiku squeezed his hand.

The old farmer sighed and reached back inside the bag. "Do you need another shot, Mimi?"

Kiku held back a scowl and shook her head. "I'm okay."

Ten minutes later, she really wished she'd taken another shot of whiskey. The farmer was gentle, but having torn skin pulled back together is never pleasant. Betsy popped in once, to bring Kiku a clean light-blue top and a pair of tan pants. "You look to be around our daughter's size," she explained before kissing her husband's cheek and disappearing back down the hallway.

When he was done, Tim washed his hands, got the whiskey bottle back down, and set it on the table. "This'll help you sleep."

Kiku shook her head and felt a little woozy. "We need to get going."

"You need to sleep," he said firmly.

Kiku poured herself a big shot and left the top off the bottle. The farmer was right: she *did* need sleep. And she and Alex needed to lie low. They might attract too much attention if they were on the road tonight. It made sense to wait.

"I'll give you a ride into Gary in the morning," Tim said. "They've got a train and a bus station. Chicago's just a hop, skip, and a jump from there." He smiled and zipped up his medical bag. "We've got a couple of spare bedrooms. Take a minute to think about it." He picked up the bag and started down the hallway.

Kiku didn't need to think about it. If the farmer and his wife drove them, she couldn't ask for a better cover. She gulped down the shot, poured herself another, then twisted the top back on the bottle.

She drummed her nails on the worn boards of the table. The whiskey she had consumed would have dulled the minds of most, but it did little to slow her racing thoughts. She inwardly swore as she went over what had happened on this mission. From the start everything had gone south, but now it was starting to make sense. The Russians had followed her to Alex's school and to the train. But they hadn't figured out her location on their own. They were led to her.

By a traitor in the Yakuza.

That was why the strike team who hit the safe house knew the exact equipment they needed to bring. They knew the layout. Kiku stared out the window at the darkness. Someone in the Yakuza had betrayed her . . . In a den of thieves, everyone is a suspect. Someone was trying to gain money, favor, or both from the Russians. Cade wanted to avenge the death of his son, so the traitor in the Yakuza was selling the intel on Alex to him. The grieving, vindictive father didn't care about DNA tests; he wanted to inflict the same pain he was suffering on Kenzo. Cade Novikov wanted Alex dead.

Kiku downed another shot, savoring the smoky taste and the burn in her throat. But when she heard the sound of Tim's boots coming back down the hall, she faked a cough and a grimace.

"Strong stuff," Tim said, picking up the bottle and looking at its now-depleted volume.

"You were right, I needed it." Kiku managed a thin smile.

"So, what did you decide?"

"We'll stay the night and gladly accept your offer of a ride in the morning."

Tim grinned. "Good. I was going to heat up some chicken pot pie. My wife makes the best in the county. Are you up for some, Mimi?"

Alex chuckled as he walked into the room.

"That would be wonderful." Kiku glared at Alex.

Alex sat down, replying with a cheery "Yes, please" when Tim asked him if he'd like some. He looked perfectly happy to be eating chicken pot pie in this little farmhouse.

But Kiku could only pretend, with the help of whiskey, that she shared his optimism. Someone in the Yakuza had betrayed them, and if they knew she was meeting Takeo in Chicago, then she was serving Alex up on a silver platter.

19

Tim and Betsy Masterson pulled into the parking lot of the bus station and Kiku and Alex got out. Kiku shook Betsy's hand through the truck's passenger-side window.

"I can't thank you enough for your kindness."

Tim leaned forward in the driver's seat and smiled. "No need to thank us. Glad to help."

Betsy grabbed hold of Kiku's wrist. "Mimi, would you drop us a note letting us know you two are okay?"

"I will. Once we're safe."

"We'll be praying for you," Tim said.

Betsy reached into her pocket and pulled out an envelope. "It's not much, but it'll be enough to get you two to Chicago and a little extra."

Kiku took the envelope but didn't open it. "Thank you. Again. Do you mind if I pray with you?"

Tim and Betsy exchanged a surprised look, but they both nodded.

Kiku grabbed Alex's hand and leaned into the cab. "Dear Lord, thank You for Tim and Betsy and the fact that they are doers of Your word. The world needs more people willing to help strangers and those in need. Bless them and their home. In the name of Your Son, Jesus. Amen."

Betsy's eyes glistened, and she squeezed Tim's hand. "God bless you, Mimi and Hwan."

"Our address is on the other side of that envelope," Tim said. "You don't have to write anything long . . . we just want to know you're safe."

"I will write." Kiku stepped away from the truck. She shot a sharp look at Alex, who was standing there looking bored to death.

"Thanks," Alex said reluctantly. He gave an awkward wave as the truck pulled away. "Are we going now, Mimi?"

When the truck was out of sight, Kiku smacked Alex in the back of the head.

"It was a joke!" Alex rubbed his crew cut and laughed.

"You could have been more polite. Those people opened their home to us."

"I thanked them like twenty times this morning. Thank you for letting me sleep over. Thank you for breakfast. Thank you for the ride. Thank you—"

"Enough. You made your point." Kiku took a map of the city from a display of tourist brochures and flyers and started walking away from the bus station.

"Aren't we taking the bus?"

"No. Too obvious. Besides, I am not arriving in Chicago by bus. I have a reputation to uphold." She opened Betsy's envelope and counted the cash.

"How much did they give you?" Alex asked.

"Two hundred dollars. It was a kind gesture, but it is not enough."

"That was good acting, praying with them. They ate it up."

"I was not acting." Kiku stuffed the envelope in her pocket. "The world needs more people like them." She unfolded the city map and studied it for a moment.

"But . . ." Alex made a face. "You don't believe in all that praying stuff, do you?"

"I do. Even the devil believes in God. He does not follow Him, but he knows God is real. Belief and obedience are two very different things. Now, would you please do me a favor? Shut up." She tossed the map into a trash can.

Alex stepped off the curb, and Kiku had to grab his elbow to keep him from pitching into the street. He yanked his arm out of her grip and gave her the finger.

Kiku resisted the urge to reach out and snap it off. "You are a very rude boy."

"Me?" Alex's voice rose. "In the last three minutes you've smacked me in the head, pinched my arm, and told me to shut up. So . . ."

Alex started to give her the finger again, but Kiku grabbed his hand. "You are making a scene." She gave his fingers a tight squeeze.

He winced. "Ow! Okay, okay. Let go."

A woman jogging by glanced back over her shoulder at them as she passed.

"We need to hurry or we'll be late, sweetie," Kiku said loudly, grabbing Alex's arm and crossing the street.

"All right, Mimi."

Kiku's claw hold tightened on his bicep. "Enough."

"Enough with you!" Alex tried to pull away but had no luck wriggling out of Kiku's grasp. When they reached the other side of the street and turned a corner, Kiku angrily swung him around to face her.

Alex held up a hand. "Whoa. Chill."

"Do *not* call me Mimi again." Her eyes blazed.

Alex glared at her and pressed his lips together. She expected him to shout, but instead he lowered his voice to a whisper. "What do you want me to call you?"

"You could keep it simple and call me by my name."

Now he shouted. "Well, guess what? I don't know it! You've never even *told* me. All you do is scream and yell and shoot people. And I've gone along with it because you said you could take me to my dad. But you know what?" He took off his hat and dropped it on the sidewalk. "*I don't care.* If my dad has someone like *you* working for him, I don't want to meet him." He spun on his heel and stormed away down the sidewalk.

Kiku grabbed the hat and quickly caught up with him. People were staring, and she didn't want him to make any more of a scene than he already had. If the street were less crowded, she'd have just knocked him out and stuffed him into a car. As it was, she settled for a softer approach.

She walked beside him, matching his pace. "Kiku," she said, holding out his hat. "My name is Kiku."

For a moment Alex was silent, then he took his hat back. "Like the bird?"

"No. KEE-koo. It is Japanese for chrysanthemum. It is an old name."

Alex stopped. "If I go with you, will you stop screaming at me?"

"I do not shout."

"But you do *that*." Alex pointed at her face.

"What am I doing?" Kiku said. She tried not to scowl.

"You look like . . . like you're going to hit me in the head, stuff me in the trunk of a car, and drive me to Chicago."

She was surprised by the accuracy of Alex's guess, and her eyebrows rose. "Keep your voice down."

"Then stop looking at me like that."

Kiku forced a smile.

Alex grimaced. "Now you look like a serial killer."

Stepping closer to him, Kiku bent down so she could whisper in his ear. "Technically, I *am* a serial killer. But I will try to be . . . nice. Now, we need to go."

Alex crossed his arms. "Where?"

"You can come with me to Chicago and I will take you to your father. We are less than an hour away." Kiku pointed down the street toward the waterfront. "Or you can take your chances on keeping yourself alive. I am not going to beg you." She gestured down at the unflattering clothes Betsy had given her. "I cannot go to Chicago like this. I need to pick up an outfit and a car."

She started walking and didn't look back. If Alex wasn't following her by the time she reached the end of the block, she'd go back to her alternate plan: knock him out and stuff him in a car. She was beyond frustrated with his teenage angst. Granted, Alex had atypical teenage problems—such as being hunted by the Russian Mafia—but still, how long would it take for him to accept that his life had changed irrevocably?

Alex jogged up and fell into step beside her. "How are you going to get clothes?" he asked. "We need that money Betsy gave you for travel."

"I have ways." Kiku grinned.

A short cab ride later, they stood in front of the Majestic Star Casino and Hotel. Given their current state of dress, Kiku thought it best to avoid the main entrance, choosing instead to enter through a side door near the conference center. That door was accessible only with a keycard, but it was easy enough to wait until two businessmen exited. Kiku smiled and batted her eyes. The men jostled each other to hold the door open for her and Alex. She had carefully parted her hair on the side and let it fall to camouflage the bruised side of her face.

"Follow me," Kiku said to Alex once they were inside.

"Can you at least tell me what we're doing?"

"Pretending to shop. You may pick something out for less than twenty dollars."

They stepped into an upscale beauty boutique in the shopping area off the hotel lobby, and Alex let out a loud huff and groaned. "I'm not going to find anything to buy here." He was loud enough to make the woman behind the register turn her head.

"I'll only be a few minutes, honey." Kiku headed to a display of lipstick near the cash register. She pretended to shop while really monitoring the other shoppers. A few women made purchases, but they all paid with a credit card or by using their phone. And then Kiku spotted what she was hoping for.

The middle-aged woman, carrying a Gucci handbag and wearing a floral-print Diane von Furstenberg dress, stepped into the store, looked around, and rolled her eyes. "Where do you hide your concealer?"

"I'm sorry, ma'am, it's right over here." The clerk hurried around the counter and held her hand toward a display.

The woman picked up a tube and waved it at the clerk. "Rochester. Room 202."

"Of course." The clerk headed back to the register. "Would you like a receipt?"

Ms. Rochester was already strolling toward the door. "Have it attached to my room. Do tell me the restaurant here is adequate."

"It's superb. They—"

Ms. Rochester cast a withering look. "When was the last time you dined there?" Her Gucci handbag swung on her forearm like a pendulum as she waited for the clerk's response.

The clerk somehow maintained her smile. "Last January. But it was fantastic."

"If that's your opinion, I suppose there's hope it's palatable."

Alex mumbled, "Don't choke on it."

Kiku, Ms. Rochester, and the clerk all turned in his direction, but Alex didn't even look up from his video game. Ms. Rochester shot Kiku a cross look and left.

Kiku held up a red lipstick and a tube of concealer. "I'll take these, please."

As she paid for her makeup, Alex dashed out of the store and toward the building's front doors. Kiku took her purchases and quickly followed.

"Stop," she called out, but the boy ignored her.

He was almost to the exit when Kiku caught him by the arm.

She dragged him close and whispered, "This is your last warning to mind me. Speak out of turn again, flip me off again, or make any other stupid move that is going to get us caught and I will give you a permanent reminder to behave."

"You could've just asked."

"I have asked. I have instructed. I have admonished, and still you are insolent, defiant, and disobedient."

Alex smiled.

"These are not compliments. This childish behavior can and will get you killed. You must take every opportunity to learn if you are going to make it."

Kiku guided her hostage/charge back to another store. The merchandise was geared to a younger market, and Kiku was confident Ms. Rochester wouldn't have done any shopping here. She picked out a stunning red dress with matching handbag and shoes, and for Alex a new shirt and pair of pants.

A few minutes later, while she kept watch on the store and the hotel's comings and goings, Alex walked out of the dressing room with a red shirt and a pair of white jeans draped over his arm. "This shirt costs a hundred and twenty bucks. Who pays that much for a shirt with nothing written on it?"

"If it looks spectacular and you feel wonderful in it, how much is that worth?"

"Not a hundred and twenty bucks, that's for sure. I could buy an old Xbox for that. And white jeans? Why did they have to be white? And there's no price on them, but they're probably overpriced, too."

Kiku winked, folded the clothes over her arm, and headed for the counter. On the way, she picked up a pair of ultra-dark sunglasses and an ornate picture frame. She handed everything to a clerk. "Would you please have these sent up to my room? Rochester. Room 202."

"Of course, Ms. Rochester. Would you like them wrapped?"

"No, thank you." Kiku smiled and started walking toward the exit.

Alex stood rooted to the spot, a puzzled expression on his face.

"Come along, honey. We don't have to wait for our bags." Kiku had to repress a smile at his confused face. He was unwittingly selling the charade. And it was important that they sell it. If the clerk suspected anything was amiss, he could ask for Kiku's room key or identification. And that was the last thing they needed.

Alex still wasn't getting it. He looked up at her, completely lost.

Kiku snapped her fingers. "Oh, that's right. We're going to meet your father and then head straight to the club." She turned back to the clerk and gave him an apologetic look. "I'm sorry, but I'll need to take those with me." She held out her hands for the bags, then shook her head and handed the bag with the picture frame back. "Please send this to our room."

"Of course."

"Thank you so much. Have a wonderful day."

Kiku strolled out of the store with Alex close beside her.

"That was awesome," Alex whispered.

"Thank you." She handed him the bag with his clothes. "Go into the men's room and put on your new clothes. Make sure you dress in a stall."

Alex stuck his tongue out and, like a recoiling vacuum cord, quickly sucked it back in for fear of Kiku lopping it off. "I'm not four. I know how to get changed."

Kiku bit her own tongue. She went to the wheelchair-accessible stall in the women's restroom. After carefully removing her shirt, she changed her bandages, using the extras Betsy had given her. Her wound still burned, but at least it wasn't bleeding. And the new dress was just the painkiller she needed. The silky fabric didn't hug her hips quite the way she liked, but she knew she looked sensational.

She walked to the sink, pushed the hair back from her face, and assessed the damage there. She was glad she had listened to Betsy and slept with a bag of frozen peas on the side of her face overnight. There was virtually no swelling, just some discoloration. She gently patted concealer on the bruise, then slicked back her raven hair into a low chignon—*sans* her favorite Korean hair pick—and applied another thin layer of concealer and red lipstick.

There was a time, back in the days when men first began to notice she was pretty, that she hid her attractiveness. She did not want that kind of attention. Now she no longer cared what men thought. She embraced her exotic beauty.

When she exited the bathroom, Alex was waiting for her. His eyes opened wide and his mouth dropped.

"Stop staring," she said with a scowl.

"I'm not staring," he protested, getting in a good, long look. "You even smell good. Were you like a model or something?"

"Remember, I am supposed to be your mother," Kiku said firmly. "Now come along."

On the way through the lobby, she stopped to pull a white gardenia from the arrangement on a table, then tucked the flower into one side of her chignon, at the nape of her slender neck. When she looked up again, she felt the gaze of every man in the lobby. They all seemed to stop what they were doing and stare in her direction. She might not care what men thought of her, but she loved having power over them. Just as a gun was a tool she could wield to make men bend to her will, so was her body.

Two doormen held the doors open as she and Alex approached. "Shall I hail you a cab?" one offered.

"No. Please have the valet get my car. Rochester. Room 202."

"Right away, ma'am." The doorman hurried over and spoke to the valet. The two men were in their twenties, and Kiku's arrival seemed to be the highlight of their day. They whispered and jostled each other, then the valet finally pushed the doorman back toward Kiku.

"I'm sorry, Ms. Rochester," the doorman said, "but do you have your ticket?"

"I'm afraid I left it in my room."

"It's a silver Audi," Alex blurted.

"Here it is," the valet announced triumphantly, lifting up a BMW key with a paper identifying tag on it. "Wait. What kind of car did you say it was?"

Kiku waved dismissively. "My son got confused. My husband took the Audi this weekend. We have the BMW."

The valet nodded and jogged off.

Kiku shot Alex a quick *shut up* glance.

Alex shoved his hands in his pockets for safe keeping.

As they waited for the valet to return, two men stepped out of the hotel behind them. One of them whistled and flagged down a cab. The other was fiddling with his phone.

Kiku walked over to him and placed her hand on his arm. "Excuse me, sir. Do you have the time?"

The man turned, and with a gentle sweep of her arm Kiku sent his phone tumbling to the ground. She and the man jostled each other as they reached to retrieve it at the same time.

"I'm so sorry." Kiku flashed a seductive smile, deftly removing his wallet from his pocket.

The man's cheeks flushed red. "My fault. Thanks." He started to put the phone in his pocket.

"The time?" Kiku gave a little wink.

"Yeah! It's, ah . . . almost seven. Five till."

The other man was holding the cab door open. "Come on, Jim!"

Kiku waited until the cab was out of sight before taking a twenty from the man's wallet. With this she airily tipped the valet when he returned with Ms. Rochester's car, and she and Alex got in and pulled away.

When the hotel had faded from the rearview mirror, Alex let out a long sigh and pulled his white cap down lower. "That was a lot of work to get a car. Couldn't you just hotwire one?"

"New cars have security features that are difficult to disable. Hopefully, Ms. Rochester will not notice her car is gone until we no longer need it. Besides, we required clothes."

"We had clothes." Alex shook his head and took out his video game. "And we didn't need a new car. It's not like we're trying to impress anyone."

Alex was wrong about that. There was no way Kiku would show up in front of Takeo looking anything less than drop dead gorgeous. And it was no coincidence that she and Alex would be clad in red and white—the traditional Japanese colors signifying the celebration of a happy occasion. Kiku was sending a clear message to Takeo. Even if Alex was not his son, the boy was *not* to be harmed.

20

The drive to Chicago passed without incident. She still had no DNA test results. Kiku needed to speak to Takeo. She had reached a decision when it came to Alex. If the DNA revealed that Alex was not his son, she would convince him to relocate Alex to another country. She would make the world think Alex Harris had disappeared and their secrets would be safe. She would personally vouch for the boy and handle the matter herself.

Kiku's fingers drummed the steering wheel. Even if Takeo agreed, there was still the matter of the traitor in the Yakuza ranks, and she still did not know the identity of the mole.

They pulled off the highway just before they reached the city limits. At Walmart, the flashy pair made a stir as they picked up a burner phone for her and a new handheld video game system for Alex. Back in the BMW, they each opened their box and started up their new gadget.

"I can't believe you let me get this." Alex's grin widened—then faltered. "You used a credit card from one of the guys on the train who tried to kill us, right?"

"Yes." Of course she'd done no such thing. She'd used the card from the man at the hotel. But Alex clearly had a moral streak, so she lied.

She held her finger to her lips as she dialed Takeo.

"Hello?" he answered.

"I am almost there. Location? Time?"

"Kiku . . ." Takeo's voice had a warmth to it she hadn't heard in a long time. He sighed, and in the silence that followed she heard someone else in the room with him clear their throat. "Meet me at the tower. Three o'clock. *Saraba da.*"

Kiku's breath hitched. "I will stop at the Thorn and Thistle."

The phone call ended with a click.

Alex was hopping up and down in his seat. "That was my dad! That's so cool. I just heard my dad's voice! What does *saraba da* mean?"

Kiku felt warmth flush her cheeks. "It means farewell in Japanese."

"I thought that was *sayonara*."

"*Sayonara* is very final. You actually do not hear that said in Japan. *Saraba da* is an old way of saying goodbye. From the samurai era."

The truth was, the phrase made Kiku hunger for Takeo—and Takeo knew that. The night he cornered her in his office, it was what he'd said to her. His eyes were so wild, at first she thought he might have been drinking. And as he took her in his arms, she warned him that the two of them making love could be the death of them both. "*Saraba da!*" he called out as he pulled her close and laid her down.

And that was what the moment felt like for her, too. Farewell to everything except him. Let the world burn, and let us kindle the fire. We will perish, but for one night nothing else matters. And nothing else did.

Not to him.

Not to her.

She started up the car again. "I need to pick something up," she said.

Alex laid his video game in his lap. "Are you okay?"

"Yes, I am fine."

"Your face is red."

Kiku powered down her window. "It is warm in here."

Alex's nose wrinkled. "How come when you speak to me you sound like a robot, but when you're pretending to be someone else you sound normal?"

"Are you back to being rude?"

Alex shrugged apologetically. "I didn't mean to sound like a jerk. I just meant . . . what's the word?" He twisted in his seat. "Contractions. You don't use contractions. You say *I am*, not *I'm*."

"That is the proper way to speak." Kiku sped up.

"Who taught you English?"

Kiku pushed the memory aside. "Play your game. We will be there soon."

"I thought you said you needed to get something."

"I do."

"What?" Alex made a circular motion with his hand like he was calling her forward. "That's another thing. You give, like, one-word answers. I've got this teacher, Mr. Murphy, and he always says that he has to drag the words out of me. He should meet you!"

Kiku scowled, but Alex just sat there with a smug look on his face waiting for her to answer. This was the issue with not striking the boy. She was certain that if she gave him even a slightly painful blow, he'd stop nagging her.

"I am getting your father a Gurkha Black Dragon."

"That sounds cool. What is it?"

Kiku laughed. "A cigar."

Alex wrinkled his nose. "My dad smokes? That's kinda uncool."

"He does not smoke often."

In fact, she'd only seen him smoke after they'd made love. As she pictured him out on the balcony with his feet up, his shirt off, and a contented smile across his face, her stomach tightened. *Saraba da*, indeed! If he had enough energy after she was done with him, she wanted to give him an exceptional cigar, and the best place to get one in Chicago was the Thorn and Thistle, on the South Side.

She pulled the BMW to the curb and kept the engine running. "I'll only be a minute. Keep the doors locked."

But Alex was already playing with his new video game, and Kiku wondered if he'd even heard her. She locked the doors herself and walked into the tobacco shop. She enjoyed the warm, woodsy smell of the place and the memories it brought back. By the time she walked out with her present in hand and the sun on her face, she was experiencing a feeling that was rare for her.

She felt happy . . .

Kiku spotted the huge man crossing the street toward her, his right eye bandaged. It was the Russian who had pretended to be a policeman and grabbed Alex from school.

His gun was pointed at her chest.

Time slowed and the world around her drained of all color. She had always known death was inevitable, and she did not fear it—but she didn't expect to be gunned down in the street like an animal. She had let down her guard—and it would be the last mistake she'd ever make.

Alex would die with her, and her sister would never be avenged.

Kiku snarled. The Russian responded with a smile . . . before he took flight.

The BMW crashed into him, flipping him up and over the roof like a rag doll. He spun in two complete revolutions before landing in a heap on the pavement not three feet away from her. Pedestrians shrieked in terror and scattered like frightened birds.

Alex was in the driver's seat, flailing his arms and screaming incoherently as if a swarm of bees were his passengers. She couldn't understand anything he was saying. It didn't matter. If one Russian was there, so were others. They were relentless.

Kiku sprinted for the car.

"Drive! Drive!" She dove into the passenger seat, and Alex stomped on the gas pedal. The BMW shot forward, ricocheting off the cars parked along the curb, sending side-view mirrors and sparks flying.

The rear window shattered as a bullet whizzed through the glass. Alex screamed, and the BMW swerved to the wrong side of the street. Kiku looked back. A blue sedan was chasing them, and a Russian was leaning halfway out of the passenger window, firing his pistol.

Horns blared, and Alex jerked the wheel, overcorrecting and heading straight for the back of a delivery van. Kiku reached across, grabbed the wheel, and fought to straighten the car out. More pieces of the BMW ripped off as they clipped the van.

"STAY ON THE ROAD!" she shouted.

"I'M TRYING! DRIVING IS WAY HARDER THAN IT LOOKS!"

Alex took his foot off the gas. As the car slowed, a bullet ripped into the dashboard and bits of plastic sprayed around the interior.

"STEP ON THE GAS!" Kiku steered with one hand as Alex jammed both feet onto the gas pedal, and the speedometer raced upward as they flew down the street. When the light ahead turned yellow, Alex kept the pedal pinned to the floor.

"Um . . . should I stop?"

"Keep going."

"IT JUST TURNED RED!"

The passenger headrest spat out stuffing as a bullet ripped through it. Ahead, cars began to move in the other direction through the intersection.

"WHAT DO I DO?" Alex said.

"KEEP GOING!"

The front left tire exploded, and bits of rubber went flying. Kiku's muscles strained as she fought to keep the car from pulling hard to the left.

A taxi crossing the intersection hit its brakes, but its front end struck the rear of the BMW. Pain sliced up her side as Kiku gripped the steering wheel as hard as she could to keep it from being ripped from her hand. The car straightened out, but they were losing speed. She glanced back over her shoulder. The intersection was partially blocked, slowing down the pursuing sedan, but it was weaving a path through the stopped cars.

"Take the wheel." Kiku grabbed her handbag. "Stop when I tell you and lie down on the seat. Okay?"

"Okay."

The car veered across the lanes like a drunken sailor as Alex turned the wheel too far in one direction and then the other. Kiku ripped open the bundled potato chip bags and exhaled as she wrapped her hand around the handle of her gun.

"STOP!" she yelled.

Alex jammed on the brakes, and Kiku kicked open her door. If she was going to die in the street, at least let it be with a gun in her hand.

Behind her, both men leaned out the windows of the sedan and fired. Kiku didn't panic and didn't rush. They were firing from a moving car, reducing their accuracy; she estimated her chances of getting hit at this distance to be about as good as getting struck by lightning. She assumed a shooter's stance and took a deep breath. Ignoring the bullets pinging around her, she took her time and focused on the driver's head.

A bullet struck the tar at her feet. She exhaled slowly and pulled the trigger. She saw the driver's head kick back. His arm went limp and the gun fell from his hand. The passenger stopped shooting and reached for the wheel.

Kiku fired four more times and watched the windshield of the sedan spiderweb and the passenger jerk and thrash as her bullets struck him. The blue sedan veered to the right and slammed into a parked car.

Kiku ran to the BMW's driver-side door and yanked it open. "Are you hit?"

"No, I'm good."

She seized Alex's arm and pulled him out. The boy was scared to death, but he still had the presence of mind to grab his new video game and clutch it to his chest. Kiku reached in and snatched the potato chip bags; she would wrap up her gun again as soon as they were away from immediate danger.

An old Honda Civic came to a stop beside them. A young man with round glasses rolled down his window. "Are you guys okay?" he asked.

"We need a ride." Kiku pulled Alex over to the Civic. "Hwan, please get in the backseat."

"What?" the man said. "You need an ambulance! I can't—"

Kiku pointed her gun at him. He stopped talking and raised his hands in the air.

"Put your hands down," she said.

The man lowered his hands and started to get out of the car. "Just take it."

"Get back in," Kiku said, "or I will have no choice but to shoot you."

"Okay, okay." The man started to move around the car for the passenger side.

"No," Kiku said. "You drive." Sirens blared in the distance. "Move." Kiku kept the gun aimed at him as he started the car. Alex climbed in the back, and Kiku slid into the front passenger seat.

"Go," Kiku said. "That way," she added, pointing behind them. The young man nervously turned the car around. "Do not try anything. I need to get my son away from here. I will let you out someplace where you cannot report the car stolen for a while. Now throw your phone in the back."

The man's hand shook as he tossed the phone into the backseat. "Okay. Okay. Just take it easy. Don't shoot me, okay? I got a baby brother to care for. I'm all he's got."

"Hwan, throw the phone out the window."

"Oh, crap no." The man started to turn in his seat, but stopped when Kiku raised the gun. "I'm not . . . Aww, I just . . . I need that phone. Can you leave it somewhere or something? Anything but busting it?"

"I could take the SIM chip out," Alex offered.

"No. He could still use Wi-Fi and call the police."

"Come on. Please?" the man begged. "My life's on that thing. Look, I don't care about the car. You can take it, or I'll drive you wherever you want. Please."

Kiku was not going to have this man drive her to Takeo. He would undoubtedly be killed. And she was not going to leave the man with his phone. He was a harmless bystander, but surely the first thing he would do was call the police. She needed to find someplace to drop him off, then ditch the car elsewhere.

"I will not destroy your phone," she said. "Do not argue."

The new burner phone she had just purchased rang. She checked the number. It was Takeo calling her back.

"Hello?"

"Kiku. Please listen."

The voice was similar to Takeo's but higher pitched. It took her a moment to place it. Takeo's brother, Jiro.

"What is wrong?"

"Don't talk to anyone or we're both dead. The DNA results came in. They matched. Alex is Takeo's son. Get the boy out of Chicago. Take him as far away as you can. They're going to kill him." The phone clicked, and the line went dead.

Kiku's heart thundered in her chest. Her feelings didn't matter. She had her orders: take Alex to Takeo. She always obeyed her orders. Dissension meant death. Slow. Painful. Dishonorable.

But Alex had saved Kiku's life—twice. For the first time in a long time, Kiku was unsure what to do.

Alex reached out and touched her shoulder. "Are you okay?"

"I am fine."

Who did Jiro mean would kill the boy? Takeo? How had the Russians found her?

Saraba da!

She had told Takeo she would stop at the Thorn and Thistle. Had he betrayed her? Had the traitor bugged Takeo's phone? Who was in there with him?

There were too many unanswered questions, but one thing was clear: she had saved Jiro's life and now he was returning the favor.

Akari was screaming in her head now. Kiku pictured her sister and the anguish on her face. She wasn't mad at Kiku, she was begging. Pleading for Kiku to do the right thing. But what was that? The right thing for her as Yakuza was to follow orders. Kiku knew that wasn't what Akari meant. Akari wanted her to do the honorable thing, the thing Akari would have done.

The driver tipped his chin up. "Um . . . what part of Chicago you want? I can get on 90 in a couple blocks."

"No," Kiku said. "Take 55 West. Head out of the city."

She would honor both her sister and her obligations to the Yakuza. Her orders were to keep the boy safe. Until she figured out who wanted him dead, she wouldn't hand Alex over to anyone.

21

An hour and forty minutes later, Kiku, Alex, and DeShawn—Alex had insisted on learning his name—got off 55 and pulled into a gas station. The driver had calmed down considerably since they left the city, but he now sat with both hands in his lap and his eyes flicking to the door handle, looking like he might jump out at any second.

"Once we travel a little farther from the city, I will let you go," Kiku said.

"You can have the car. Just don't take me someplace and put a bullet in the back of my head. I'm the only one left to take care of my baby sister."

"I thought you said you had a little brother," Alex piped up from the backseat.

DeShawn's mouth opened and closed several times. "I got—I got both." He exhaled. "A baby brother *and* a sister."

"Stop worrying," Kiku said. "Do not make a scene, and I give you my word I will leave you alive." She turned to Alex. "Tell the clerk, pump number four. Economy. Here is thirty dollars."

"Can I pick up a couple of snacks—"

"Four waters and two protein bars. Nothing more."

DeShawn's hand rose timidly into the air. "Can you get one for me?"

Kiku nodded. As Alex got out of the car, Kiku told DeShawn, "I will drive now."

"Sure." He reached for his door handle, but blanched when Kiku raised her gun.

"I will walk around. You will slide across the seat," she said.

"Can't I at least stretch my legs? I haven't moved for a couple hours. I'm all cramped up."

"It will not be much longer and you will be free to do as you wish."

Kiku took the driver's seat, and a few minutes later Alex handed her a bag through the window. He stared at the gas pump with his hands on his hips, then turned and stared at the car.

"Oh," said DeShawn. "Miss, could you pull the lever for the gas tank? It's beneath the steering wheel."

Kiku popped the handle.

Alex opened the little door and tried to twist the gas cap. "How do you open this?"

"Just turn it."

"It won't move."

"Counterclockwise?" DeShawn said.

"Oh. Okay. Got it."

"You never pumped gas before?"

"Sure I have." Alex removed the cap, then looked uncertainly at the pump.

"Pick up the lever," DeShawn said. "Not that one. That's diesel."

"What's the difference?"

"Diesel will kill this car. Use the other one. Stick it in the tank and squeeze the handle."

"I know," Alex muttered. He started to pump. When the gas started flowing, he smiled, then gave DeShawn a conciliatory nod.

"Kid's okay," DeShawn said to Kiku.

She knew she was scowling, but she couldn't help it. DeShawn's simple act of walking Alex through pumping gas had made her realize how neglected the boy had been. She thought about Takeo's garages filled with sports cars and she felt her blood boil.

DeShawn stared straight ahead and folded his hands in his lap. "Sorry. Just making conversation."

When the tank was filled, they pulled back onto the small road. After another five miles of alfalfa and soybean fields, Kiku turned onto an unmarked dirt road. DeShawn sat up straighter. Sweat formed on his brow and his eyes kept darting to the door.

"Do not do that," Kiku cautioned.

Alex sat forward in the backseat. "She's going to let you go."

DeShawn shook his head. "No, she ain't. You don't bring someone out here to cut them loose."

"I will not shoot you. Although it would be best."

"Best?" Alex and DeShawn said in unison.

"Shooting you would minimize the chances of the police stopping us. But I gave you my word. I will set you free in another mile."

DeShawn's legs started shaking. "Like I said, take the car. I won't say a word. Just don't kill me."

Kiku stopped the car and raised the gun. "What is the PIN for your phone?"

DeShawn hesitated for only a moment before blurting out, "One-two-three-four-five-six."

Alex shook his head. "You've got to be kidding me, dude." He punched in the numbers. "Terrible passcode. We could've just guessed it."

"I'm not good with remembering numbers. Keep the phone, too." DeShawn's lip trembled.

Kiku aimed the gun at his chest. "Get out. Slowly."

DeShawn grimaced. "Come on. Come on. Please?"

"Get out of the car, take off all of your clothes, and hand them back through the window."

"Oh, hell no." DeShawn raised his hands.

"We are driving back the way we came. We will leave them for you at the side of the road a mile from here." Kiku raised the gun. "I need to slow you down before you contact the authorities, as I am sure you will do. My other option is to shoot you in the leg."

"Whoa. All right." DeShawn got out of the car, stripped down to his underwear and shoes, and handed the rest of his clothes through the window.

"Everything."

DeShawn's cheeks flushed, but he complied.

Alex tossed a small umbrella out of the car.

"What's that for?" DeShawn asked.

"To cover up your junk." Alex chuckled.

DeShawn gave him the finger but immediately started waving his hands. "I didn't mean that. Ha-ha. Funny. He's a good kid; I said that before. What a kidder."

"I will leave your phone with your clothes." Kiku put the car in reverse and turned around.

Alex dropped a bottle of water out the window as they drove off.

"Can you stop and let me in the front seat?" he asked as Kiku flew down the dirt road, the car jostling them back and forth like a carnival ride.

"No. We need distance because you asked me to keep him alive."

Alex climbed over and unceremoniously flopped down in the front passenger seat. "You weren't really going to kill him, were you?"

"At the least, I should have tied him up and knocked him out. Your kindness will get you killed someday. We did not need to know his name either."

"Kindness? The guy has to walk, like, five miles down a gravel road naked. We'll be long gone."

"Maybe. But I do not like leaving anything to chance."

"We should probably drop off his clothes," Alex said. "You said you'd drop them off after a mile."

"That is what I told him, but it is not what I will do. I will leave his clothes at the end of this road."

"You're gonna make him walk down the whole road naked? That is a total jerk move."

Kiku glared, and Alex shut his mouth.

"Being naked will make him go more slowly," Kiku said, "and so will looking for his clothes. I did not shoot him. Be grateful for that."

"So, you just straight-up lied? Wait. You're not even going to give him his phone back, are you?"

"Giving his phone back would be equivalent to driving myself to the police station and turning myself in. Do not be foolish."

They rode the rest of the way down the road in silence. Before they got back to the two-lane highway, Kiku pulled over and Alex got out of the car with DeShawn's clothes. He reached into the car and grabbed another bottle of water.

"Leave that water for us."

Alex frowned. "He can have mine." He carried the clothes and water over to the grass at the side of the road, set them down, then stomped back to the car. He started to get into the backseat, but Kiku pointed to the front.

"It will raise suspicion if you ride back there. Ride up front."

Alex slammed the back door, climbed in, then slammed the front door.

Kiku's eyes narrowed. The boy was getting under her skin again. "If you do not like the front seat, there is another place in this car where you can ride for the rest of the trip." She glanced back at the trunk.

Alex's eyes widened. He shook his head, pulled his seat belt on, and stared straight ahead.

Kiku jammed the transmission into drive, and rocks pinged off the car's undercarriage as she pulled out and doubled back the way they'd come, her thoughts focused but offering no clear solution.

She got on the interstate, heading southwest. "Give me the phone," she ordered Alex. The boy sat unmoving, not even looking at her. His breathing sped up. Hers slowed down. "Give me the phone."

"I can't," Alex whispered. He shifted closer to the door.

Kiku's nails ticked off the steering wheel. He'd left the phone behind with the clothes. She checked the rearview mirror, half expecting to see blue lights behind them. She exhaled slowly. The damage was done. She would have changed cars anyway. Now it was simply a matter of sooner rather than later. And the police were the least of her problems. The Yakuza had a mole. With no one to trust, there was only one place she could turn now.

She ran the prosthetic end of her pinky against the steering wheel. He'd cost her a part of herself. He was the last man she thought she'd speak with again. But if anyone could help her, it was Daichi.

22

They drove through the night and into the next day. The pain in Kiku's side was a constant dull throb, but when she'd last changed the bandage, at a gas station, the wound appeared to be healing well—though *well* was a relative term. She wouldn't be dying from an infection, but the scar would be quite noticeable.

Kiku cut off a car as she took the exit ramp. The driver laid on the horn and flipped her off. She resisted the urge to get back on the highway, pull the guy over, and work out all her frustrations on him with a tire iron. Cutting him off in the first place had been foolish. She needed to get a grip on her emotions and fly under the radar.

They were now driving a dark-blue Toyota Camry, freshly stolen from a fleet of company cars, all fifteen exactly alike. Today was Saturday, so it likely wouldn't be reported stolen until Monday. Alex was sleeping peacefully in the passenger seat. Or pretending to, anyway. They hadn't spoken more than a dozen words since leaving DeShawn behind. Alex had spent the entire ride playing his video game or staring out the window.

She couldn't bring herself to tell him the results of the DNA test. At least Alex wasn't asking where they were going. She could not tell him anything at this point that would not endanger him—or herself—

further. And she appreciated the quiet time to let her subconscious mind meditate on her dilemma.

She followed the curves of the seemingly endless highway until they reached Texarkana. From here, anyone who needed to disappear could take their pick of Oklahoma, Texas, Arkansas, or Louisiana. Kiku could see the usefulness of that, but why Daichi had chosen the town of Fairhope was beyond her. It was like a completely different planet from Hong Kong or any other big, flashy city where Daichi could have moved easily in anonymity. There was no way he could ever blend in here. Even if he weren't missing an arm, the tall Japanese-Chinese man couldn't help but stick out among the locals. But he had put down roots here and earned the respect of the community.

Seven years ago, she'd checked up on him. For hours she observed him from a distance, trying to understand how the hard-partying playboy and fearsome assassin, Kenzo's half-brother and Alex's great-uncle, had taken up farming. After watching him among his beans and turnips and carrots, feeding his animals, fetching his tools, whistling the whole time, she had left more mystified than ever. He seemed completely at ease, in harmony with his surroundings, and without fear—though she had no doubt that if he had caught even the slightest whiff of her presence, she would have quickly found out where he hid his sword or dagger among the rakes and hoes.

Kiku made sure to observe the speed limit as they passed through Fairhope. The small town hadn't changed much. She was surprised that all the little shops in town were still open, especially given the current economy, but then again, she had noticed that people in rural areas tended to watch out for one another.

She was reminded of that as she saw the people watching them go by. A few people waved or gave a curt nod. Most just looked on, keeping an eye on the strangers passing through their town.

Now, as she pulled off onto a dirt road, Alex opened his eyes and sat up.

"We are almost there. You will wait in the car."

"Whatever." Alex crossed his arms and turned away from her.

A rusted metal gate blocked their way. Thick trees on each side and a well-placed boulder made it impossible for her to go around. Kiku put the car in park and grabbed her gun, leaving it wrapped, for now, in the chip bags. She was about to shut off the engine, but hesitated. Her history with Daichi was complicated.

"If I am not back in half an hour," she said, "leave."

Alex looked puzzled.

"If I come back, I will whistle twice. If I do not, or if anyone else comes first, drive away and do not return." She told him a phone number and made him repeat it several times. It was the number for the emergency burner phone she'd given Jack Stratton on a previous occasion. "Drive to that town we passed and call that number. Tell the man who answers that I am dead. Lie and tell him you are my son. Tell him you need to disappear. He will help you."

Alex rubbed his right eye with the palm of his hand. "Sounds like maybe you shouldn't go do whatever you're about to do."

Kiku weighed Alex's words. There was wisdom there. But she had no choice. She needed Daichi's counsel. He was the only man she knew of who had made it out of the Yakuza.

"Half an hour."

She got out of the car and walked around the gate. The day was beautiful and the sun was just starting to set. After a hundred yards, the woods gave way to a view of a two-story farmhouse and an old barn where chickens pecked at the ground, goats pranced, and three cows lazily chewed the grass.

Kiku continued on, neither advertising nor hiding her presence. As she stepped onto the porch of the farmhouse, a fat Yellow Lab wearily raised its head, disturbing the gray cat nuzzled up against it. The dog huffed once, lowered its head, and closed its eyes, while the cat shook itself and then stalked off indignantly.

Kiku raised her arms. "We need to speak," she called out.

"Drop what's in your hand." The gruff voice, which came from directly below her feet, would have made most people jump, but Kiku grinned.

Daichi was waiting for her arrival, hidden underneath the porch.

"Well played," she said, dropping the bag with a thump that brought the dog to its feet.

"Back off the porch and into the driveway. Fingers interlaced."

Kiku complied, walking backward down the steps. A wooden door opened on the side of the porch decking and a shotgun appeared. Kiku couldn't see the face of the man holding the gun, but she saw the metal prosthetic cradling the shotgun's barrel. It was Daichi all right. Kiku noted that he'd switched to a left-hand-dominant position.

I guess I didn't leave him much of a choice.

"The passenger is still in the car," called a voice from a second-floor window. A woman's voice, Swiss accent. "We're clear."

"You checked the perimeter feed?" Daichi shouted.

"One second." Pause. "Clear."

Daichi ducked as he exited from under the porch, but kept the shotgun leveled at Kiku.

"You have a new look," Kiku said.

She smiled at his salt-and-pepper hair. There was a time when Daichi could have been the spokesperson for hair products. Back then, he had thick, lustrous, black hair, and he pampered it. But now his locks were in need of a cut and brushed back.

"I need your help," she said simply.

"Who's in the car?"

"I will tell you later. There is a mole in the Yakuza."

Daichi rocked his head to the side and flashed the smile that had once made the teenage Kiku melt. His laughter boomed across the yard, and the animals responded to it. The chickens came closer and the goats pranced happily toward the fence. "There are many in the Yakuza who would sell information for a price. Why come to me?"

"It is not information they are selling." Kiku kept her hands interlocked behind her head, but gestured with her elbow back down the road. "They have targeted me and the boy who is with me."

Daichi's eyebrows rose. "You have a son?"

Kiku's stomach clenched. Perhaps because of her wound. She started to lower her arms.

"Nope." Daichi raised the shotgun and shook his head. "You still haven't answered my question. Who is he?"

"He is Takeo's son."

23

Daichi chuckled and pointed the shotgun at the ground. "So, the good son has some bad boy in him." Slowly, he raised the shotgun back up and aimed it at Kiku. "Since when did Takeo have a kid?"

"He didn't know about the boy until recently. He sent me to get a DNA sample."

"And you just took the whole kid? You know saliva or blood would work?"

"I got his DNA, but the Russians came after him. It's complicated. The test came back positive."

Daichi lowered the shotgun again. "If you want my help, I need to see the boy with my own eyes."

Kiku frowned, but she saw she had no choice. "Fine."

Daichi held up his good hand toward the house and made a couple of motions that Kiku recognized as sign language. Then he gestured toward the driveway and said to Kiku, "After you."

Kiku glanced up at the house. Someone was still watching them from the second floor. And a curtain on the first floor moved, too.

This farm is big. Daichi would need help to run it. How many people are inside?

As her shoes crunched the gravel, Daichi fell into step alongside her. His face was lined with age and his hair was now streaked with gray, but those things weren't what made him look so different. It was something else about him. An attitude, a feeling.

He seemed happy. The Daichi she remembered was always smiling, but it hadn't been a smile of joy. It was more of a roguish grin. A challenge to the universe: he was here, and he would run his life how he wanted to—and he'd smile while he was at it. But his eyes . . . it was said that people didn't want to look him in the eyes, afraid of what they'd see. As a teenager, Kiku had ignored that advice—and when Daichi finally noticed her, she found his brown eyes as inviting and tempting as melted chocolate.

Until the day they worked together for the first time.

She thought it was to be a simple money drop. The men they went to see were his friends. She had no idea they had skimmed money off the top—or that Kenzo had ordered a hit. But that was the way of the Yakuza: at any moment a simple task might turn into a bloodbath.

Daichi slaughtered everyone in the restaurant. Kiku had seen horror before, but never executed with such fluidity, grace, and absolute lack of emotion. That was the first time she had ever seen Daichi not smiling. And she understood then what people said about his eyes. They still haunted her dreams.

As did his words: *"Every time you pull the trigger, you blow away a piece of your own soul."* After that, Kiku never saw him the same way again.

"He let you live," Daichi said, walking beside her. His words snapped her out of her memory. "And you kept your hand."

Kiku tapped the severed pinky with her thumb. "Most of it."

"I'm surprised by Kenzo's restraint."

"Of course, he *wanted* my whole hand. Takeo talked him out of it."

"I told you Kenzo would be furious when you didn't bring back my noggin'. You should have taken it."

"Your head was worth a bit of a digit."

They walked in silence for a moment, then Daichi said, "I've gotta ask. Where did my brother bury my hand? I figure it wouldn't be in the main family plot, but is it in the cemetery at Kamakura?"

"No. He fed it to the dogs."

A range of emotions washed over Daichi's face. "Seriously? Dog food?"

Kiku laughed.

"It isn't funny." His grip tightened on the shotgun, but not in a threatening way. "Some mutts ate my hand."

"No, not mutts." Kiku grinned. "Purebred Kai Kens."

He stared at his prosthetic and pouted. "I liked that hand."

"It was the only way."

Daichi's smile returned. "So, your pinky tip was their appetizer and my hand the main course. We must have made a great meal." He laughed.

Kiku was glad to hear him laugh again. She didn't tell him that Takeo had cremated her fingertip and spread the ashes in his private garden.

They approached the bend in the road, and through the trees they could see the car waiting just beyond the gate, no more than fifty yards away.

"Do not speak to the boy," Kiku said. "I do not want him learning of his heritage from you."

"I don't want him learning of me, period. I will stay in the shadows of the trees, where he can't see my face." Daichi shifted the shotgun in his grip. Although it was still pointed at the ground, he was clearly prepared to shoot. "You continue forward down the drive."

Kiku nodded and started back toward the car. Daichi moved off the road and kept pace with her in the woods.

As Kiku came around the bend, in view of the car, Daichi ordered, "Stop. Call him out."

Kiku whistled twice. "Hwan? Come out."

Alex got out of the car and started to walk around the gate, but Kiku held up her hand.

"Stop."

"What?" Alex froze.

Kiku waited a moment before saying, "Get back in the car."

"What?" Alex looked around, puzzled. "Are you just messing with me?"

"I will explain later."

Alex rolled his eyes before getting back in and slamming the door behind him.

Sticks crunched in the woods, and Kiku spun. Daichi came strolling toward the edge of the trees with a huge grin on his face and his chest puffed out. "I'm a great-uncle!" he said, beaming. "That boy's the spitting image of my grandfather. He's Takeo's son all right. You don't need a DNA test for that."

"Will you help?"

Daichi stayed under the trees, out of Alex's sight. "I'll listen. Tell the boy to wait here."

Kiku ran back to the car and grabbed the water bottle Alex had been drinking out of. "Stay here until I come back. Same drill."

"Are you okay? How long are you gonna be?"

"I do not know. When I come back, I will whistle." She held up three fingers. "Understand?"

Alex nodded.

Kiku turned and started back toward the farmhouse. After she was out of sight of the car, Daichi fell into step beside her, the shotgun resting on his shoulder, his expression darkened in thought.

"The traitor is targeting the boy?" he said.

Kiku nodded. "They've been tracking me and Hwan."

Daichi chuckled. "You're selling that fake name a little too hard. You said they're tracking you. How?"

"They put a locator in my gun. I wrapped it in aluminum to block the signal."

"You need to tell me everything. Talk."

Kiku ran down everything that had happened, leaving no details out. The war with the Russians. Dr. Rogoff. The pursuit of the boy. The safe house, the attack on the train, the interception at the Thorn and Thistle, Jiro's call.

Daichi didn't ask a single question. He walked beside her as calmly as if they were heading off to go fishing, but she knew he was taking in every word. Daichi was the best tactician she knew, and right now she prayed he had some advice that could help.

When they reached the farmhouse, Daichi grabbed a metal pail with a lid. "First, put your gun in here. I'm not taking any chances with a tracker."

Kiku retrieved her gun, which was still lying on the porch wrapped in the potato chip bags, and put it in the pail. Daichi covered it with the lid and set it off to the side.

He crossed his arms and shook his head. "Kiku . . . you didn't just step in it. If someone on the inside wants both you and the boy dead, you're neck deep. Do you have any kind of plan?"

"That is why I came here," Kiku admitted. "I need your advice."

Daichi frowned. "The Russians could tell you who is behind this. Do you have something you could offer them? Besides the boy, of course."

"I will not bargain with the Russians."

"You sound just like my brother. Well then, my advice would be to take that kid far away and drop him off on the side of the road. There's no life for him if you take him to Kenzo. Only a walking death."

"I cannot just drop him off. They know who he is. He will not be safe."

"You came here asking for my advice, yet you reject it," Daichi said. "Perhaps it would be better for you to tell me what your best idea is, and then I can go back to minding my own business."

Kiku scowled. "I thought I would use the tracker to lure the Russians into a trap. Then I would make them give me the name of the one who is betraying me. But I lack the firepower to deal with the numbers that would likely descend upon me."

Daichi smiled approvingly. "Now I see your plan. I think I can help you with that. Follow me." He led her inside the barn and walked to the stall at the end. He swept aside the straw to uncover a door in the floor, then opened it, revealing steps leading down. He grabbed a flashlight, flicked it on, and handed it to Kiku. "After you."

Kiku played the flashlight beam around the room, taking everything in. The cellar contained enough weapons and ammo to open a gun store. When the light landed on several large bags of cocaine, her face must have shown her surprise.

"It's not mine," Daichi quickly explained. "The Correa-Cabrera cartel has a route that ran straight through Fairhope. I like this town, so I convinced them to relocate their pipeline."

Kiku turned her attention back to the weapons. "This will work, Daichi." She nodded. "Yes, this will work quite nicely." She walked over to a table, picked up a Glock 45, and smiled.

Daichi laughed. "I know that look, Ōkami. You're getting ready to hunt."

Kiku's smile widened, exposing the prominent canines that were one reason Daichi had nicknamed her Ōkami—the Japanese word for wolf. But there was another similarity between Kiku and the *ōkami*. Like Kiku, the small, fierce wolves indigenous to Japan are known for doing one thing exceptionally well.

Bringing down their prey.

24

"I'll get you some food to bring back to the boy," Daichi said, opening the door to the farmhouse. Just inside, a plump blond woman with a round face was sitting at the kitchen table. Alex was seated next to her.

The woman smiled sheepishly. "Whoopsie-doodle."

Kiku moved to step in front of Daichi to hide his face from Alex's view, but Daichi strode inside, walked right up to the table, and frowned down at the woman. He shook his head, his face stern.

"It wasn't my doing," she said.

"It was me," a voice called from the pantry.

An elderly Japanese woman, bent with age, stepped into the kitchen holding a colander filled with mushrooms. "I went out to pick mushrooms. The boy's so skinny I thought he was one. We haven't used any names if that's what you're worried about. I may be old, but I'm not dense. What else was I going to do? I caught him peeing on my mushrooms and he got so scared he ran right for the house."

"That's not true!" Alex stammered, turning beet-red. "I . . . I was . . ."

"I told you to wait in the car," Kiku snapped.

"I had to go—"

"Ha!" the old woman said, dumping the mushrooms into a pot on the stove. "I told you, he was watering the mushrooms."

The blonde made a face. "You're not using those in the soup, are you?"

"I washed them." The old woman winked.

The blonde huffed, but Daichi laughed. "She's kidding," he said. "I think." He shot a questioning glance at the cook.

The old woman stirred the pot and sipped the liquid. "Of course, I would have used them if I wasn't planning to eat some myself . . ." She chuckled and added some salt. "Dinner will be ready in half an hour. Will you be joining us, *Mimi*?" Her eyes gleamed impishly.

Kiku—showing restraint—smacked the back of Alex's head. Inside, she was seething. And not because of "Mimi," but because Alex had seen Daichi's face. That should never have happened. It posed a danger not only to Alex but to Daichi. And perhaps most of all to Kiku, because if Kenzo found out his brother was alive, he would burn this town to the ground. And then he would mount Kiku's head on a spike.

25

Kiku stared out the passenger window of the truck as Daichi drove. They exited the highway. The signs with the icons for food and gas both listed only one store: Big K.

"It's a dot on the map," Daichi said, as if reading her mind.

They'd driven through several towns and past endless fields of green since leaving Fairhope, but Kiku wondered if it was far enough to keep Daichi's secret safe. She would have preferred to go farther, but Daichi had insisted they spring her trap here. She hated to have to rely on anyone, but she had no choice. She was the one looking for help, so she had to trust him—for now.

"The Russians will bring at least four well-armed men," she said. "And considering that I have already taken out a number of them, there could be many more, all heavily armed. Can the police from this small town handle that?"

Daichi flashed the roguish grin he was famous for. He looked as though they were merely driving to the store to pick up bread, his window down and the wind blowing his hair back. Fear never seemed to stick to the man. Or if it did, he never showed it.

"I've got it covered," he said. "The police chief's a friend of mine. But getting them arrested is only half the plan. Are you certain you can pull this off?"

Kiku forced her mouth to tick up in a slight mischievous grin. She wanted Daichi to wonder what trick she might have up her sleeve. She was certain she would make her part succeed. But the truth was, it wasn't her role she was concerned with. If Daichi's half of the plan failed . . .

They drove through the tiny town, which seemed to be composed of a feed store, a church, and a few shacks clustered around the railroad tracks, and kept going. Kiku wondered once again how Daichi had gone from the lights and noise and bustle of Hong Kong to . . . this. Maybe it was like someone who overindulges in a particular food and never wants to eat it again. Kiku couldn't imagine ever living a farming life. Once all this was over, she'd go home, pick up a bottle of wine, and take a two-hour bath.

"We don't want this to end in a shootout," Kiku said.

"It's going to be fine. But I still think it would have been better if we grabbed one and killed the rest of them. Then we could have made him talk at the house."

"He would lie."

Daichi chuckled. "Then you've lost your edge."

Kiku rolled her eyes. "I have not." If anything, the years had hardened her. "These Russians are tough. I can make anyone talk, but the truthfulness of their confession is always in doubt. He could give me a dozen false names. I need to be certain. We will stick to my plan."

Daichi turned into a long driveway. An incongruously huge, well-kept house sat back from the road, a *For Sale* sign in the yard. "Here we go."

"You are positive the house is vacant?"

"It's been on the market for three years. Guy who owned the house built a mini-mansion to enjoy quiet living in Norwell, until he realized it was *too* quiet. His wife called it Snorewell and begged to leave."

Kiku scanned the wide-open fields surrounding the house. The nearest trees were over a hundred feet away. Perfect line of sight.

Daichi parked out front. Kiku grabbed the duffel bag from the backseat and hopped out. She started to head around back, but Daichi shook his head.

"Go in the front."

"I can get in the back door more easily than picking the realtor's combination lock."

"No need. A while back I asked the realtor lady to show me the place." Daichi punched in a code, and the lock clicked. He grinned. "She wasn't too careful about hiding the combination from me."

Kiku headed for the stairs. "The most difficult part will be the timing."

"I've got a friend in air traffic control. They monitor all flights, commercial and private. I also have people watching the interstate, just in case. Once they spot the Russians, that'll start the clock ticking. Trust me. The police chief here knows me."

"That is what worries me."

Kiku sought out the most interior room in the house—a huge bedroom. She set down the duffel bag and unzipped it. Inside were two dozen packages of cocaine and her gun, still safely encased in the potato chip bags.

She unwrapped the gun, wiped it down, and set it on the floor. Then she took out three bags of cocaine and zipped up the duffel. The trap was set.

"I wouldn't take any with you," Daichi cautioned.

"I will plant them in the study far from where they can flush the evidence."

"Good thinking."

"We need to make sure the police can hold them."

"They will. Now what?" Daichi asked.

Kiku felt a little charge of electricity travel up her legs. "As you said, the clock is ticking. Now we wait."

26

Sitting in the driver's seat of his truck, well hidden in the woods, Daichi unwrapped a mint and popped it into his mouth. He held out another to Kiku.

"No, thank you." She went back to staring at the house.

"You don't have to worry about putting on weight. You look in better shape than when I last saw you." Daichi opened the glove compartment and started rooting around like a squirrel digging for a nut.

"We just had a large dinner. I see that you have gained twenty pounds."

Daichi scowled. "Thanks for reminding me." His scowl disappeared as he triumphantly raised a candy bar.

"I take it back. Twenty-one."

"For that, you don't get any." He leaned against the door and opened the wrapper, expertly using his single hand.

Kiku ignored him and sipped her water. "You are certain no one is coming home?"

"I told you, the house has been vacant for three years. The realtor told me all about it. Everyone's pretty transparent around here."

"Pretty foolish, you mean."

"People call it honesty."

"If they knew who you really are, would they be so honest?"

Daichi chewed happily. “I think they’d surprise you. They’re a forgiving lot out here. Besides, I’ve changed. I’m honest now.”

“Who is the blonde? Is she living with you?”

The candy bar stopped halfway to his mouth. He paused before taking a bite, then took his time chewing, as if considering how to answer. “Lilly is my wife. I bet when you pictured my wife, you never thought she’d be short, plump, and blond.”

Kiku smiled ruefully. The truth was, she had never pictured Daichi with a wife because she’d never believed Daichi would live long enough to get married. He was a man who lived on the edge and burned white-hot. She thought a fire like that could only burn for so long.

“She seems nice. And when did you become a polygamist?”

Daichi coughed on his candy bar and reached for his water. “Baba? She’s not my wife. I’m . . . She stays with me.”

Kiku regretted her weak attempt at a joke. Of course she knew who the old woman was. Baba and her husband owned a small restaurant outside of Hong Kong. Or at least, they once did. Daichi and Kiku had dined there often. Until Baba’s husband was killed—by Daichi.

She recalled the hit. A local politician had reneged on a deal; it was Daichi’s job to exact the price. He took the sniper shot from over half a mile away. It was a perfect shot, except for one thing. Bullets don’t always stop when they hit something. The bullet killed the target, whizzed by the security guards behind him, and struck Baba’s husband. Kiku couldn’t remember the man’s name, but she would never forget the sound of Baba wailing. Daichi might as well have killed her that day.

Which was why it made no sense that she was with him now.

“Does she know it was you who took the shot?” Kiku asked.

Daichi winced, then nodded.

Kiku tensed. “And—”

“The boy is safe with her,” Daichi said firmly.

“What about you? How do you sleep with her in the house?”

He chuckled. “Not very well at first.” His chuckle grew into joyful laughter. He laughed so hard he needed to wipe his eyes. Then he took a deep breath and regained control of himself. “How could anyone forgive that? You know, I think she was only joking when she said she washed the mushrooms."

Kiku made a face.

"I'm kidding!" He laughed again. "Seriously, Lilly's the one who convinced me to try to make amends. I can't, of course. The truth is, I thought Baba would run straight to Kenzo. But she didn't."

"I cannot believe you took such a risk."

Daichi rolled down his window, took a deep breath, and shrugged. "When's the last time *you* slept well?"

Kiku kept her mouth closed. She knew the silence would provide the answer. *Not for a long, long time.*

Daichi's phone buzzed with a text. "It's my friend in air traffic control." He read it. "SIX MEN LANDED IN SHREVEPORT IN A PRIVATE PLANE." He held up his phone. "From the picture, they're either here for a body-building convention or the Russians have landed. The clock's ticking."

As Daichi had predicted, eighty minutes later, two cars—the only cars they had seen so far—slowed down at the driveway of the mansion and pulled in.

Kiku motioned for Daichi to start the truck. "None of them can get away."

"Relax. They won't."

"The house is completely exposed on all sides. The lookout could rabbit."

Daichi just smiled and tapped his watch. "Any minute . . . now," he said, looking up to see her face. From the left and right, lines of silhouetted vehicles appeared—at least half a dozen cars from both directions, their headlights off. In the distance, the heavy beat of helicopter blades filled the air. "I told you. I called in a favor."

"Impressive."

Daichi posed with his one hand hanging over the steering wheel. "It never hurts to get the law on your side, so I've tipped off the chief here about a few scores. Turns out they were some of the biggest drug busts in state history. Now I'm his hero."

The house lit up like the Fourth of July as two helicopters aimed their spotlights at it and a dozen vehicles hit their lights and sirens.

"Where did they all come from?" Kiku asked. "This little town looks like it doesn't have a dozen residents, let alone cruisers and helicopters."

"No, they don't. But they're firm believers in interagency cooperation around here." Daichi smiled broadly. "You said you needed firepower . . ."

Kiku bowed. "*Arigato gozaimasu*, Daichi." The trap had been sprung.

27

Texarkana, Arkansas

Kiku strolled through the front doors of the Texarkana, Arkansas, police headquarters. For someone in her line of work, it was like walking into the lion's den, but she didn't hesitate. She headed straight for the bulletproof information window, and instead of breaking a sweat, she smiled as the familiar glow of adrenaline rushed through her veins.

Beats jumping out of a plane any day.

The recent arrest of six Russian mobsters was the biggest news drama this town had ever seen. Daichi had chatted up his friend the police chief, who had let slip the name of the group's leader—Dima Kuznetsov. Daichi had also said the chief was so happy he could burst, but he was fighting tooth and nail to keep jurisdiction, and that was a fight Daichi said he wouldn't win. Which meant Kiku needed to work fast.

She handed her freshly printed business card along with her new fake ID to the young policeman. Kiku was impressed with not only how fast Daichi had gotten her the fake ID but also how flawless the quality of the product was. She hadn't seen a forger of that caliber outside Tokyo.

"I'm Attorney Ji-woo Kim, representing Dima Kuznetsov," she said. She'd opted for a dark-gray business suit with a pencil skirt. A brunette wig, coiffed in a high bun, and a pair of thick, round glasses completed her disguise. "I'd like to see my client," she said in a tough Chicago accent.

"You need to fill this out." The officer pushed a clipboard over to her and pointed behind him. "I'll be right back."

After another forty-five minutes and a pat-down she found herself sitting at a metal table in a bare room. The door opened, and two burly policemen escorted in a hulking Russian, who froze when he saw Kiku's face. She had never seen Dima Kuznetsov before, but there was a high probability that he had seen at least a photograph of her. Her thick glasses were sure to distort her eyes and her low-cut blouse was sure to divert his. He scowled but gave no indication that he recognized her. His massive bald head tilted forward and his shoulders pulled back.

Before he could speak, Kiku turned to the guards. "Remove my client's restraints. They're not necessary." She hoped that appearing at ease in Dima's presence would both lower his defenses and sell the lawyer act.

The two guards looked at her like she was out of her mind, but Dima's face lost some of its tightness. One officer unfastened the Russian's handcuffs; the other rested his hand nervously on his nightstick and said, "We'll leave the leg restraints on, ma'am."

"Thank you, Officers. I'll let you know when we're finished. We won't be long; I'm aware of the time limit," she added, cutting off any potential protest.

The men gave her a sideways glance that seemed to say, *I hope you know what you're doing*, but they left her alone with her "client."

Kiku motioned to the chair across from her. "I am Ji-woo Kim and I will be representing you."

Dima remained standing, looking at her suspiciously. Did he recognize her?

Kiku's face hardened. "If you want to see the light of day sometime before twenty years from now, you'll sit down and listen to everything I say."

"How do you know who I am? Maybe you're with whoever set us up." Dima pushed the chair out of the way and placed two large hands down on the table.

Kiku resisted the urge to take a defensive posture. "You and your men walked right into a trap."

Dima just glared at her.

"Will you please stop the drama and sit down?" Kiku demurely crossed her legs. "This is at most a minor inconvenience, unless you choose to make it a major one."

"Minor? I was arrested in possession of over fifteen pounds of cocaine. Add in the weapons charges, and they'll crucify me."

"Not if you listen to me." Kiku held a delicate hand toward the chair across from her.

Dima's hands flexed as he pressed them down on the table, and veins stood out and grew like vines up his forearms and through his neck, until they throbbed at his temples.

Kiku sighed. "Very well. Stand, sit, it doesn't matter to me as long as you listen. Before I tell you how we are going to make all of this go away, you need to answer one question. Have you said anything to the police? Given them any reason for your presence in the house?"

Dima scoffed.

"Excellent," Kiku said. "You and your team work for Robert Bennigan, an internationally famous antiquities dealer and author. You were hired to recover an antique statue that was stolen from him in New York last week. As we speak, all the necessary paperwork to corroborate those facts is being sent to the DA's office."

Dima straightened, and Kiku paused until she saw the network of veins in his arms deflate as his blood pressure went down.

"As a security precaution," Kiku continued, "a tracking device was placed inside the statue. You and your team followed it, and that is how you arrived at the house."

Dima finally pulled the chair back and sat down. "How are you going to prove that?"

Good. He trusts me.

"Your travel records. You flew into Shreveport and went directly to the house. I need the exact route you took so I can pull security footage and prove that you arrived minutes before the police. Mr. Bennigan has confirmed that he hired you and that the tracking chip the police found in the gun was originally placed inside his statue. Just remember, you and your team were hired to track a—" Kiku folded her arms across her chest and waited.

Dima shifted uncomfortably in his seat.

"On second thought," she said, "keep your mouth shut and let me do all the talking."

Dima's chair scraped the floor as he leaned in menacingly. "So, you work for Bennigan?" His breath was hot and rancid on her cheeks.

Kiku let her eyelids flutter in faux exasperation. "Once you and your men have been released, your services are no longer required."

"That's not the deal."

Good. Getting closer.

"Three strikes, Kuznetsov. I'm not a miracle worker."

Dima's veins blossomed once more, and his face turned a splotchy red. "I know who you really work for." He leveled a thick finger at Kiku and lowered his voice. "The Yakuza killed Cade Novikov's son. The only way this ends is an eye for an eye. Tell Shin to deliver the kid. Until then, I'm not done."

Kiku's head spun. She somehow managed to keep her breathing even and steady, but she could feel the color draining from her face. Did the Russian just say what she thought he said?

Tell Shin?

Shin Uchihara was Takeo's head of security. He had been groomed from childhood to protect Takeo, the seventh generation of Uchiharas to serve in the role of protecting the head of the Yakuza. She was as certain that Shin would never betray Takeo as she was that the sun would rise tomorrow. Shin would never dishonor his ancestors by disobeying Takeo. So, if Shin knew . . . Takeo knew. Takeo had authorized Alex's death. And hers. Takeo was appeasing the Russians. The price of ending the war was killing his own son.

Like a shark smelling blood in the water, Dima sensed her weakness. "Tell Shin we still want Takeo's dog, too. She killed a lot of my men."

Kiku maintained a neutral mask despite the pain in her chest. A deal like that . . . it made a sort of sick sense. Give up your son—the son you don't want anyway—to avoid the carnage of war.

But she had to be sure.

"I'll relay the message," Kiku said coolly. "When was the last contact you had with Shin?"

"Yesterday. Chicago. A burner phone."

"Did you have it on you when you were arrested?" Kiku asked.

"It's a burner," Dima repeated.

"The police will get a warrant to trace the calls. We'll have to wrap the number into the cover story. Do you remember it?"

Her hand shook slightly as she wrote down the number he repeated. Like the fool that he was, Dima was grinning. He thought her hand was trembling because he was intimidating her. In reality, it was all she could do to keep her rage in check and not stab him to death with the writing utensil in her hand. Her fury burned inside her like molten lava. She wanted to unleash it on anything and anyone; Dima was closest. But besides the temporary relief, what would she gain by killing him?

Kiku inhaled slowly and envisioned herself holding in her hand all the pain raging inside her. She closed her fingers, crushing the emotions into a bullet that she would save for later.

She motioned to summon the officers. "Don't speak to anyone," she said as she calmly placed the pen in her pocket. "And tell your men the same thing. I don't care who it is or who they claim to be."

As the key rattled in the door, Dima's lip twisted into a sneer. "Remind Shin that if anyone is thinking about backing out, Takeo's head will suffice to make peace."

She refrained from looking at him, but she heard him chuckling as the cuffs were snapped on him.

As she left the police station, a thousand emotional daggers stabbed at Kiku from all sides. She had been wrong about Takeo. Wrong about their connection. Takeo had betrayed her.

Her lip bled as her canines bit into her flesh. She tasted the metallic tang of blood on her tongue. Takeo had made a grave mistake scorning her. He had once even taken her to see the play with the famous line, in Vienna, at the Opera House. Takeo seemed to have forgotten that lesson: "Heaven has no rage like love to hatred turned, nor hell a fury like a woman scorned."

Kiku would have to teach him.

28

Daichi was leaning against the pickup with his arms crossed. "I take it things didn't go well?"

"Drive." Kiku circled around and climbed in. Her temples throbbed and her mouth was as dry as sand. Her brain struggled to organize the storm inside—lightning bolts of anger that made her want to scream. Or shoot something.

Daichi knew better than to argue with her and he pulled out of the parking lot, the front tire clipping the curb. They rode in silence, except for the creaks and groans of the old truck, until Daichi's phone buzzed. He picked it up and frowned.

"What is it?" Kiku asked.

"Lilly asked when I'm coming back. I'm not usually gone overnight. She's probably just worried." Daichi texted something back, then put his phone on the seat. "Are you going to tell me what happened?"

Using as few words as possible, Kiku recapped her talk with Kuznetsov. When she mentioned Shin, the muscles in Daichi's jaw tightened. She finished her story, and waited.

The miles stretched on.

In Kiku's experience, most people underestimated Daichi. Certainly, his father and brother always had. Maybe because Daichi was the perennial playboy, people just assumed he was shallow. But Kiku knew he was a brilliant strategist, and she waited for his wisdom. She never expected the response she got. A tear rolled down his face.

"I believed Takeo would be different," he said softly.

Kiku turned to look out the window. So had she.

Daichi had done more to raise Takeo and Jiro than their father had. The two young boys were naturally attracted to their dashing uncle, and he showered them with not only presents but also his time, and took the brothers all over the world with him. Until now, though, even Kiku hadn't known just how strong the bond was that they forged.

"You believe Takeo agreed to the deal with the Russians?" she asked.

Daichi nodded. His expression was grim. "If it was anyone but Shin Uchihara, I would hold out hope I was wrong." The truck struggled to keep up the speed Daichi pressed it to. He eased back on the gas. "Shin is a fanatic, like his father. He thinks the Uchiharas' sole destiny is to guard the head of the Yakuza. He'd never come after the boy unless Takeo approved it."

"But his own son?" she asked. "How could Takeo do that?"

Daichi shrugged sadly. "The Yakuza welcomes all, but the Nakumora clan does not. The histories claim to trace Kenzo's lineage back to the Kamakura period. Their blood is said to be pure. For that reason, I suspect Takeo doesn't view the boy as a son. He sees him as a stain on his family's legacy."

Kiku burned with anger. She and Takeo had discussed the old ways. He professed to be different. He had told her he believed that a person was an individual soul, unbound by the baggage and trappings of lineage. Had he been lying? Or did he change his mind when the existence of a biracial son tested his beliefs?

"It was the same with me," Daichi said. "I am half Chinese. You are aware that I'm the firstborn?"

Kiku's eyes widened slightly. "I knew you and Kenzo were close in age, but I always assumed Kenzo was older because he became boss."

Daichi chuckled ruefully. "My father called me to his home and explained it to me. He was dying and we had sake. He drank a little too much. He wanted to explain why a half-breed was ill suited to leading a group of outcasts. He talked about getting my mother pregnant. I should have killed him for the names that he called her. He didn't say it with malice; he simply viewed her as trash. Then he told me that he loved me—even if I was a dog. That's why I figured you and Takeo would never work," Daichi said. "You're not pure Japanese."

Kiku closed her eyes and remembered Takeo's finger tracing down her neck, over her breast, and coming to rest on her stomach. His eyes, always clouded by stress, were soft and clear. So was his voice. "If we had a child," he said, "I wonder what it would look like."

She pictured a newborn cradled in her arms. Their child. It would have been beautiful. But even her imagination could not support such a possibility. Takeo appeared in the vision in her mind. He leaned over, carefully lifted the baby out of her arms . . . and kept lifting. He raised their child over his head, his handsome face twisting in disgust, ready to slam the baby to the floor.

Kiku's scream of rage filled the cab of the truck and shook the windows. Almost insane with fury, she wanted to throw Daichi out onto the road, turn around, and drive straight to Chicago and storm Takeo's office tower. She'd slaughter anyone who got in her way. She'd certainly die, but she'd take Takeo to Hell with her.

Daichi rolled down his window and rubbed his ear with his forearm. "Can you give me a little warning next time you're going to scream? It's not easy to plug your ears when you're missing a hand."

Kiku scowled, and Daichi kept his arm raised as if afraid she would strike him.

"What are you going to do with the boy?" he asked quietly.

Kiku exhaled slowly, letting her anger cool to a slow simmer. She turned to stare at the desert outside her window. Alex's choices were as barren as the land. He would be hunted now. Both by the Russians and the Yakuza.

Daichi's phone buzzed. He picked it up with his good hand, his prosthetic clicking as he laid it against the steering wheel. He read the text, then tossed the phone onto the seat and jammed the gas pedal to the floor.

Kiku grabbed his phone and read the text. It was from Lilly.

COME HOME. THEY HAVE BABA AND HWAN.

29

The truck barreled down the road, but just before they reached Daichi's driveway, Kiku laid a hand on his arm.

"Pull over." She drew her gun. "I'll cut through the woods and flank the house."

He ground his teeth, glared at her, and kept driving. "Lilly's alone at the farmhouse."

The truck groaned as it struggled to turn sharply into the driveway. Just before ramming into the closed metal gate, Daichi jammed on the brakes, kicking up a cloud of dust. She'd never seen him flustered like this.

"Use your head, Daichi. You do not know what we will find. Give me four minutes." She slipped out of the truck and raced into the woods.

Branches ripped at her clothes as she sprinted between the trees. She let her anger build, using the pain of Takeo's betrayal to power her on. And how deep did that betrayal go? Was it possible that they had found Daichi's farm? Had Shin somehow tracked her and Alex here?

How?

Kiku ducked under a branch and dashed along a small creek. The lip of the bank gave her an open route and she flew. The wound in her side was healing, but the deep muscles burned. She pushed herself forward, but she was drained from lack of sleep and blood loss. Like an engine running on fumes, her muscles shook and sputtered. Her energy was at its lowest, so she switched over to her alternative power source —hatred.

Conjuring up an image of Shin laughing as he killed Lilly, Kiku pushed herself to run faster. Every fiber in her body shrieked in protest, but Kiku dashed through the woods like a wolf on the hunt. Bounding over rocks and sprinting across the open stretches, Kiku ran with a singular purpose: to reach the farm and kill every threat there.

The farmhouse appeared between the trees. She wanted nothing more than to rush in and kill Shin and all his men—but she'd have to harness her temper. She had to live today . . . in order to kill Takeo tomorrow.

At the same moment, she heard the old pickup barreling down the road. Daichi hadn't waited.

Old lovesick fool.

She'd intended to circle the farmhouse under the cover of the woods, but that would take time. Thanks to Daichi, instead she'd have to use the distraction of the approaching truck and cut across the open area alongside the woods. It was less than ideal, but if all eyes inside the house were on that truck . . .

If? This is Shin you're dealing with.

Shin wasn't someone to be underestimated. He was ruthless and thorough. Kiku's grip tightened on her pistol. She crouched low as she sprinted across the open space, using the shed and a vine-covered pergola for cover as she dashed toward the back of the house. She scanned the windows, the woods, and the outlying structures. For all she knew, the Russians or Shin himself were lying in ambush and would kill Daichi before he even reached his front steps.

The truck skidded to a stop. She was too far around the house to see it, but she knew Daichi would be running madly for the front door. Even in his best days, he'd have been foolish to take on Shin and all his men head-on. And now, because of her, he was shooting lefty.

Kiku bolted for the back porch, grabbed the railing, and jumped.

The front door slammed open—*Daichi.* A woman screamed. It sounded like Lilly.

Kiku kicked open the back door, sending splinters flying. Lowering her gun, she stepped inside and swept the empty kitchen.

Sobbing erupted from the hallway. Kiku sidestepped through the living room. As she neared the front door, she saw Daichi, his arms wrapped around Lilly, paying no attention to his surroundings. His entire focus was on his wife.

Fool.

"Daichi," Kiku whispered harshly. "Get her to pull it together. Or I will."

Daichi glared murderously at Kiku. But he needed a slap across his face, and her threat did the trick. "Lilly." He gently shook her shoulders, and she turned her tear-stained face up to his. "Start at the beginning. Who was here?"

Lilly shook her head, a sob racking her frame. She wiped her nose with her sleeve and dissolved into another fit of crying, pulling Daichi to her like she was drowning. He stroked Lilly's back with his hand.

Kiku didn't have time for this drama. "If you do not tell us what happened, Baba and Hwan are going to die."

Lilly cried harder, and Daichi shot Kiku a mystified look. "That is *not* helpful." He leaned his face against Lilly's and whispered something in her ear. Though she continued to sob, she began to speak in fits and starts. She was almost unintelligible, but Kiku heard enough.

Food. Dinner. Town.

"Tell me Baba wouldn't have taken Hwan into town," Kiku snapped.

"And why the hell not?" Daichi shot back. He wrapped a protective arm around Lilly's shoulders.

"Because she should have known better than to expose a well-hidden target, and we told her to stay here."

A muffled buzzing interrupted them. Lilly held her phone out to Daichi with a trembling hand.

"Hello?" Daichi answered. His lip curled as he listened. "When?"

Kiku angled her head, but it was impossible to hear over Lilly's continued crying. The distraught woman was trying to choke down her sobs by covering her mouth with both hands, but it was still loud. Kiku debated about shoving her out the door but thought better of it.

"I need more time," Daichi said.

Kiku considered grabbing the phone away from him, but when his eyes locked on hers, she knew there was no need. The fierce focus in his gaze said it all—the old Daichi was back; he could handle this.

"Dogwood Park. Four o'clock. Bring them both or no deal." Daichi's face remained an expressionless mask, but the deepening of his crow's-feet gave him away. He was worried.

So was she. Kidnappings almost never ended well.

"I want to speak with them," Daichi said.

The man on the other end hung up.

"Who was it?" Kiku asked.

"They're not Yakuza or Russians. The Correa-Cabrera cartel grabbed Baba and Hwan when they went into town. They want their drugs back."

Kiku's grip tightened on her pistol. They didn't have the drugs anymore. The police did.

30

Daichi had cleared off a table and nailed a piece of canvas on top of it. In black marker, he now drew a square outline and indicated a rough area surrounding it. He pointed. "Dogwood Park. It's on the edge of town."

Kiku pulled down an AK-47 and checked the magazine. It was full. "How many of them do you expect?"

"They've never had more than four guys. It used to be just two-man teams that made the drug runs."

"When did you decide to protect Fairhope and become Batman?"

Daichi's lips curled into a smile.

"I did not mean it as a compliment." Kiku put the AK-47 back in the rack and took down a sniper rifle.

"You can't compare a guy to Batman and not have it be taken as a compliment." Daichi nodded at the gun. "That's a better choice. This is going to take finesse."

"Explain how you got involved in stopping the drug trade." Kiku walked over to a workbench and began breaking down the sniper rifle.

"The son of a friend of mine was killed. Kid was only twelve. He was looking for a sheep that wandered off and he stumbled into a deal. They hacked him to pieces."

Kiku raised an eyebrow. "The Daichi I knew would have said it was someone else's problem."

"That Daichi is dead." He placed his good hand on the table and went back to staring at the map. As his focus intensified, so did his crow's-feet and the wrinkles in his brow. "Lilly taught that kid in Sunday school. He was a good kid. I went to the funeral. And then I'd see his grieving parents every Sunday in . . ." He cleared his throat.

Kiku sighed.

He leveled a finger at her. "Don't give me that look." He stomped over to a shelf and picked up several small glass jars filled with nuts and bolts. "I'm serious."

Kiku smirked. "I'm surprised you didn't burst into flames going into a church." She grabbed the oil and began cleaning the gun.

"Lilly goes to church. I go sometimes because of her and . . ." He set the jars on the table and began placing them like chess pieces on a board. "Not every Sunday or anything."

"I was teasing you. What you do is your business." Kiku wiped down the barrel. "I only care about whether you can get the job done. So, can you still kill a man, or are you a man of God now?"

"I didn't become Amish."

"Then you are okay with killing?"

Daichi's prosthetic tapped the bottle in his hand. He seemed to be looking at his reflection in the glass. "If there's no other choice."

"There is none. You know what they will do to Hwan and Baba."

His prosthetic cracked the bottle. "I know."

"Finish what happened with the cartel."

"There's not much to say. I found the men responsible for killing the boy, and I did the same to them." He pitched the bottle into the trash and grabbed another. "They sent more drugs, and I sent more bodies back. They finally stopped sending people."

Kiku started reassembling the sniper rifle. They didn't have much time. "How many of their men did you kill?"

"Twenty-six."

Kiku saw no need to question Daichi's resolve further. Or his willingness to kill. "And you did not think they would try to retaliate?"

"They have tried. I thought they'd given up and picked a different route that wouldn't cost them as much."

Kiku finished with the rifle and began breaking down the Glock she'd selected as her sidearm. Something didn't add up. "One of them saw you?"

Daichi nodded. "I winged one. He took off on a motocross bike. I found the bike and a blood trail that led out to the desert. I didn't think he'd make it."

"It seems he did. And he told the cartel that an Asian man killed their people. They came looking for their drugs, saw Baba and Alex, and grabbed them because two Asians were their only lead back to you."

"That's what I think happened, too."

"What is your plan?" Kiku looked down at his makeshift map.

"It's weak." He placed four glass jars at the end of the table. "They'll make the swap at the end of the park. We have no way of knowing how many they'll have as backup." He placed another jar at the entrance to the park and two more in the corners. Then he picked up two old beer bottles and put one on the edge of the table. "There's a World War Two monument outside the park on a hill. You'll be there." He placed the other bottle in the middle. "I'll bring the bag."

Kiku tapped his prosthetic hand with her pistol. "I should carry the bag."

Daichi rolled his shoulders. "I've been practicing. Besides, you'll have my back."

"I can take the man on Hwan and maybe the one on Baba before it becomes a shootout. You will not make it out alive, and if there are more men than you estimate, I will not be able to provide enough cover fire for Hwan and Baba to do so either."

Daichi opened a trunk and pulled out a bulletproof vest. "Don't count me dead so fast."

"If they bring six men, spread out in the park, and you walk into the middle, you are dead."

He tapped his phone. "I made a call to a friend in town and got us some backup."

"Tell me you did not call the police. Law enforcement would make it an instant hostage situation, and the cartel *always* kill their hostages."

"I didn't call the police. I called a friend. We'll have enough firepower for this to work."

Kiku didn't care for the plan. It gave them a window of opportunity to rescue Alex, but Daichi didn't stand a chance. He wasn't Kiku's responsibility, but still . . .

She crossed her arms and frowned. "Adding one farmer friend of yours with a pitchfork will not make a difference. With this plan, you will die."

The familiar grin spread across his face—the one that had once made her think he could leap over tall buildings in a single bound. "Trust me."

31

Dogwood Park

As Kiku jogged up the hill to the memorial, the bag slung over her shoulder, her focus was on the park below her. Dogwood Park, on the outskirts of town, was obviously a popular spot for locals. She stared down at a picture that was completely foreign to her—normal life. At least a dozen people were in the park. A husband and wife pushing a baby carriage waved to an elderly couple sitting on a bench. The older man and woman were holding hands as they fed a mother duck and her skittish ducklings. Three men jogged side by side as they circled the outer walking path. People were scattered all over the park, taking advantage of the beautiful day and enjoying life. It would make a great tourism commercial—at least for the next ten minutes.

Kiku hadn't counted on the civilians. Inside, her two selves battled. The cold, calculating side saw the benefit: the presence of people would temper the cartel's reaction and add to the confusion once the shooting started. But the sliver of good in Kiku wished they weren't there and vividly pictured the downside: once the bullets started flying, the innocent civilians would be caught in the middle of a fierce gunfight. Daichi would have taken the civilians into account. After what happened to Baba's husband, she knew he didn't want more innocent blood on his hands. She would trust him.

She hurried the final few yards to the peak, adjusted her earpiece, and took three deep breaths. She had an ideal perch with an unobstructed view. It was a clear run down the hill from the monument to the rest of the park. A row of trees protected her back and provided an exit that she wouldn't take. Once the shooting started, she'd be racing toward Alex.

The entire park was about the size of two football fields, with a paved walking path around the perimeter. The areas to the left and right were flat scrubland that ran along the road, but across the park sat an ice cream parlor, coffee shop, and art gallery. Two cars were parked on the road in front of the coffee shop, a white van and a dark sedan with tinted windows.

Kiku looked up at the monument, a statue of World War Two soldiers. As she unzipped the bag and began assembling the long gun, she studied the statue, looking for the best place to rest her rifle. She was so tired, she was surprised she was still thinking straight. Grateful for muscle memory, she moved like a machine as she assembled the sniper rifle. Once she was done, she swept the park again for any sign of the kidnappers.

"Any visual yet?" Daichi asked in her earpiece.

"None. A van and sedan are parked across the way."

"Entering the parking lot now." Daichi's truck rounded the corner. "Lots of cars."

"A dozen civilians." Kiku again searched the faces of the people in the park. "No sign of— Wait."

The van door slid open and a short man exited, yanking Alex behind him. The side of Alex's face was red, but he held his head high. Baba came out next, and she didn't look as good. The old woman's right eye was swollen shut, and she limped as a chunky woman pushed her forward. Three more men piled out of the van behind them, bringing the total to five.

Daichi's plan had a chance of working with four. With five kidnappers, success without casualties was a long shot.

"Five targets." She resisted the urge to say four men and one woman. Gender didn't matter to a gun.

"We've got this." She heard Daichi's grin in his voice.

She did not share his optimism. Her chest tightened as the sedan's doors opened and four more men stepped out, stuffing miscellaneous arms under their clothing.

"Four more. Nine total. Heavy firepower."

The speaker in her ear crackled as Daichi exhaled. "That's going to make it a little more interesting." She heard his car door open.

"Abort." Kiku kept the sniper rifle trained on the man holding Alex's elbow with his left hand and prodding the boy forward with his right. She assumed there was a pistol in that hand.

"That's a negative." Daichi got out and walked back to the truck bed.

"Daichi, abort now." Kiku swung the sniper rifle around and aimed at Daichi's foot. "There are too many targets for us. You are going to get Hwan killed."

"Don't forget about Baba." There was a ring of mirth in Daichi's voice as he lifted the heavy bag out of the back of the truck.

"Last warning." Kiku pressed her left eye closed.

Daichi froze. "Don't tell me that you have such little faith in me that I'm in your crosshairs?"

"Get back in the truck. Your plan failed."

"It hasn't started, Ōkami. You forget, that is my nephew's son. My nephew may consider him garbage, but to me, he is blood. He will live today. I swear it." Daichi started walking. "And you forget, I called a friend."

Kiku zoomed in on the kidnappers. They had only fanned out a little, but their numbers made it impossible for Daichi's plan to succeed. She could take out at most four of them before they turned their guns on Alex and Baba. Daichi could take out maybe two before he was cut down in a hail of bullets.

Sweat rolled down her back. During all of the missions with Daichi he had never failed. Not once. If there was anyone who had a chance of getting out of this, it was Daichi. He had been the best.

Until Kiku.

"I'm going to bring them more into the middle of the park," Daichi said. "Kiku, your target is the man on Hwan."

Daichi strolled into the park like he was meeting friends for a picnic. The people continued with their activities, oblivious to the storm that was about to be unleashed, while the kidnappers moved into the park like wolves in a loosely formed pack, with Alex and Baba in the middle.

"On my signal," Daichi said. His voice had dropped to a whisper.

Kiku stopped breathing. She'd done this over a dozen times with Daichi. She knew his methods. He wouldn't say a word—and he always struck first.

She glanced back at Daichi and saw that he had shifted the bag to his good hand. It would be impossible for him to shoot with his prosthetic.

What is he doing?

Daichi raised his prosthetic in a sign of surrender. "I'm not armed! Get it?" He laughed.

Kiku zoomed in on the man holding Alex. She exhaled quickly and prepped to take the shot. Daichi had *never* spoken in negotiations before now . . .

Daichi dropped the bag at his side and held up his other arm. "The bag is empty. I'm not stupid enough to bring your drugs with me." The pack of men shifted restlessly. "But I have something to offer you for the old woman. Something that's much more valuable."

Kiku's breath slowed, and she exhaled twice before closing her left eye.

"If you guys give me another hour, I promise you, you won't be disappointed."

He is stalling. Why?

The people in the park started to react to all the shouting. The three joggers slowed to a stop. The young couple pushing the baby carriage had been walking directly toward the kidnappers but now changed direction and started to circle behind them toward the exit. Even the old couple feeding the ducks had gathered up their bags and shuffled over to see what all the noise was about. The only people not paying attention were the two sets of older men playing chess at the cement tables, ignoring the world around them.

The kidnappers exchanged puzzled glances. The short man holding onto Alex shook his head. "We told you to bring the stuff with you."

Kiku zoomed in on the kidnapper's face.

"I was right in the middle of something when you called," Daichi said. "Look, I promise. You give me one more hour and you'll have exactly what you want."

The crowd watching stopped moving. Even the chess players now paused their game and stood up, craning their necks to view the spectacle. Kiku prayed that the young couple with the baby carriage had the sense to keep moving, but they stopped only yards away from the kidnappers, on their right.

Kiku's finger moved closer to the trigger. Once the shooting started, she'd do what she could to draw the fire away from the child.

The short man holding Alex sneered. "Which one dies while we wait?"

Daichi shrugged. "You." He dropped his arms and Kiku fired.

Her shot was the first in a sudden hail of bullets as it seemed everyone in the park now drew a weapon and opened fire. The three male joggers had pistols in their hands and killed the kidnappers holding Baba. The old couple, who had been hiding their weapons in the bags of birdseed for the ducks, were now blasting away, too. The chess players wielded rifles that they had pulled free from beneath the chess tables. Even the young couple with the baby carriage were in on it, pulling two machine guns from the carriage and mowing down the kidnappers closest to them.

Kiku didn't even need to fire a second time. All nine kidnappers were dead. Daichi was giving orders now, and everyone was moving quickly and purposefully. A truck in the parking lot tore across the grass, and Daichi's army of "civilians" began loading the bodies of the kidnappers into the back.

Kiku broke down the sniper rifle as she struggled to piece together what had just happened. Daichi said he'd made a call. But how did he get so many shooters? Judging by the elegant lethality of the operation, these people were all hardcore professionals.

Kiku glanced back into the park and kicked herself for not recognizing it earlier. She had scanned these people's faces, looking for the kidnappers, and had failed to notice that they all had one trait in common: they were all Asian. She had been too busy looking for South Americans.

"What's taking you so long?" Daichi called over the microphone. "Come on down. I want to introduce you to some old friends of mine."

32

As Kiku stood staring out the window of Daichi's second-floor bedroom, Alex's laughter filtered up from the kitchen. The boy was far more resilient than she'd given him credit for. She'd expected him to fall apart after the park, but he had been more concerned about taking care of Baba.

Of course, the old woman didn't need care and absolutely refused to be pampered in any way. She allowed Lilly to bandage up her face, and that was it. Now she was talking about what she would make for dinner.

As for Lilly, she hadn't left Daichi's side since they'd returned. She'd even tried to follow him into the bathroom once, but Daichi drew the line there. Which was why Kiku was surprised when he knocked at her door and peered in, alone.

"You got a second?" he asked.

Kiku smiled and nodded as he strutted in and shut the door. Though she could tell he was puffed up, he wasn't crowing about his heroic rescue the way he used to. A good part of the legend of Daichi's past exploits was due to his shameless self-promotion. In the old days, when a mission went well, he'd throw a party—more like a traveling festival that lasted for days and migrated through various cities, where Daichi would retell tales of his achievements, their grandness growing each time.

Now his eyes were searching hers. He was looking for something, but she couldn't figure out what.

He rubbed the back of his neck and gazed sheepishly at her. "You must think I'm an old fool."

Kiku laughed. "Do you really think that I would agree with your decision to tell over a dozen people that you are alive? Let alone bring them to your new hometown." She doubled over in laughter. Her side throbbed, but it couldn't dampen her amusement. "You *are* an old fool. Who are they?"

Daichi shrugged. "Ghosts of the past. Some were Yakuza and wanted to get out, too. Some are like Baba. I owed them for a wrong I could not right."

Kiku shook her head. "How can you trust them?"

Daichi walked over and stared out the window. "Because they are like me. They just wanted a normal life. All of the people in the park . . . they were broken, each in their own way. I only showed them the door. It was their decision to come and theirs alone to stay."

"You trust them but not me?"

"That's not true." Daichi straightened up.

"Then why did you hide your plan from me?"

"You would have spent all your energy watching them instead of the cartel." A small smile appeared on his face. "Besides, I knew you would trust me. It all worked out in the end."

"Thank you, Daichi, but that was a walk in the park, pun intended, compared to what I am facing. I need to deal with Takeo."

"I'm working on that." Daichi crossed his arms. "I'm thinking—"

"Daichi!" Lilly called out from the first floor. "Daichi!"

Daichi rolled his eyes. "Just give me, like, twenty minutes."

Kiku angled her head. "Go. I understand."

"We'll figure something out," Daichi said before opening the door. "Coming, honey," he called.

Kiku turned and looked out the window to hide her smirk.

A minute later, footsteps came thundering up the stairs and Alex appeared in the doorway, a smile on his face, his cheeks flushed, and evidence of ice cream and chocolate sauce on his upper lip and shirt. "Are you coming down?"

"In a moment. How is Baba?"

"Great! She keeps pretending to be a pirate with her eye all bandaged up. She's really funny. She made you a banana split."

Kiku couldn't remember the last time she'd had ice cream. "You talked me into it."

"Sweet. How long are we staying? Baba said she'd take me fishing tomorrow, but I didn't know when we're leaving to see my dad."

Kiku opened and closed her mouth. She wanted to lie, but none came.

Alex's expression darkened like the sky outside. "Did you call him when you left? Is that why you were gone so long?"

"No. But . . ."

Alex crossed his arms and planted his feet. The fresh bruise along his cheek reddened.

"I spoke with some associates of your father," Kiku said, "and right now he does not think it would be safe if—"

Alex's eyes blazed. "I want to talk to him. Call him. Call my father."

"Alex—"

"No." He shook his head. "I've done everything you've said, and now some 'associate' is telling me to stay away?" Alex swore. And not just once, but a steady stream that rose in volume until he was screaming profanities at the top of his lungs.

Baba appeared behind him. "Wow. That even made me blush." She narrowed her good eye at Kiku. "You certainly have a way with children."

"Me?" Kiku bristled. "His actions are not a result of anything I have done."

"Everyone all right up there?" Two more sets of footsteps on the stairs heralded the arrival of Daichi and Lilly. "We've had a bit of a rough day. Maybe everyone should just dial it back."

"Thank you, Captain Understatement," Baba muttered. "Now, if you'd call off your attack dog." She jerked a thumb at Kiku.

Kiku stepped menacingly toward her, and Alex jumped in front of Baba, as if to defend her. "Back off!"

Kiku forced a smile. "Watch your mouth, Baba."

"Are you threatening an old woman?" Baba held her hands to her chest, made a face like she was about to cry, then stuck her tongue out at Kiku so no one else could see.

Kiku turned to Daichi. "Did you see that?"

Baba held her hands up innocently. "See what, Mimi?"

Daichi frowned.

"How about some more ice cream?" Lilly offered, placing a restraining hand on Daichi's shoulder.

Alex stomped to the middle of the room. "I don't want any more ice cream, and I'm not going anywhere until Kiku calls my father. I want to talk to him."

Kiku glared at Alex for using her real name.

"Everyone just needs to calm down," Daichi said. "Hwan and I are—"

"You know my name's not Hwan," Alex said. "It's Alex. I'm your great-nephew. My father is Takeo Nakumora, son of Kenzo Nakumora, the head of the Yakuza."

Both Kiku and Daichi turned on Baba.

The old woman shrugged. "The boy had a right to know."

"That wasn't your place, Baba!" Daichi fumed.

"It was *yours*," Alex said, pointing an accusing finger at his great-uncle. "Don't blame her. She thought we were both going to die and I should know who my real father is."

"You have just signed his death warrant, Baba," Kiku snarled.

"No. Alex's father did," Daichi said.

Kiku's shock must have shown on her face as she turned to Daichi.

Alex's face twisted in horror. He stepped right up to Daichi, toe to toe, his breath coming in short puffs. His voice was a whisper. "What did you say about my father?"

Daichi's eyes glistened. "I'm so sorry. But someone has to tell you. Your father—"

"Daichi!" Kiku stepped forward.

"Alex is right," Daichi said. "It is my place to tell him."

"Alone," Baba added. She took Lilly by the hand and scowled at Kiku.

Kiku wanted to stay—if only to defy the woman—but Baba was

right. Alex should hear his family story from family. So she followed the two women out of the room.

"The boy needs to know the truth," Baba said loudly to Lilly as they walked down the stairs.

Kiku vaulted over the railing and stepped in front of the two, blocking them on the staircase. "All of you are in danger now. If Shin finds Alex, he will make him talk. Then all your lives will be forfeited."

"Then . . . you have to make sure that doesn't happen. *Please*," Lilly pleaded.

"I cannot stop it. You need to move. Disappear. That is the only way you will live." Kiku turned and headed for the kitchen.

Baba followed right on her heels. "What about the boy? What's going to happen to him?"

"If you are so concerned about Alex, you should ask Daichi if he can stay with you three."

Lilly clapped her hands together, but an icy glance from Baba cut her off. "Daichi has worked hard to get away from that gangster life . . ." Baba's chin lifted as she studied Kiku. "That was your plan all along, wasn't it? That's why you really came here. You knew Daichi wouldn't turn his great-nephew away."

Kiku hid her surprise that Baba had figured it out. "No, but with circumstances the way they are, that would seem the most logical path now."

"I agree," Lilly said.

Kiku leaned against the kitchen counter while Lilly sat at the table and Baba paced the floor. Kiku's outward calm belied her inner turmoil. The annoying old woman had raised a pertinent question: *What will I do with the boy if Daichi will not keep him?*

The hands of the clock slowly inched forward as the three women waited. Baba made several trips to the pantry, each time hauling out an armful of ingredients and dropping them off at the table, only to change her mind and drag them all back, grumbling the whole time. Now and then she would mutter *Kiku*, and Lilly would wince and flash an apologetic smile.

Finally, footsteps came stomping down the stairs—loud, angry footsteps that echoed like thunder in the little kitchen. Then came the crash of the front door hitting the wall. The screen door rattled loudly before shaking into silence.

Daichi appeared in the kitchen and went to the sink to fill a glass with water. “Give the boy some time,” he said. “He’ll be back.”

“Is he going to stay with us?” Lilly asked, looking hopeful.

Daichi shook his head. “It’s complicated.”

Lilly visibly deflated.

Daichi’s water glass clicked against the counter. He wiped his trembling hand, took out his phone, and handed it to Kiku. “I’ve been trying to figure out what Shin’s next move will be. After we got Alex and Baba back, I did a little digging. I started at the beginning and looked into the doctor who first approached Takeo about Alex.”

Kiku stared down at the screen. Daichi had pulled up a news article about a recent drive-by shooting in Washington Heights, NY. There was a picture of the victim, and Kiku instantly recognized Dr. Rogoff—the therapist who had contacted Takeo. He had been struck three times in the head. That didn’t happen in a random drive-by. It was a hit.

“You can’t deliver the boy to Takeo,” Daichi said, “and as you can see, he can’t go back to New York either. I tried to convince Alex that he isn’t safe in either place.”

The front door banged open and Alex ran into the kitchen. He slid to a stop in the doorway, planted his feet, and lifted his chin. “They killed Dr. Rogoff. I know where they’re going next. California. They’re going to go after my mom. I have to warn her.”

33

Daichi led Kiku down a farm road to a second, older barn that she had not been aware existed. The tin roof was heavily rusted, the worn sideboards showed only the faintest remnants of paint, and the whole building leaned at a twenty-degree slant. Daichi had to put his back into it to drag the door open.

"I still think I should go with you," he said.

Kiku stepped past him into the barn. The huge space was empty except for a row of vehicles covered with dusty tarps. Part of her wanted Daichi to come with her—but she knew he had to stay here and guard Lilly and Baba. He knew it, too. He just couldn't admit it.

"You know that Shin could send another squad here," she said. "He must have spoken with the Russians by now. He may not believe that I was just passing through on my way to California."

"My friends can handle it."

Kiku turned back to him. "Your friends are capable. But would you leave and put Lilly and Baba's lives entirely in their hands?"

The look on Daichi's face answered her question. He would stay and protect his family.

"Besides," Kiku said with a smile, "I will only be a whisper. A warning and I am gone."

"You sure about taking Alex with you?"

"Unless I bring him, his mother may not believe me. And you know he would not stay here quietly. He would try to go on his own to warn his mother, and he would be at far greater risk. Even if you allowed me to chain him up, he would get free and find his way to California."

Daichi laughed so hard that several birds scattered from the rafters. "He's a Nakumora all right."

She stared at his smiling face. He had changed.

"What?" He scratched the back of his head with his prosthetic.

"The risks that you are taking. Everyone in that park knows who you are."

Daichi's expression hardened. "None of them would betray me. They'd be signing their own death warrant. And warrants for their families as well."

"Why did you bring them here?"

Daichi laughed again. "You still don't get it, Ōkami. They came here because they all want to live. Really *live*. What you're doing . . . it's not living."

"You overestimate them. Taking down untrained drug dealers is one thing. Shin is another."

"Shin won't give this place a second thought. If he does, we will gladly fight him. But my money's on him heading to California. So"—he gestured to the vehicles—"you need to pick your ride."

Kiku looked at the dusty tarps. "I hope you have something faster than an old pickup without air conditioning."

Daichi grinned as he walked down the row of vehicles, pulling the tarps off one by one, and Kiku smiled as well as he uncovered two BMWs, a Corvette, two Audis, and a Dodge Hellcat.

Daichi shrugged. "I kept the good ones. Spoils of war."

Kiku didn't hesitate. Her friend Jack Stratton was a fan of the Dodge Charger, and the Hellcat was like the Charger's wild, untamed sister. "I will take the Hellcat."

"You'll need to stop often with that one," Daichi cautioned. "She guzzles gas."

"A price I am willing to pay. I have a friend who would be disappointed in me if I picked any other. Besides, this is the car I will take back to Chicago. It is appropriate that I arrive in a Hellcat."

34

California

Kiku powered down the windows as they closed in on the California coast. The fresh air was a welcome change, but it provided little comfort to her spirits. Shin was thorough and fast—there was a good chance Alex's mother was already dead. Or, at the very least, being watched.

"How are we going to find her?" Alex asked.

"I have a friend working on that." Kiku pulled out the burner phone she'd picked up before crossing the California border. She still didn't have a signal.

"Why are you so sure your friend can find my mom?"

"Because she can find anyone."

The Hellcat hugged the road. She'd been averaging well over one hundred miles per hour, thanks to the long line of sight in the desert—and police cutbacks.

Kiku tried to focus on driving, but her thoughts wandered to the last thing she wanted to think about. She had a meeting at Mount Hicks Cemetery she couldn't pass up. Jack had tracked down the mystery man who had left her the note.

She looked over at Alex. The fingernails of his right hand were digging into the flesh of his left arm, leaving fresh, bright-red streaks.

She smacked his hand.

"Ow!" Alex jumped, seemingly more stung from the rebuke than the actual strike.

"Stop doing that," Kiku ordered.

"Doing what?" The teen attitude was back.

"Hurting yourself. If you need to take your pain out on something, focus on hurting someone else."

Alex coughed, started to smile, and coughed again. He opened and closed his mouth twice before he said, "I don't think any therapist would *ever* recommend that."

"It works for me." Kiku blew by an eighteen-wheeler. The truck driver beeped and gave her a thumbs-up.

Alex grabbed the safety handle. "Why are you helping me?" he asked.

The question caught Kiku off-guard. She didn't know the answer. Her mission was done. Takeo wanted her dead, which released her from any personal oath. Still, she couldn't leave the boy on his own.

She shrugged. "I do not know."

Alex's face scrunched up. "Thanks," he said sourly.

"What? That bothers you?"

"I was kinda hoping to hear it's because you like me. Or even that you're doing it out of pity." He shifted in his seat to face her. "Or how about because I saved your life? *That* would be a good reason for helping me."

"When did you save my life?"

Alex was hopping up and down in his seat. "On the train! That guy was choking you. Your face was purple."

"As I recall, you accidentally ejected the magazine from the gun."

"Yeah, but I still shot him."

"You left him alive. I killed him."

Alex threw up his hands dramatically. "I still saved your life."

"Marginally."

"Oh, oh—" He snapped his fingers. "Outside the tobacco store. That huge guy had you in his sights! I guess you forgot about how I hit him with the car."

Kiku scowled. She had not forgotten, but she'd hoped he had. She was more than aware that Alex had saved her life twice, and she loathed being indebted to anyone. But as hard as it was to admit the fact to herself, the boy had earned her respect through his acts of courage.

"Thank you."

"Ha!" Alex sat back proudly in his seat. "Ha!" he said again as he crossed his arms and puffed out his chest.

Kiku opened her mouth, but the buzzing of her phone cut her off. She checked the screen. *Alice.*

"What do you have?"

"I found Karen Harris." Alice's voice had a smile to it. "I texted everything to your phone, along with Jack's data. Karen lives in a suburb outside San Francisco. She's married. They're both doctors. No children."

Alice's warm voice made Kiku suddenly want to unburden herself of her feelings. Pain, betrayal, fear—they all rushed to escape, and Kiku slaughtered every single one.

"Thank you." Her voice was calm and aloof. "Please give my thanks and regards to your soon-to-be husband. I will be sending your wedding present shortly, but do not open it until the wedding. And I would do so privately."

"Is everything all right? Do you need us to come to you? We will in a heartbeat—just say the word."

Kiku's hand tightened on the steering wheel. She knew if she asked, her two friends would travel to the ends of the Earth—even to Hell if they had to, to find her, because they fought on the side of angels.

"My apologies, but I need to go. Thank you again."

She ended the call, switched to her text messages, got the address, and punched it into the GPS. She sped up, the Hellcat roaring as it greedily devoured the additional fuel and thirsted for more. She needed to warn Alex's mother before Shin got to her. She hoped they weren't too late.

35

A little after four o'clock, Kiku and Alex stood at the front door of Alex's mother's house, a modest-sized contemporary in an upscale neighborhood, with a two-bay garage and a nicely landscaped lawn. From studying the GPS, Kiku knew that the houses on the block had sizable backyards, and at the other end of the street was a cul-de-sac.

Alex rang the doorbell a third time.

They're both doctors. They think they're indispensable. There's no way they're going to fly their well-feathered nest or their lucrative practices. Not even to save their own lives. Like people clinging to their possessions as they try to outrun a fire, their pride will drag them to the grave. They'll stay, thinking the police will protect them. They're wrong. To the Yakuza, they're disposable.

Alex was shifting from foot to foot like he had to go to the bathroom.

"Stand still," Kiku whispered.

"I'm nervous. How do you know she's home?"

"It is Sunday. It is the only time she is likely to be home. Do you want to leave?"

"No."

"You get one chance to make a first impression."

Alex threw his shoulders back, squared his jaw, and stood tall.

The door was opened by a uniquely beautiful woman with green eyes and shoulder-length brown hair.

"Dr. Harris. My name is Lan Sano. There is no way to buffer this news. Please allow me to introduce you to your son, Alex."

Alex waved awkwardly. "Nothing like ripping the Band-Aid off, huh? Ha-ha. Get it, Doc? So, hello. I'm your son."

Karen Harris glanced back at Kiku before focusing all her attention on Alex's face. "Well . . . hello. This is a surprise." She looked over her shoulder back into the house, then turned to gaze at Alex and chewed her bottom lip.

"We need to speak with you," Kiku said. She held out her hand and Karen shook it. "May we come in?"

"Of course. Of course." Karen shot another glance back into the house, but she didn't move out of the way. "It's just . . . I . . . Could you give me a few moments, please?"

"Certainly."

Karen disappeared inside, shutting the door behind her.

"I sounded so stupid," Alex groaned. "Do you think I look like her?"

Kiku held up a calming hand. "Slow down. We have just given her a lot to process. I think she is telling her husband who is at the front door."

Alex's face scrunched up. "Wait. He might not even know I exist? Why would she not have told him about me?"

Kiku placed a comforting arm around his shoulders.

After waiting five minutes, Alex started to nervously pick the leaves off the shrub next to the door. After ten minutes, Kiku kicked the small pile that had formed at his feet off the walkway.

"Remember, first impressions. Smile."

The front door opened once more. This time Karen was not alone. A tall, much older man stood behind her with his hand on her shoulder.

"Lan. Alex. This is my husband, Richard."

The expression on Richard's face as he studied Alex was one of barely hidden shock. He tried to plaster on a smile, but it didn't make the moment any less uncomfortable. "Nice to meet you both," he said stiffly.

"Won't you come in?" said Karen.

The house was open, bright, and immaculately clean. Karen led them to a large living room with a patio that overlooked the sparkling San Pablo Bay in the distance.

"You have a lovely view here," Kiku said as she and Alex sat on the couch.

Karen pointed at the BMW motorcycle on the patio. "It's nicer when there isn't a motorcycle blocking it."

"That's my fault." Richard rubbed the back of his neck and sat next to Karen on the loveseat. "It's a hobby. Something to keep my hands busy when I'm not in surgery. I take it that's your Hellcat in the driveway?"

Karen placed a silencing hand on his thigh. "I don't think they came all this way to talk about cars."

"That is correct." Kiku sat on the edge of the couch, her feet flat on the floor. "I assume you have talked to Richard?"

Karen nodded, and Richard took her hand. She locked eyes with Kiku. "Have you . . . adopted Alex?"

"I am his guardian."

"It's kind of a long story," Alex said, staring intently at his mother. Kiku didn't think he'd taken his eyes off her since they'd come inside.

"Why don't you start at the beginning?" Richard suggested.

"All right," Alex said. He took a deep breath and jumped into his life story.

Kiku was relatively certain that wasn't what the doctor had intended, but when Kiku saw the excited look on Alex's face, she wasn't about to shut him down. Besides, Kiku wanted the opportunity to study the boy's mother. Something about her didn't seem right. Richard was fine; he didn't set off any of her internal alarm bells. But Karen had Kiku's whole system on red alert, and she couldn't figure out why.

There was a definite similarity to Alex; Kiku had no doubt this woman was his mother. The boy was fortunate in that he seemed to have inherited the best facial attributes of both Takeo and Karen. As Alex spoke, Karen listened attentively. She nodded in the right places, frowned when she should, and even chuckled softly at his attempts at humor. Her actions were exactly what Kiku would expect . . . but something about the woman bothered Kiku.

Alex was nearing the part of his life where Kiku entered the picture when Richard held up a hand. "I'm sorry to interrupt, but can I get anyone a drink?"

Alex cleared his throat. "Yes, please," he said.

Kiku gave a polite smile. "I am fine." She hated to cut Alex's time with his mother short, but Shin could be on his way. "We need to be going soon."

Alex shot Kiku a panic-stricken look but nodded.

"If you'll excuse me as well," Karen said with a strained smile, "I need to dash into the bathroom. I'll be right back."

Richard went into the kitchen and returned with two bottles of water, offering one to Alex and taking one himself. "We don't have any soda, but this is flavored with juice." He looked down the hall to make sure his wife wasn't within earshot, then gushed, "I can't believe you got your hands on a custom Hellcat!" To Alex he said, "I just put a new muffler on the motorcycle. You want to see?"

Alex's eyes lit up. "Yeah!" Then he looked at Kiku and asked, "Do we have time?"

Kiku rose from the couch. "Yes. I think I will have some water after all. Don't worry, I'll get it." She headed for the kitchen.

"There are cold bottles on the top shelf in the refrigerator," Richard called out as he slid open the door to the patio. "Alex—it's Alex, right?"

"Yes, sir."

In the kitchen, Kiku rolled her eyes at the boy's newfound manners before returning to the living room.

"Well, I used to have a smaller motorcycle, but I wanted to get something to tour the coast, so I thought some German engineering would be a better fit." Richard went on and on, with Alex nodding deferentially, but when Richard started up the motorcycle, Kiku frowned.

"Sorry." Richard gave a small, apologetic wave. "Karen hates it when I start the bike, too," he whispered to Alex, who chuckled.

Kiku nodded politely. The noise had bothered her because she was straining to hear any sound in the rest of the house. Karen had been gone seven minutes.

Richard and Alex came back inside. Richard cleared his throat. "Sorry about all the awkwardness. I'm really unprepared for this. Karen and I decided long ago not to have children. This has thrown me for a loop."

"You are doing fine," Kiku said. "It's a lot to process."

Richard chuckled. "You're a good liar."

Alex opened his mouth to say something but snapped it shut. He was nervously rubbing his hands together.

Karen came downstairs and strolled into the living room. "Sorry I was gone so long."

Alex took a deep breath and blurted out, "Mom. The Yakuza are on their way to kill you."

Karen and Richard stared, slack jawed, at the boy.

Kiku stepped forward and placed a hand on Alex's shoulder. "Maybe you should stop ripping the Band-Aids off."

"What is he talking about?" Richard's voice rose and he glared at Karen.

"That's ridiculous, Alex," said Karen. "Wherever did you get an idea like that?"

"It is true," Kiku said. "Both of your lives are in danger. You need to get out of here, now."

Karen glanced at Richard and gave a dismissive shake of her head. Then she turned to Kiku. "Alex's father would never hurt me."

Kiku drew her pistol and aimed at Karen's chest.

Richard dropped his water bottle, sending liquid jetting across the floor.

Karen started shaking. "Please, please don't—"

"What the hell is wrong with you?!" Alex screamed.

"Takeo *never* told Karen he was Yakuza."

"He did tell me. Please tell her to put the gun down," Karen begged Alex, her face twisted in fear.

"Take out your phone and unlock it," Kiku ordered.

"What are you doing?" Richard asked. His voice was unnaturally high.

"Silence, Doctor. Take out your phone now, Karen."

Karen's hand shook as she pulled her phone from her pocket.

"Unlock it."

"I don't understand," Karen said, trembling.

"Yes, you do. Unlock the phone now." Kiku raised the gun to Karen's eye level.

Staring down the barrel of a gun had the intended effect: Karen unlocked her phone and held it out.

"Take the phone, Alex. Read the last text—aloud, please."

Alex took the phone and said, "It's from an unknown caller. It says, WE'RE ON OUR WAY. KEEP THEM THERE."

"Read the text before that one."

"THEY'RE HERE. COME NOW." Alex's voice cracked. "I don't understand."

Richard started to move, but when Kiku aimed at him, he froze. "Look. We don't want any trouble. They said they were looking for Alex. Karen told them she didn't want anything to do with him. They offered us a little bit of money to tell them if he came here."

Alex was scrolling through the messages now. "They offered you a hundred grand. *You* wanted a quarter of a million dollars." Alex's eyes glistened as he stared at his mother. "Why?"

Karen's face twisted in scorn as she looked at her son. "You should have just stayed in New York. I gave you away for a reason."

"Mom?"

"Don't call me *that*," Karen snapped. "I terminated my parental rights. That means that I am *nothing* to you. I don't owe you anything. I carried you for nine months because my mother begged me, and my father said he'd cut me off if I had an abortion. I *never* wanted you."

Alex stiffened, but he didn't cry.

Part of Kiku wished he would. The other part wanted to put a bullet through Karen's head before she hurt her child any more—if that was possible.

Alex stepped between Kiku and his mother and stared down the barrel of Kiku's gun. He shook his head. "Don't. Please."

As Kiku lowered the weapon, headlights swept the front window.

Kiku grabbed Alex, dragged him onto the patio, and pushed him onto the motorcycle.

Richard and Karen ran to the front door and yanked it open.

"In here! They're in here!" Karen yelled.

Kiku hopped on the motorcycle in front of Alex and fired up the engine. The front wheel lifted as they raced off the patio just as the first spray of bullets tore through the living room.

36

Steering the BMW across the wet grass was like driving on ice. Compounding the problem was Alex's shifting weight and the bullets flying past their heads. The bike almost slid sideways as she crossed into the neighbor's yard and headed for the road.

Above the crackle of gunfire and the roar of the motorcycle, shouted orders and squealing tires announced that the hunt was on, and in the rearview Kiku saw three sets of headlights snap on behind her. She wondered if Shin himself had decided to come to the party.

As soon as the motorcycle's tires gripped tar, Kiku pinned the throttle back. The main street out of the subdivision was a straight shot—effectively a quarter-mile drag strip. Kiku shut off the headlight.

"Hold on!" she shouted. Alex's hands tightened around her waist.

They passed a huge black Escalade parked on the curb, and Kiku instantly locked the brakes and shifted all her weight to the right. The motorcycle spun one hundred and eighty degrees and came to a stop behind the car, completely hidden from their pursuers.

Three cars shot down the road toward their hiding place. Kiku drew her gun, leaned out, and fired three shots into the driver's side of each. As the third car approached, she saw Shin's bald head and fired two rounds at the passenger seat before forcing herself to refocus and aim at the driver. Without taking time to observe the results, she holstered her gun, pulled a U-turn, cranked the throttle, and raced back in the direction from which they'd come. Behind her, tires screeched, metal crunched, one gun fired.

Shin survived. Anyone but Shin would have needed more time to wonder what had hit them.

"Are you going back for my mom?" Alex shouted. The boy still didn't realize there was nothing left for him at his mother's house—that there was never really anything there for him to begin with.

Kiku said nothing, but her actions made her answer clear. Instead of turning down the road to the Harrises' home, she headed for the cul-de-sac at the other end. Calling on her memory of the GPS images, she barreled down the driveway of the last house and across the backyard, then flicked the headlight back on. Down a small grass slope lay a soccer field beside a high school, as she'd remembered. The bike slid down the hill, then Kiku sped up again, chewing through slick grass. In the distance, metal glinted as her headlight beam sped along a tall chain-link fence. Kiku crossed over to the running track and searched the fence for an opening.

Behind her, a car barreled down the slope and started across the soccer field.

"There!" Alex pointed at a narrow gate.

Kiku revved the engine and maneuvered through the tight opening, losing a lot of speed in the process. Shin, on the other hand, didn't slow down and slammed through the fence right behind them.

Kiku kept the throttle pinned and tensed her back—as if that could somehow offer protection from the force poised to mow them down. The car came within inches of her rear tire, but the bike pulled away just in time and quickly gained momentum. She felt Alex try to turn to look at the monster chasing them.

"Head down!" Kiku shouted.

A bullet pinged off the tar beside them. Kiku glanced in the rearview mirror, hoping to see only one shooter. The driver's left arm was outside the window, holding a pistol, and she saw the explosion of another shot that disappeared into the night. And then Shin leaned out with a submachine gun.

Kiku cut the wheel and headed down a sidewalk toward the main school building. Ahead stood a row of closely placed lights mounted on cement poles, like lighthouse beacons beckoning her to safe harbor. But as she got close, she suddenly doubted the span between the columns was wide enough for them to pass between them.

And it was too late to stop.

Alex screamed. Kiku's forearms flexed as she made a minor course correction, avoiding a horrible crash by millimeters. Alex shouted again —this time in celebration.

Tires screeched behind them and bullets pinged off brick. When Kiku rounded the corner of the building, a flame of pain shot through her right calf, and her leg flopped limply into the bike like someone had hit it with a bat. She didn't need to look to know she'd been shot.

Reaching the main road, Kiku shifted gears, then opened up the throttle once more, grateful the bullet had hit her right leg and not her left. They reached a section of homes that were small and tightly packed, in sharp contrast to Karen Harris's wealthy subdivision. Kiku stuck to the main road; taking side streets was too risky. She didn't know which road would be a dead end or a loop that would bring them back full circle.

Shin's car appeared on the road far behind them. Kiku blew through a red light and took a right into a commercial district of old brick-front buildings.

"Are you okay?" she shouted.

"Something's leaking!" Alex said. "It's all over my leg."

Kiku took a deep breath through her nose and was relieved not to smell gas. But her relief was short-lived. The bike chugged twice, sputtered, and went into a death shake. The engine powered down and Kiku steered over to the curb. She looked at the sign above the nearest door and smiled at the irony: motorcycle repair.

The street was deserted and there were no parked vehicles to duck behind. As Kiku dismounted and put weight on her leg, pain shot up her thigh, turning her muscles to jelly. She stumbled sideways and leaned against the building to catch herself.

Alex swore. "You've been shot."

"You need to run," she said. She pointed at an alley across the street. "Go. I will hold them here."

"No!" Alex ground his teeth. "I'm not a coward."

"I know you are not." Kiku smiled as she smashed the shop's huge glass window with the butt of her pistol. "That just set off the alarm. The police will come, arrest us all, and take me to the hospital. A hospital is a lot easier to escape from than a police station." She forced out a chuckle that was meant to be reassuring.

Tears ran down Alex's face, but he tried to smile. "That's smart. You're so smart."

"I will find you. What is the phone number I gave you?" Alex repeated the number for Jack Stratton's burner phone. "Call him. He will help you. Now run, and do not look back. Promise me."

Alex nodded. "I promise." He turned, raced across the street, and disappeared down the alley.

Kiku wondered what Daichi would think of her now. Probably that she'd gone soft. And he would be right. The boy was Shin's primary target. Her best chance for survival was to give Alex to Shin.

But there are some things worse than dying.

37

Kiku removed her bra and tied it around her bleeding calf. Gritting her teeth, she pulled it tight, wrapped it around, and tied it again. Then she put one leg through the store's broken window and waited until Shin's car came roaring through the intersection toward her. When its headlights hit the BMW and Kiku was sure they had seen her, she disappeared into the store.

The floor space was mostly taken up by three gleaming, new high-end bikes. A long counter and display case stood in front of a doorway in the rear wall. An open box on the counter turned out to contain a headlamp surrounded by shipping peanuts.

Kiku dumped the shipping peanuts in front of the rear doorway, opened the door a crack, and slipped into a garage big enough for a small airplane, closing the door behind her. A dozen or so motorcycles were scattered throughout in various states of disassembly. Safety lights provided a little dim light, but the garage was otherwise quite dark. If she weren't burning with pain, she would have smiled. Under the circumstances, she couldn't have hoped for a better place to make a last stand. She liked her chances of holding Shin off until the police arrived.

She scanned for other entrances. The garage had no windows. There were five bay doors, all of them closed. A red glow indicated a fire exit. Far away, something dripped, making a faint metallic chime as it landed. She limped behind a stack of tires to wait, keeping her aim on the door and trying to calm her breathing.

She counted off three minutes before she sensed movement and the shipping peanuts crunched. Kiku immediately fired five shots through the closed door. Her thumb tapped the magazine release, the empty container bounced off the cement, and something big and heavy crashed to the floor on the other side of the door, causing a slight tremor under her feet. Kiku swapped her magazine and kept her gun aimed at the door. The faintest crunch of glass sounded from the front room. *They are regrouping.*

Kiku crept farther back into the garage, hoping to find something else to use as a shield. She settled on a thick steel rack used to hold engines. It was now Shin's move—and she couldn't guess what it would be. The police had to be on their way. She doubted the garage had a direct alarm to the police station, but a shop of this size would most likely have a connection to an alarm company. That would increase response time, but the police would still come.

How many men did Shin have? She'd only seen the one car approaching down the street, and she'd just taken out one man, probably Shin's driver, in the doorway. That left just Shin—but there had been two more cars behind her when she left Alex's mother's house. Still, she doubted Shin would have brought the kind of firepower he'd used to attack the safe house. He had always looked down his nose at Kiku and underestimated her. She would make him pay for that today.

Suddenly, Shin shouted from the front room, "If you shoot, you'll kill your little friend."

Kiku kept her aim on the door and her mouth shut. She prayed Shin was bluffing and Alex was long gone.

She could hear Shin now, but his voice was low and she couldn't make out what he was saying. Then a scream of sheer agony echoed off the ceiling of the garage, piercing her heart. The cry was Alex's—of that she was certain.

Kiku stepped out from behind the engine rack. "Shin! Get in here."

The door was kicked open and Shin marched through the doorway, holding Alex in front of him. Like a boa constrictor around the boy's throat, his tattooed left arm held Alex tightly against himself, shielding his own chest. With his right hand he pressed his gun against Alex's temple. Alex's eyes were wide open, pleading with Kiku. She returned his gaze unflinchingly.

The shipping peanuts in the doorway rustled across the floor as a gentle breeze swept into the garage, and the hairs on the back of Kiku's neck rose. She couldn't see it, but the presence of death hung in the air, and it wasn't just from the dead man lying on the floor in the front room.

Shin sensed it, too. His eyes were wild and bright. There was no fear there. In fact, he looked like he was in rapture. Beads of sweat ran down his bald head and he licked his lips. Shin was an addict, all right. But he wasn't addicted to adrenaline or drugs. He was hooked on death.

Both Shin and Kiku realized someone was about to die.

Alex had tears running down his cheeks and he was trembling, and not just with fear . . . with pain. The boy's hand was bloody. His pinky had been cut off. Shin must have ordered Alex to call out to Kiku and he had refused.

"Put down the gun, Kiku," Shin ordered.

"Not a chance."

With the boy held tightly in front of Shin, Kiku didn't have a shot.

Shin smiled. "I'll kill the boy."

"You will kill him no matter what. And when you do, I will kill you." Kiku chuckled. "Is this really your plan?"

Shin's thin mouth twisted into a snarl. "You will not hurt the boy." He jammed the pistol hard against Alex's temple.

"Do you think my seeing his brains splattered across the floor will make me choose not to do the same to you?"

"More men are on their way."

"They will not arrive in time to save you." Kiku aimed for Shin's forehead.

He crouched lower behind Alex, tightened his grip on the boy's throat, and shifted the barrel of his gun to just under Alex's jaw. Alex's eyes met Kiku's. The pain was still there, but the fear was gone. He gave her a little wink. Then he grabbed Shin's hand holding the gun.

"DON'T!" Kiku shouted.

The magazine fell from Shin's gun and bounced once off the floor before Alex kicked it away into the darkness.

Shin smashed Alex in the face with the butt of his pistol. Something in Alex's mouth cracked.

"You fool," Shin hissed. "There's still a bullet in the chamber."

Alex spat out a couple of broken teeth and flashed a bloody grin. "I know. But now, you only have one bullet. After you shoot me, Kiku's definitely gonna kill you."

Kiku nodded. He was right about the last part, but she could not let the brave, stupid boy sacrifice himself for her.

Shin started to drag Alex backward toward the door.

Kiku caught Alex's eye and said, "I am sorry." She aimed at the meaty section on the outside of his thigh and pulled the trigger.

Alex screamed and pitched forward.

Kiku put five rounds in Shin's chest. Shin's single shot whipped by Kiku's ear and ricocheted off somewhere in the garage.

Alex rolled on the floor, grasping his thigh and swearing. Five feet away, Shin lay on his back.

Kiku limped past Alex and pointed her gun at Shin's face. His eyes blazed with hatred, and blood stained his teeth.

"You're dead," Shin said. "Kenzo will hunt you to the ends of the earth."

In spite of herself, Kiku gasped. *Kenzo?* She had missed the truth. Shin Uchihara may have protected Takeo since childhood, but the Uchiharas were sworn to serve the *head* of the Yakuza—and Takeo was only the leader of the American Yakuza.

Takeo had not betrayed her.

Shin's eyes widened. Too late did he realize his mistake in revealing his true master. His *last* mistake. His eyes were already dimming, but she didn't want him to go peacefully. She emptied the clip into his body.

"STOP! STOP! STOP!" Alex shouted, lurching awkwardly to his feet, putting all his weight on one leg. "He's dead. He's totally dead."

Panting, Kiku grabbed the wire snips off a cart next to her, bent down, and cut off Shin's pinky. She pointed to the ground where Shin had pistol-whipped him. "Are those your teeth? Pick them up. I need them."

Alex did as she asked, and dropped three bloody bits into her hand with a look that hovered between disgust and awe.

"Where is your finger?" She slammed the butt of her gun into Shin's mouth.

"I don't know. I guess it fell on the floor up front."

"Find it. I'll meet you there."

Kiku quickly went through Shin's pockets and found what she was looking for. She transferred it to her own pocket, grabbed a gas can, and dumped the contents onto Shin's body. Sirens approached from about three blocks down, the whine rising in pitch.

"What are you *doing*?" Alex asked as he handed her his severed digit.

"Killing you."

38

Alex leaned heavily against Kiku as she helped him to Shin's car. "Did you really have to shoot me?" he asked. His lips pulled back, revealing a gap on the left side where two of his teeth had been.

"Yes. Don't scream." She clamped her hand over his mouth and shoved him down into the seat. Her fingers muffled his cries. She waited impatiently until he stopped screaming and glared up at her. The police sirens were almost at the motorcycle shop.

Kiku supported herself on the hood of the car as she circled around to the driver's side. She got in, started the engine, and awkwardly used her left leg to operate the gas. As she drove away in the opposite direction, she pulled out her burner phone and dialed.

"Who are you calling?" Alex asked.

Kiku held up a silencing hand.

"Nine-one-one. This is a recorded line. What is your emergency?"

Kiku started crying into the phone. "Help! He needs help!"

"I need you to calm down, ma'am, and tell me exactly what's happening."

"I saw a man drag a boy into the motorcycle store. I heard gunshots. The man ran out, but not the boy."

"Gunshots? What is your exact location, ma'am?"

Kiku's sobs softened as she relayed the address. "It was . . . Oh, no! No! Fire! The store is on fire!"

"Ma'am, did you see where the man went?"

"He got on a motorcycle and headed north. But where's the boy? There are so many flames! I can't see the boy! He's still inside!"

As the wails of fire engines ripped through the night, Kiku hung up and placed both hands on the wheel. She was as calm as could be. She could have been an ordinary mom driving her son to a soccer game as the first police cars sped by.

"That was cool," Alex whispered. "Now you've got the cops going in the opposite direction from us. But I still don't get why you cut off Shin's finger."

"Your grandfather wants you dead. I need to convince him that you are."

The boy's eyes widened. "My . . . grandfather? *Not* my father?" The desperate hope in his voice was heart-wrenching.

"Your grandfather sent those men to kill you. I do not think your father knew." Kiku felt shame washing over her. But all of the information had led her to believe that Takeo wanted his son killed. "Shin was sworn to serve the head of the Yakuza. If Kenzo gave him an order, Shin would obey, regardless of what Takeo told him to do."

The boy sat quietly, processing this information. His eyes glistened. In a few short days, he had found his father and mother, lost his mother, and lost all hope of ever meeting his father. Now perhaps he had hope again.

"But . . . there's no way that the police are going to think Shin's body is mine," he said at last. "Even if he's missing a pinky. Don't you watch TV? They'll do DNA and bone analysis and all kinds of science stuff."

"No, they will not." Kiku dialed another number.

"Hello?"

"Daichi. It went south. Shin is dead. Kenzo is the one who gave the order to kill Alex."

"Kenzo!" Something in the background broke. "Alex? Where's Alex?" Daichi shouted so loudly that Alex heard him, and the boy's eyes teared up again.

"He is fine."

Alex held up his bloody hand, gestured down to his leg, and said loudly, "I'm *not* fine. She freakin' shot me!"

"What did he say?"

"Nothing." Kiku's icy stare cut Alex off. "Alex is missing a pinky—"

"You cut off his finger!"

"Shut up. Shin did it. He is dead, and I torched his body. I need to cover Alex's tracks. I need you to come out here and persuade the ME to match Alex's finger and teeth to Shin."

"Teeth? What the hell did you do to Alex?"

"She shot me!" Alex yelled, then held up his wounded hand as if to show Daichi.

"Both of you calm down and listen. Daichi, I need you to get out here."

She gave him the address of the motorcycle shop and all the details. When she had finished, there was a long pause.

"It's a long shot, Kiku. And even if it works, what about Takeo? What are you going to tell him?"

"I cannot tell Takeo that his father was behind this. Takeo would go after Kenzo and he would lose."

Daichi swore. "I agree. You can't tell him. Not yet."

How could she lie to Takeo about all of this? Wouldn't that put him in *more* danger? Would he ever forgive her?

As if reading her thoughts, Daichi said, "Don't worry. My brother won't do anything to harm Takeo. The Nakumora dynasty is too important to him."

"So, you will handle the ME?"

"Lilly is packing my bag now."

"I will handle Takeo. Thank you, Daichi."

Kiku hung up and turned to Alex. "Alex, I need to make another call, and it is essential that you keep your mouth shut. I need you to promise that you will not utter a sound while I am on this call—no matter what you hear me say. Do you understand?"

Alex nodded.

"I need a verbal response."

He whispered, "Yes."

As Kiku punched in the number, her finger trembled. She tried to tell herself the tremor was due to pain, but she knew better.

"Kiku?" Takeo answered. His voice sounded tense.

"Takeo . . ." Kiku swallowed. "Shin has gone rogue. He has been working with the Russians. You need to switch your security."

"Where are you? Where's my son?" There was a panic in his voice that she'd never heard before.

Alex jumped slightly in his seat but honored his promise and managed to stay quiet.

"The Russians attacked us in Chicago, so I went underground and radio silent." She didn't apologize; she had followed protocol. "They attacked us again as we fled, and I suspected they were tracking us. They were. Shin planted a tracker in my gun and was feeding the location to the Russians. I set up an intercept for them. The Russians indicated that they were working with someone. I went to San Francisco to interview Alex's mother."

Two fire trucks barreled down the street, their lights flashing and sirens blaring.

"Karen Harris is dead," Kiku continued.

Alex dropped his head, any doubt in his mind about his mother's survival now gone.

"Shin killed her and her husband. I fled with Alex, but . . ." Kiku pictured Takeo on the other end of the line, gripping the phone, his handsome face twisted in pain. "Alex is dead. Shin killed him. I have failed you."

Alex savagely bit his lip to keep himself from crying out to his father.

With each thump of her heart, Kiku felt colder. The yellow line of the road was a blur that Kiku's brain instinctively followed, but the image of Takeo filled her mind. The seconds stretched on to minutes and the distance turned to miles.

Wounded things did nothing to soften her heart or resolve.

Until now.

A voice inside her pleaded with her to say something to Takeo. She ached to hold him, and since that was impossible, she yearned to wrap soothing words around his pained spirit. It would be the feeblest of bandages, but still, it would be something to ease his loss. But she said nothing. If this lie was what it took to protect Takeo and Alex, then she would lie. She would rip Takeo's heart out and grind it under her heel. She had to tell him the truth at a time that wouldn't get them both killed.

Takeo finally spoke. "I will be at my summer house." Then he hung up.

Kiku set down the phone.

Alex cradled his hand and rocked slightly. "I . . . I heard what he said. And I don't know how you can do . . . some of the things you do . . . but you can't go there. My grandfather will say you failed to protect me, and he'll use that as a reason to kill you. Right?"

The boy was sharp. She sometimes wished he didn't see things so clearly. And in this case, he'd seen it all.

She would go to Takeo's summer house. Kenzo would order her maimed or worse.

39

Arkansas

Kiku sat on the edge of Daichi's kitchen table as the country doctor finished bandaging her leg.

The old man smiled warmly. "Well, I think that should do it. But you're going to need to stay off that leg for a couple of weeks. Have to let it heal."

"Thank you, Doctor. And thank you for helping Hwan as well."

"I'll need to see you both again . . . let's see . . ." He squinted up at the ceiling like his schedule was etched into the rafters. "Same time next Tuesday?"

"That is very kind of you. We will see you then."

It was a lie, of course. Or a partial one. Alex would be there; she would not. The doctor smiled, gave a little wave, and almost stumbled into Daichi as he turned to leave. The two men spoke in hushed tones as Daichi escorted the doctor out.

When Daichi returned, Kiku asked, "How is Alex?" She winced as she attempted to put on her shoe.

"He's upstairs, propped up in bed, eating ice cream and getting pampered like a fat cat. I wish I had it so good. And he only lost a pinky." He held up his prosthetic.

"A reasonable cost, under the circumstances."

Daichi handed her a set of crutches. "Nothing I can say to change your mind?"

Kiku ignored the question. "I need one more favor." She handed him a padded envelope addressed to Tim and Betsy. "I need you to place two thousand dollars in here and mail it."

Daichi nodded. "I'll drop it in a box a couple of towns over."

"Good. Did you take care of everything in San Francisco?"

"It cost me a hundred grand and one of the Audis, but the assistant ME has two kids in college, so . . . yeah, she'll do it. The official result will take weeks, but they already ID'd the fingerprint off Alex's juvie record."

"That is a relief. *Arigato*."

"You do realize that buying off the ME is the easy part. Convincing Kenzo is an entirely higher degree of difficulty."

"I will take care of that. I need him to believe Alex is dead."

"Either way, if you go there, he'll kill you. If Kenzo thinks you figured out his plan, you're dead. If you manage to convince him that Shin killed Alex, he'll blame you for Alex's death. Takeo won't be able to save you."

"I need to warn Takeo."

"Kenzo will be watching you both closely. Takeo's phones will be tapped," Daichi said.

"I will get him alone."

"If Kenzo doesn't kill you first."

"If I don't go to Takeo's summer house, then Kenzo will know I discovered the truth. There is no other way. I must warn Takeo."

"Kiku . . ." Daichi rubbed the back of his neck. "Takeo may not want to talk to you right now."

Kiku nodded. Takeo believed that she had disobeyed his orders and failed to keep his son alive. He must despise her.

Daichi reached into his pocket, took out a set of keys, and handed them to her. "I brought a car around back. The Corvette. You can keep it."

Kiku started for the door. "Thank you again, Daichi. I should leave now."

"You're not even going to say goodbye to the kid?"

"I am not."

Daichi's expression was stern, but the fire that had once burned there was absent. There had been a time when Kiku would not have disobeyed him if he had so much as raised an eyebrow in her direction. That Daichi was gone—and she was still unsure if that was a good thing. If Kenzo ever found Daichi, she feared that this new, kinder version of the man would not stand a chance against his savage brother.

Kiku gave him a single, quick bow. Daichi returned the gesture. Silently, they spoke a thousand words. He knew her plan. He understood she would die. He also knew that he could not persuade her from that path.

Kiku limped down the back steps. The Corvette's engine hummed when she fired it up. A curtain on the second-floor window drew back, and Baba peered out. A moment later, Alex's badly bruised face appeared.

Kiku turned away and hit the gas, but the boy's voice sounded in her ears. He was screaming her name.

It is better this way. What could either of them say? How do you thank someone for dying for you?

Besides, his thanks would be misplaced—she wasn't going to sacrifice her life just for Alex.

She would die for Takeo.

40

Takeo's summer house

It is a beautiful place to die.

The irony of being back in the traditional Japanese garden at Takeo's summer house was not lost on her. Here Kenzo had tasked her with saving Jiro, under the penalty of death for failure. How could he not render the same verdict for her failure to rescue his grandson? But if she was condemned to death, she would ask to speak with Takeo alone first.

The last of the cherry blossoms had fallen to the ground and the leaves were a deep, somber green under the swirling gray clouds overhead. With each step, her crutches settled softly into the pea-stone path, punctuating the murmur of the waterfall cascading into the koi pond.

Seven men stood at the back, all dressed in dark suits. Two of them stood apart from the others, their backs to her, their faces hidden. But she was certain the one closest was Kenzo.

Her one regret was that she was going to miss the meeting in Mount Hicks, Virginia. Her sister Akari's murderer would go unpunished—at least by her. Another favor she would owe Jack Stratton.

She continued at a steady pace, placing her crutches carefully on the wooden slats of the little bridge. The pain in her calf was a dull throb. She'd practically glued the bandages on and then wrapped it all in a flexible plastic sheath. Kenzo's security had taken her gun and her knife. They'd even taken her favorite hairpin, which was the smartest thing they could have done. The seven-inch titanium spike would've been the last thing Kenzo saw . . .

Still, they had not been smart enough; they had let her keep her crutches, as she had expected. With the weights that she had inserted in the underarm supports, they made passible bludgeoning weapons if the need arose.

She recognized a couple of the men in suits as part of Kenzo's personal security force. The biggest one, Ryder, a hulking man with no neck, eyed her carefully. She'd met the Australian only once, but he had a reputation as a focused, ruthless sociopath. Kenzo, hypocrite that he was, hired foreigners for security and switched them out frequently because of his paranoia. But Ryder was different, a truly loyal pawn.

She scanned the other men and several faces were noticeably absent. There were no Uchiharas present. What had Shin's betrayal cost his family? She could only guess, but she would be surprised if any still drew breath.

At the sound of her approach, Kenzo and the man beside him turned. Her hands tightened on the grips of her crutches. It wasn't Takeo standing beside Kenzo but his brother, Jiro. Kiku lifted her chin as she limped forward.

Her heart thundered in her chest. Takeo had said he would be here. If Kenzo ordered her death now, her petition to speak with Takeo would be denied. She had a backup plan, a video explaining everything to Takeo, but she wanted to be there to tell him. She needed to convince him not to attack his father in a blind rage. What would Takeo do when he learned his father had had both Takeo's son and lover killed?

Jiro appeared thinner than when she'd last seen him. She searched his face for a hint of what was to come, but his expression was a neutral mask. One cheek—on the same side as his hearing aid—bore a small, puckered scar from his run-in with the Russians, making him look older and a little rougher. She had tried to reach out to him again, but he had not returned any of her calls. Jiro had warned her to flee Chicago, but she knew she would get no assistance from him now.

"Kiku." Kenzo's voice cut through the silence of the garden like a deep gong.

Kiku stopped when Kenzo spoke, as custom required, and stood seven and a half feet from him. She had to repress a smile; the distance was almost perfect for one lunge, swinging the weighed crutch around and caving in Kenzo's skull. But her task today was not to kill him. She had to convince him that Alex was dead and the secret that Kenzo himself had ordered Alex's death was still safe.

Kenzo stood there studying Kiku. His eyes bore into hers, examining her face and searching for a hint of deception.

Kiku met his steely gaze with an iron stare of her own.

"Thank you." Kenzo bowed deeply, at almost forty-five degrees—a gesture of the highest apology, and unheard of for Kenzo.

"My sincerest apologies to the entire Nakumora family for your loss." Kiku returned the gesture, making sure to bow even lower.

Kenzo straightened. "My son should have been aware of Shin's betrayal. Thank you for protecting the honor of my name."

Kiku remained in her bow until he motioned for her to rise. Jiro's eyes now met hers. Behind his glasses, a frost had chilled his usual warmth. He bowed stiffly.

"Jiro will be overseeing operations in the States." Kenzo motioned, and Ryder stepped forward. "Ryder has taken over as head of security."

Ryder puffed out his massive chest. His stance was misleading. From his upper body, it would appear that his weight was on his heels, which would make his response time slow—but Kiku saw that the balls of his feet were depressing the pea stones. The Neanderthal was smarter than he looked.

"Take as long as you need to recover from your injuries," Kenzo said, starting to bow once more.

"Where is Takeo?" The question broke free from her lips.

Jiro's eyes narrowed.

Kenzo frowned. She'd broken protocol, and he was clearly displeased. "My son is in Japan. Mourning and contemplating the reasons for his failure."

For a split second, his eyes flicked down to her hands on her crutches. She wondered if Kenzo realized the mistake his security had made in letting her keep them.

Ryder slid his right foot slightly back. The sound of the shifting pea stones was almost drowned out by the murmur of the waterfall, but not quite. He was on guard.

Jiro bowed again as well. “I also thank you for dealing with Liev. You promised to avenge the death of Samantha, and you kept your word.”

Kiku exhaled. She returned his bow, bowed again to Kenzo, and spun on her heel. She forced herself to walk slowly as she made her way back through the garden, even pausing for a moment on the bridge and pretending to glance at the koi.

She would not die today. She had been prepared for death, but now she needed to prepare for another fight. Takeo needed her help. She was certain of it. Jiro had told her as much: the girl whose death she had vowed to avenge for him was named Jessica, not Samantha.

41

Chicago

Jiro sat at the large table in the back of the restaurant. For the last two hours he had been eager to keep the meeting short, but now he was desperate to leave. Positioned at the head of the table, he was surrounded by security and advisers, but everyone knew that Kenzo was the one in charge—even in his absence. He had returned to Japan with Takeo and left behind his men and one rule for Jiro to follow: don't do anything without asking him. Kenzo may have declared Jiro in charge of the American Yakuza, but he was only a figurehead, a puppet controlled by Kenzo.

Ryder must have told another raunchy joke because the whole table erupted in laughter. Ryder eyed Jiro with a look that bordered on disgust. It was clear Ryder held him in very low regard. Jiro was tempted to speak with his father about it but knew it would make him look weak. Takeo would have put Ryder in his place himself. Or sent Kiku.

Jiro swirled his single-malt Scotch and stared at the little whirlpool in the glass. He needed to get in touch with Kiku but hadn't found a way yet. He was certain Ryder had hacked his phones and Internet, and the huge Australian had a detail following Jiro everywhere. His father had forbidden him to speak with Takeo. There was no one he could trust. Nowhere he could turn.

Jiro pushed his chair back and stood up. Ryder's glass stopped halfway to his lips and he lifted an eyebrow. Everyone at the table stopped talking and looked up at Jiro. He felt like a kid asking for permission to go to the potty. He mumbled, "Restroom," dropped his napkin on his plate, and headed for the back of the restaurant, with two security guards following him.

He walked past the kitchen and down a hallway. A woman with long brown hair was exiting the ladies' room. He smiled at her, but one of the security guards stepped in front of him and made her shuffle around them. She shot the guard an annoyed look and kept walking.

The guard opened the door to the men's room, peered inside, and motioned for Jiro. Casting a last glance at the departing woman, Jiro stepped inside. His father's new security measures were tanking his personal life.

After finishing his business, he scrubbed his hands in the sink. The faucet was the type that turned on just long enough to get your hands damp but not long enough to wash the soap off. His frustration growing, he glared in the mirror.

The reflection staring back at him surprised him, and his mouth ticked up as a memory of his uncle Daichi flashed through his head. Daichi would have known what to do. But Daichi had defied his father and paid the price with his life. Takeo now seemed to be following in Daichi's footsteps.

Jiro got one last trickle out of the faucet and began to dry his hands. Would he share the same fate?

Inside the restaurant, an alarm blared to life. The bathroom door burst open and another of Jiro's guards called out, "There's a fire! Let's go!"

Smoke was already billowing out of the kitchen and filling the hallway as Jiro followed the men.

The kitchen staff surged out of the double doors, yelling and jostling. The gray smoke was turning black, its tendrils obscuring the ceiling and dimming the lights. Just as Jiro passed the kitchen doors, a hand coiled around his waist while another clamped over his mouth.

"Come with me," Kiku whispered in his ear as she dragged him into the kitchen and through the thick smoke. Her hand slid from his waist and seized his wrist as she pulled him toward the back.

Jiro was coughing and his eyes burned. He could barely breathe, let alone see, but Kiku was undeterred. They made their way to the door by the dishwasher and down a short hallway.

Kiku cracked open the fire exit door and stuck his face near the opening. He gulped in air and wiped his eyes.

"Where is Takeo?"

Jiro shook his head. "Supposedly Japan, but I don't know for sure."

She shook him so hard his teeth clacked. "Focus. Think. Where?"

"I heard Ryder talking to this guy, Zane. Zane is guarding Takeo. Ryder said Zane was going to be in Hong Kong at the end of the week."

"You think Takeo is in Hong Kong?"

"My father doesn't tell me much. But . . ." Jiro grabbed Kiku's arm. "You have to get Takeo. Our father found out Takeo defied him by trying to turn the American Yakuza legit. And then he found out about Alex. He wants a grandchild to honor Takeo's mother." Jiro let go of her arm. "The marriage is all arranged."

"Marriage? Takeo would never go along with an arranged marriage." Kiku's canines flashed pearly white.

"Kenzo plans for me to take over, but Takeo is the firstborn. The heir should come from him. After Kenzo has his heir, he will have no more use for Takeo."

Kiku stuffed a burner phone in Jiro's pocket along with a folded sheet of paper. "Take this."

"What are you going to do?"

"I will go to Hong Kong in three days. I will get Takeo."

"Why three days?" Jiro coughed. The smoke in the kitchen was thinning.

"You said it yourself: Kenzo will not harm Takeo until he has his heir. I must take care of a piece of personal business first."

Kiku gave a curt bow, and disappeared out the door.

42

Mount Hicks Cemetery

Cold rain fell from the dark sky, pinging off Kiku's umbrella and dripping onto the grass-covered grave. The tombstone was inscribed with a fake name, but the bodies entombed beneath the soil were as real as the orchids in her hand.

Kiku wasn't looking at the grave, however; her focus was on her phone screen, where she was monitoring the security cameras she had placed around the cemetery. At the appointed time of 7:00, headlights approached and a car entered through the main gate, with only a driver inside. Gary Dunn. The man who had delivered the letter about the girl from Jayu-ui Maeul.

When the car parked behind her, Kiku slipped the phone in her pocket and took the flowers into her right hand. It was awkward holding both the umbrella and the orchids, and she frowned at the bent stems.

"Excuse me." Gary stopped at the bumper of his car to open up his umbrella, shaking slightly. "Ma'am?"

Kiku didn't turn fully around. She could see well enough with her peripheral vision, and she wanted him to come closer.

"Ma'am?" Gary walked up until he was only a few feet behind her. "I don't mean to interrupt. Are you visiting . . ." He read the name off the tombstone. "Brian Miller?"

"Yes and no. In a way, it is funny that you selected this cemetery for a meeting. I doubt you were aware I had any connection to it. But the flowers are not for him." Kiku turned and laid the orchids on the grave next to Brian's.

"Are you the girl from Jayu-ui Maeul?"

"I am."

Gary held out a trembling hand like he was calming a dog that might run away. "I need to make amends. I came to apologize."

Kiku waited. Wind shifted the rain sideways and a cool spray brushed her cheek.

"I was there. I was there when your sister . . . It was your sister, wasn't it?"

"Yes."

"I was in the room. I didn't do it, I didn't do anything, but . . . I should have. I should have at least said something."

"My sister was shot. Why?"

"She overheard a name."

"Whose name?"

"I can't . . . I can't tell you that." Gary sighed. "I made a mistake. I'm the one who said the name." His hand shook so much he almost dropped his umbrella. "I'm so sorry. I didn't shoot her. I swear."

"I believe you. But you said the name then. And you will say it again now."

He backed off a step. "No, I'm sorry. You don't know these men. They're *monsters*. They'll kill me."

Kiku's umbrella swung out in an arc and struck Gary's right knee. His cry was cut off as a kick slammed into his other knee, causing him to lurch forward. He would have landed face-first in the grass if Kiku hadn't grabbed a handful of his hair.

She dragged him forward until his face was inches in front of the tombstone. "You do not know what a monster is. If you did, you would never have summoned *me*." She pressed his face against the wet marble. "There is no Brian in this grave. There are several men entombed here. I am the one who killed them all. I left the flowers as an apology to the poor soul stuck next to them. These men were evil. They were monsters. But I am far worse." Kiku yanked Gary's head back, forcing him to look up at her. His eyes were filled with terror. "The name."

Gary shuddered. "You can't threaten me. I'm already dead. Stage four cancer. You can't do anything to me. I just needed to make things right. But if I tell you and they find out, they will come after my family."

"Your name is Gary Dunn. You live in Highland Falls, New York, with your wife, Susan, and three children: Patrick, Mary, and Jennifer. I thought of bringing one of them here tonight. Well . . . a piece of them at least."

Gary jerked his head away and threw up on the grass.

Kiku stepped on his hand. "I am a monster, and *you* created me. Tell me the name, or I leave now and bring back the tongue of your son to loosen yours."

"Jeff . . . Jeff Klein. He was my boss."

"Where is he now?"

"Washington State. North Ridge. It's way up the coast. But he didn't shoot your sister either."

"Did he stop it? Did he go to the police?" She yanked his head around, and Gary started crying. "Who else was there at the meeting in the restaurant?"

"I don't know. They didn't use names. None of them did. I knew my boss's name. That's it. There were twelve of them, I remember that."

"What was the meeting about?" Kiku pulled him up until he was on his knees.

He sobbed. "Drugs, I think. Or weapons. I really don't know. I thought . . . I thought . . ."

Kiku put her face right in front of his. "Go ahead. Lie to me. Give me another reason to slit your throat here and now."

"It was a lot of money. I know it was something illegal, but I was just out of college and . . ." Gary broke down.

Kiku punched him in the face, knocking him onto his side. She stood over him. "Your mother is still living, as are two of your aunts. You have three brothers and a sister, and they all have children. Defy me in any way and I will end your bloodline in the goriest way possible."

"Please, just kill me. Take it all out on me." Gary crawled to her and grabbed for her boot. "Please."

Kiku placed her foot on his shoulder blade and pinned him to the ground. "Did my sister beg? Did she?"

Gary sobbed and nodded.

"And yet you did *nothing*. I will give you the mercy she begged for. I will not kill you today. You may recall more details later." She pressed harder, and he flailed on the ground. "Under the right circumstances, the mind can recall many things. You live—for now. You live until every man who was in that room dies."

Kiku lifted her boot, and Gary, clutching his arm to his chest, curled into the fetal position and whimpered. There was no pity for him in Kiku's heart. She'd found her sister's body in the same position.

The skies opened up and the rain poured down.

"The day I kill the twelfth man," she said, "I will come for you. Do what I have said, do not run, and I will spare your family. Run . . . and I will slaughter them all."

Gary sobbed and nodded.

Kiku stepped over him and walked calmly to her car.

The man was a fool. He feared those monsters.

But she was the beast that monsters fear.

43

Arkansas

Alex grimaced as he set the post-hole digger against the back of the old pickup truck. "Are you going to at least help with one of these?" he called up to the cab as he sat down on the tailgate.

"How can I?" Daichi yelled back.

"I'm missing a finger, you know!" Alex said good-naturedly.

"You've got nine others." Daichi held his half-full glass of sweet tea out the window as he gestured down the long row of new fence posts. "I only have five fingers, and as you can see, they're all quite busy."

Alex laughed.

His laughter stopped when he saw the large man walking down the road toward them. Daichi's glass fell from his hand, shattering on the gravel. He shoved his door open and stepped out with a shotgun clutched in his good hand. Alex scrambled around the truck, undid the straps beneath the front bumper, and pulled out the sawed-off shotgun, just like he'd practiced with Daichi.

"Stay down," Daichi ordered. His tone left no room for argument. To the approaching man, he shouted, "That's far enough!"

Alex peered beneath the truck. He couldn't see the man's face, only his legs and a duffel bag in his hand.

"Kiku sent me," the stranger called.

"I don't know the name," Daichi answered.

"I've come a long way and—"

"Turn around and head back the way you came."

"But . . . Kiku said you could help. She's got a message for you, too."

"I told you. I don't know *a* Kiku. And I don't know you."

"Wait." The man dropped the duffel bag at his side. "Alex knows who I am."

Alex's heart pounded in his chest. He thought he recognized the voice, but it couldn't be. His friend was dead. He peered over the hood and through the windshield. Standing in the road with his legs apart, ready to fight if he had to, was Hwan. The ever-present smile on his face was wavering—understandable, given the shotgun pointed at him—but it was there just the same.

Alex raced around the truck. "You're alive!"

Hwan took one look at Alex and started to jog forward, but Daichi's shouted order froze them both in their tracks.

"STOP!" Daichi kept the gun leveled at Hwan. He glanced at Alex. "Get behind the truck, Hwan."

Hwan took a step forward.

Daichi shifted into his shooting stance.

"Hwan, stop!" Alex shouted.

"But the guy with the gun just told me to move."

"He's talking to me," Alex said with a grin.

Hwan's raised eyebrows looked like a bunched-up caterpillar. "Huh?"

Alex motioned for Daichi to lower his gun. "It's okay. I know him."

Daichi kept the shotgun pointed at Hwan. "I don't."

"Really. He saved my life. Kiku's, too." Alex smiled at Hwan. "What happened? I thought they killed you in the safe room."

"You'd be surprised how inspirational bullets can be in convincing a fat man that he can fit into a tight space. I lost a lot of skin and had to shift a few internal organs, but I made it through the vent into the crawlspace. By then you and Kiku were gone. I heard Shin and his men.

I knew it was them. There was no way I was going back to the safe house after that."

"Then how did you find Kiku?" Daichi asked.

"I didn't. She found me. She checked the morgue, and when they didn't have any bodies as good-looking as mine, she came looking."

Alex pressed his hands together and gazed pleadingly at his uncle. "I'm telling you, Hwan saved our lives. He's a *good* guy."

"I'll believe Kiku. Where is she?" Daichi asked.

Hwan's smile vanished. "She's going to Hong Kong. To help Takeo."

At the mention of his father, Alex ran for the driver's side of the truck.

Daichi grabbed his arm and pulled him to a stop. "Where do you think you're going?"

"We can catch her!" Alex said. "We can get to her before she reaches the airport!"

Daichi turned back to Hwan. "How does she plan on helping Takeo?"

"She said that Kenzo is waiting for something, and once he gets it, he's going to kill Takeo. And she heard that the Russians want Takeo dead to settle the debt. Shin killing Alex didn't satisfy Cade Novikov. Cade was bitten by a dog as a child and to this day he kills any dog that gets within arm's reach. The man has an unquenchable thirst for vengeance. They're coming at Takeo from all sides. He doesn't stand a chance."

"So Kiku's going to Hong Kong against those odds?" Daichi said.

Hwan nodded.

"She doesn't stand a chance," Alex said.

Daichi laughed. "Don't forget, it's Kiku we're talking about, kid. Kenzo and the Russians are the ones who should be afraid."

KIKU - YAKUZA ASSASSIN

ACTION-THRILLER NOVELS

Award-winning, *Wall Street Journal* bestselling author Christopher Greyson breaks the mold for action-thrillers. Join Kiku as she criss-crosses the globe from Chicago to Hong Kong, the streets of Japan, and the frozen tundra of Russia and takes on the mob, Yakuza, black market, and anyone else who stands in her way!

A BEAUTIFUL PLACE TO DIE

Protector. Lover. Assassin. — ***Kiku.***

Orphaned as a child and taken in by the Yakuza, Kiku swore an oath to serve and protect the organization. But, when Kiku discovers that the 13-year-old boy she has been assigned to guard may be the son of her lover and heir to the Yakuza throne, her pledge is put to the test. With a price on the boy's head and a target on his back, Kiku must not only save him from the ruthless Russian mob but possibly from a traitor in the Yakuza itself. Torn between love and honor, Kiku must snatch the boy from the crosshairs before it's too late.

KINDLE THE FIRES OF WAR

She's outnumbered 100 to 1.
They're going to need more men.

Kiku has gone rogue. Now hunted by the Russian mob and the Yakuza, Kiku heads to Hong Kong's underbelly to rescue her lover. Faced with impossible odds, Kiku must outwit, outfight, and outrun everyone trying to capture her and collect the two-million-dollar bounty. Rats fueled by greed or vengeance, driven by ruthless leaders, run rampant, all hoping to score. The mob, Yakuza, and Hong Kong's black market—they all wanted to fight. Kiku started a war.

DANCE OF DEATH

To save the one she loves,
she'll kill them all.

Kiku's quest to rescue her lover has gone disastrously wrong. With the odds stacked against her, her enemies think she'll run and hide to save herself. They're wrong—dead wrong. Kiku decides to take the fight to them instead. Now the hunter, Kiku, will stop at nothing to protect those she loves.

JOIN THE FREE PREFERRED READER PROGRAM

Join the Preferred Reader program and get your *exclusive* copy of *FIRST PATROL*

Preferred readers enjoy:

- Advanced Notification of New Book Releases
- The Christopher Greyson Newsletter
- Special Appreciation Giveaways
- The exclusive short story: FIRST PATROL!

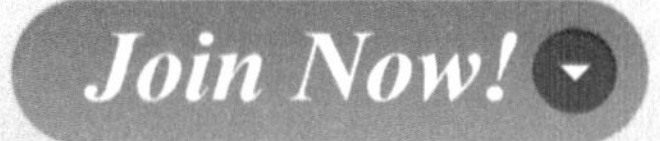

Visit ChristopherGreyson.com to sign-up!

ALSO BY
CHRISTOPHER GREYSON

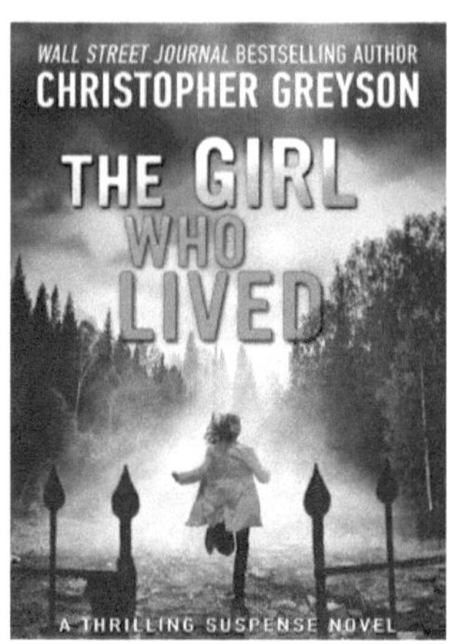

THE GIRL WHO LIVED

Ten years ago, four people were brutally murdered. One girl lived. As the anniversary of the murders approaches, Faith Winters is released from the psychiatric hospital and yanked back to the last spot on earth she wants to be—her hometown where the slayings took place. Wracked by the lingering echoes of survivor's guilt, Faith spirals into a black hole of alcoholism and wanton self-destruction. Finding no solace at the bottom of a bottle, Faith decides to track down her sister's killer—and then discovers that she's the one being hunted.

ONE LITTLE LIE

A LIE IS A WELCOME MAT FOR THE DEVIL...

Kate had high hopes when she moved to her husband's hometown, but her domestic bliss was short-lived. Blindsided by her spouse's public affair with his high school sweetheart, everything she worked for begins to unravel, along with her sanity. Confused, alone, and afraid, can Kate untangle the web of lies and unmask her stalker, or will she lose everything—including her life?

One Little Lie is a riveting suspense novel set in an idyllic town where money talks, gossip flows, and the court of public opinion rules. Jump on for a fun, fast-paced ride with a book you can't put down!

The Detective Jack Stratton Mystery-Thriller Series

The Detective Jack Stratton Mystery-Thriller Series, authored by *Wall Street Journal* bestselling writer Christopher Greyson, has 5,000+ five-star reviews and over a million readers and counting. If you'd love to read another page-turning thriller with mystery, humor, and a dash of romance, pick up the next book in the highly acclaimed series today:

And Then She Was GONE

A hometown hero with a heart of gold, Jack Stratton was raised in a whorehouse by his prostitute mother. When his foster mother asks him to look into a missing girl's disappearance, Jack quickly gets drawn into a baffling mystery. As Jack digs deeper, everyone becomes a suspect—including himself.

GIRL JACKED

They say a dangerous man is the one who had it all and lost it. But they're wrong, it's the one who lost everything but has a chance to get it back...

Guilt has driven a wedge between Jack and the family he loves. When Jack, now a police officer, hears the news that his foster sister Michelle is missing, it cuts straight to his core. The police think she just took off, but Jack knows Michelle would never leave her loved ones behind—like he did. Forced to confront the demons from his past, Jack must take action, find Michelle, and bring her home... or die trying.

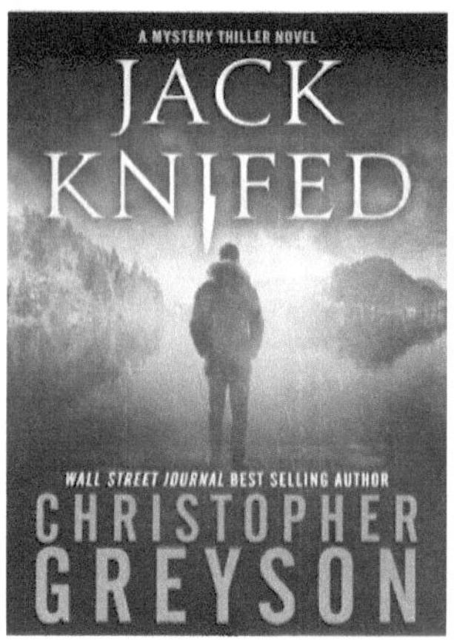

JACK KNIFED

How far would you go to uncover the truth of your past?

Constant nightmares have forced Jack to seek answers about his rough childhood and the dark secrets hidden there. The mystery surrounding Jack's birth father leads Jack to investigate the twenty-seven-year-old murder case in Hope Falls.

A heart-rending mystery-thriller about lost love, betrayal, and murder that will keep you on the edge of your seat.

JACKS ARE WILD

As the body count rises, the stakes are life and death—with no rules except one—Jacks are Wild.

When Jack's sexy old flame disappears, no one thinks it's suspicious except Jack and one unbalanced witness. Jack feels in his gut that something is wrong. He knows that Marisa has a past, and if it ever caught up with her—it would be deadly. The trail leads him into all sorts of trouble—landing him smack in the middle of an all-out mob war between the Italian Mafia and the Japanese Yakuza.

A strong hero, smart women sleuths, and more twists and turns than a piece of licorice.

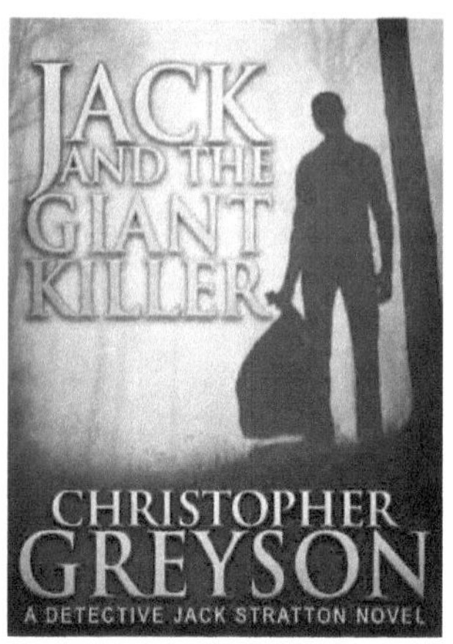

JACK AND THE GIANT KILLER

A serial killer is stalking Jack's town--and no one's safe. But they don't know Jack.

Rogue hero Jack Stratton is back in another action-packed, thrilling adventure. While recovering from a gunshot wound, Jack gets a seemingly harmless private investigation job—locate the owner of a lost dog—Jack begrudgingly assists. Little does he know it will place him directly in the crosshairs of a merciless serial killer.

An action-packed thrill ride until the very end!

DATA JACK

Can Jack and Alice stop a pack of ruthless criminals before they can Data Jack?

Jack Stratton's back is up against the wall. He's broke, kicked off the force, and his new bounty hunting business has slowed to a trickle. He thinks things are turning around when Alice gets a lucrative job setting up a home data network.When the computer program the CEO invented becomes the key tool in an international data heist, things turn deadly. In this digital age of hackers, spyware, and cyber terrorism--data is more valuable than gold. The thieves plan to steal the keys to the digital kingdom and with this much money at stake, they'll kill for it. Can Jack and Alice stop the pack of ruthless criminals before they can *Data Jack*?

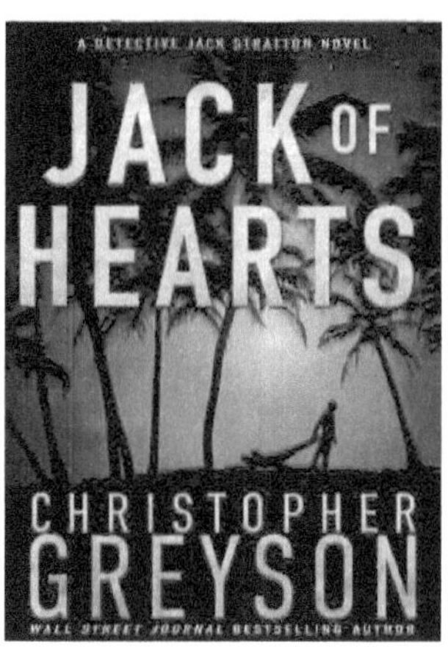

JACK OF HEARTS

Jack Stratton is heading south for some fun in the sun. Already nervous about introducing his girlfriend, Alice, to his parents, the last thing Jack needed was for the dog-sitter to cancel, forcing him to bring Lady, their 120-pound King Shepherd, on the plane with them. The dog holds Jack responsible and wants payback. On top of everything, Jack is still waiting for Alice's answer to his marriage proposal.

When his mother and the members of her neighborhood book club ask him to catch the "Orange Blossom Cove Bandit," a small-time thief who's stealing garden gnomes and peace of mind from their quiet retirement community, how can Jack refuse?

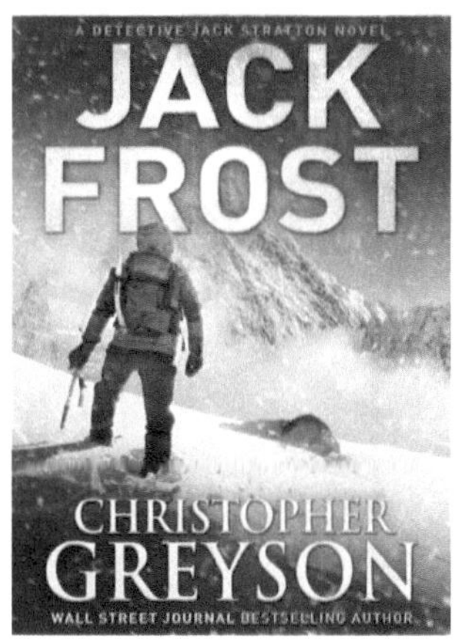

JACK FROST

What do you get when you mix the blockbuster television show Survivor with Agatha Christie's masterpiece And Then There Were None...

Jack has a new assignment: to investigate the suspicious death of a soundman on the hit TV show *Planet Survival*. Jack goes undercover as a security agent where the show is filming on nearby Mount Minuit. Soon trapped on the treacherous peak by a blizzard, a mysterious killer continues to stalk the cast and crew of *Planet Survival*. What started out as a game is now a deadly competition for survival. As the temperature drops and the body count rises, what will get them first? The mountain or the killer?

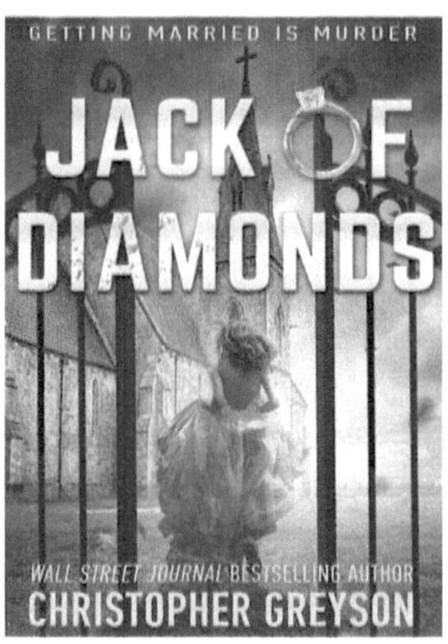

JACK OF DIAMONDS

All Jack Stratton wants to do is get married to the woman he loves—and make it through the wedding. It seems like he is finally getting his wish until he responds to a police distress call and discovers his old partner unconscious in an abandoned house. Investigators insist it was just an accident, but Jack fears there may be more to it. Sketches of women cover the walls, and among them is one sketch that makes Jack's blood run cold—a sketch of Alice, pinned up beside an invitation to a very special wedding—his own.

This time, "till death do us part" might just be a bit too accurate!

CAPTAIN JACK

Looking forward to some fun in the surf and sand, newlyweds Jack and Alice Stratton are determined not to let something like a hurricane upset their honeymoon plans. But the storm's winds and churning tides unearthed a secret long hidden beneath the turquoise waters of the island paradise.

A local tour boat captain discovers a lost submarine and offers to sell the location to a man known only as the Dyab—the Devil. When the captain is murdered, the police suspect Jack and Alice and confiscate their passports. Trapped between the Devil and the deep blue sea, the handsome young detective and his blushing bride have nowhere to turn and everything to lose as they set out to prove their innocence and find the real killer.

Hear your favorite characters
come to life in audio versions of
the Detective Jack Stratton
Mystery-Thriller Series!
Audio Books now available on Audible!
Listen Now

Novels featuring Jack Stratton in order:
AND THEN SHE WAS GONE
GIRL JACKED
JACK KNIFED
JACKS ARE WILD
JACK AND THE GIANT KILLER
DATA JACK
JACK OF HEARTS
JACK FROST
JACK OF DIAMONDS
CAPTAIN JACK

Fantasy Adventure

PURE OF HEART

Orphaned and alone, rogue-teen Dean Walker has learned how to take care of himself on the rough city streets. Unjustly wanted by the police, he takes refuge within the shadows of the city. When Dean stumbles upon an old man being mugged, he tries to help—only to discover that the victim is anything but helpless and far more than he appears. Together with three friends, he sets out on an epic quest where only the pure of heart will prevail.

THE ADVENTURES OF FINN & ANNIE — MINIMYSTERY SERIES

In these heartwarming short stories, join Finn and Annie as they investigate their way through murder, arson, theft, embezzlement, and maybe even love, seeking to distinguish between truth and lies, scammers and victims. A Mini-Mystery series that will touch your heart and leave you craving more!

ACKNOWLEDGMENTS

I would like to thank all the wonderful readers out there. It is you who make the literary world what it is today—a place of dreams filled with tales of adventure! Word of mouth is crucial for any author to succeed. If you enjoyed the novel, please consider leaving a review at Amazon, even if it is only a line or two; it would make all the difference and I would appreciate it very much.

I would also like to thank my amazing wife for standing beside me every step of the way on this journey. My thanks also go out to my two awesome kids—Laura and Christopher, my dear mother and the rest of my family. Finally, thank you to my wonderful team, Anne Cherry, Maia McViney, Michael Mishoe, Charlie Wilson of The Book Specialist, and the unbelievably helpful beta readers!

ABOUT THE AUTHOR

My name is Christopher Greyson, and I am a storyteller. Since I was a little boy, I have dreamt of what mystery was around the next corner, or what quest lay over the hill. If I couldn't find an adventure, one usually found me, and now I weave those tales into my stories.

My love for tales of mystery and adventure began with my grandfather, a decorated World War I hero. I will never forget being introduced to his friend, a WWI pilot who flew across the skies at the same time as the feared, legendary Red Baron. I love to hear from my readers. Please go to ChristopherGreyson.com and sign up for my mailing list to receive periodic updates on new book releases. Thank you for reading my novels. I hope my stories have brightened your day.

Sincerely,

Find out more about the author and upcoming books online at www.Christopher-Greyson.com.

v.2.10.22

www.ingramcontent.com/pod-product-compliance
Lightning Source LLC
Chambersburg PA
CBHW020324030826
48979CB00022B/1022

* 9 7 8 1 6 8 3 9 9 5 0 3 6 *